T0164661

THE BOOK OF MINAB

BETTY T. KYLER

iUniverse, Inc.
Bloomington

The Book of Minab

iUniverse books may be ordered through booksellers or by contacting:

*iUniverse
1663 Liberty Drive
Bloomington, IN 47403
www.iuniverse.com
1-800-Authors (1-800-288-4677)*

*ISBN: 978-1-4620-1684-6 (sc)
ISBN: 978-1-4620-1686-0 (dj)
ISBN: 978-1-4620-1685-3 (ebook)*

Library of Congress Control Number: 2011906641

Printed in the United States of America

iUniverse rev. date: 05/17/2011

This is dedicated to my best friend,
the love of my life, my husband and soul supporter,
Harv Kyler.

CHAPTER ONE

DR. KEETS CHECKED OVER the equipment and the other supplies as they were loaded onto the plane. It was to be a two-week expedition to the North Pole. They would land in northern Canada. From there, they would head 'true north' to the pole. Breena Keets had begged her father for months to allow her to go. She had worked hard during the last few semesters of school and with her private tutoring and extra studies she would be entering university this fall to major in social psychology. Her father was proud of her. She was only three weeks shy of her seventeenth birthday but she had matured beyond her years. She had every part of her life planned out. She would major in psychology and minor in geology. Her minor would be easy sailing. Her father and brother were both geologists and sociologist. Dr. Keets was a professor at the university Breena would be attending. Breena lived geology every day of her life. She knew about societies in deepest, darkest Africa that others never even heard of. Her knowledge of the history of various civilizations was better than that of her own genealogy. She had studied earthquakes and had been to the mountains of Turkey and India. She had even been to Kilimanjaro. Breena loved the different characteristics in the human race. They were as varied as fish in the sea.

Breena's family consisted of her father, Alexander Keets, her mother Karen, who was full-time homemaker, Jonathan, who was her older brother and her father's colleague, and herself. Although Breena's IQ was higher than most people her age, she enjoyed the same activities others did in school. She was a track star and could play the piano very well. To look at her you would think she was just another dizzy teenage cheerleader. She had blond hair like everyone else in her family but she inherited her distinct pale blue eyes solely from her father. Her frame was deceiving. It looked delicate but Breena was strong for her size and had endurance that wouldn't quit.

"Breena, did you pack extra underwear?" Her mother was always worried she'd forget something.

Breena mouthed that she took the underwear she ordered from the sexy catalogue her brother used when he bought things for his wife. Her father laughed. She had a wonderful relationship with her father. They talked for hours about everything, like friends instead of daughter and father. She didn't get along well with her mother though. She was a stay at home mom, at Dr. Keets request, but Breena thought she was way too passive and missed out on the real thrills of life. Breena thought it was exciting to barter in the streets of Hong Kong and to debate women's issues with men from Asia. To her, her mother was dutiful and unrealistic. Breena's plan was that after she had earned her master's degree in social psychology and had gone into research, she would then marry. Maybe by the time she was thirty, she would take a year off and have a child. Until then, she would take men for what they were - good associates, information sources, and great surfing buddies.

"Alex, I really don't feel good about Breena going this time. Maybe you should reconsider. You know she hates the cold."

Breena groaned. Her mother was going to ruin everything. Breena had spent too many hours changing her father's mind so she could go. He wanted her to take the extra studies needed to get a head start on the fall's university semester. Her mother wanted her to visit her grandparents in Montana. The last thing Breena wanted was to be on some remote farm feeding cows and chickens.

"She'll be fine, Karen. Breena is a hardy little trooper. She's been to Kilimanjaro. This will be a picnic. We're spending most of the time in the airplane."

Breena's mom hugged and kissed everyone, then cried as they stepped into the plane. Breena gave her a casual wave and turned her attentions to her father who was sitting beside her.

"Thank you so much for not giving into Mom's worries. I thought maybe next year we could go to China." Breena liked to watch the ground as the plane took off.

"Why China?"

"I was doing some research and found out there is a small culture in north-east China where the women are great matriarchs. I could do a thesis on them."

Dr. Keets nodded. He'd do just about anything to make his daughter happy.

They landed in Edmonton, Alberta, refueled and headed on to the Queen Elizabeth Islands. Once they landed at a refueling station there, they readied themselves for the final leg of their journey. It was summer and they were truly heading for the land of the midnight sun. It would stay light all twenty-four hours of the day for six months, and then the opposite would be true, because of the angle of the earth towards the sun. Breena wondered what it would be like if they lived in a land that had sun, or darkness, for six months of the year, like that. Her goal in life was to search the world for some place with a completely different culture, one that books could be written about and modern society could not touch. Her father told her one did not exist anymore and even if it did, she could never survive in it. One word, he would joke, against the abilities of women compared to men and they would have a war on their hands. He would tell Breena she was a man's dream of a woman's-libber. She was for equality yet there was nothing she loved more than men. Breena would giggle and agree. After all, she would say, what would the world be without men?

Dr. Keets' expedition to the pole wasn't a new thing or even a big deal. It had all been mapped out before, but Dr. Keets' childhood hero was Robert E. Peary, who was the first man to reach the North Pole in

1909. Dr. Keets had won a bet with Max Jared, who owned an Arctic supply company. He won the privilege of flying to the pole.

As they approached the position where their compasses would go haywire, because of the magnetic forces, they switched to the use of their altimeter to help them fly at a correct altitude and then they headed for true north.

Max Jared kept moving back and forth from the cockpit to his seat beside Dr. Keets. He seemed agitated and worried. A terrible storm had just suddenly appeared. It was the likes of one, Jared had never seen before. All the instruments on the control panel were going crazy and the turbulence was tossing the little plane about as if it was on a trampoline. Max Jared finally took his seat and told everyone to buckle up their seat belts. They were going to attempt an emergency landing. The storm was getting worse and they had no idea where they were. Breena was now sitting beside her brother, and he held her hand tight.

"Don't worry little sister. It'll be all right." Jonathan told her but Breena was unusually calm.

"I know Jon. I'm not worried. We can handle anything together." Breena looked out the window and saw nothing but white.

The storm continued and the little plane was bouncing around so much Breena began to feel nauseated. She closed her eyes. Jonathan suddenly yelled for Breena to look out the window and when she opened her eyes, she saw bits of green through the thick clouds.

"What's that? Why is it green?" She asked but before anyone could answer, she heard a loud crash and the plane began to spin. Untied Items were thrown in every direction. Breena was hit in the head by a small camera bag. She heard her father cry out her name and she felt she was on the worst roller-costar ride of her life. Suddenly everything stopped and her mind went blank, or her mind went blank and everything stopped.

As Breena opened her eyes, she could see daylight through the gaping holes in the fuselage. There was no sense of panic within her nor was there any form of sadness at the sight that surrounded her, as if she was observing through someone else's eyes. In the seat beside her was her brother. He looked to be asleep but the whiteness of his skin and the almost dried blood on his shirt and in his hair, told her otherwise. In the other seats in front of her were the bodies of her father and Max Jared. They too, were abnormally still. Breena unfastened her seat belt and moved towards them. Mr. Jared's eyes were open, in a stare that was empty. He too, had blood on his forehead that had dripped down to his shirt. Her father was sitting in the seat closest to the window, or where the window had once been. It, along with her father's arm, was now gone. Breena couldn't see anyone in the pilot's seat even through the wide hole in the door that once separated the passengers from the pilot. Slowly, Breena moved along towards the exit door that was at the front near the cockpit. The door was still intact but there were two large cavities on either side of it. Still, Breena moved the latch that opened the door of the airplane. It seemed to be stuck and took an effort on her part just to open it enough to squeeze through and escape the fuselage.

Once outside and on the grass, Breena knelt down and examined her own injuries. She had a few bruises and scratches, nothing else. It seemed unfair to her that she would survive and everyone else that remained in the metal body of the plane was silent. Except the pilot, she thought, for he must have exited far before the plane had found its permanent resting spot. Breena stood on wobbly legs to return to the fuselage but everything turned dark once more and she fell to the ground.

This time, when Breena woke, she found herself lying on a cot, inside a room with large brick walls. There was a table, two wooden chairs; and a couple of old trunks in the opposite corner. The window had thick curtains that were pulled apart barely covering the wooden shutters that were half opened. There was no glass in the windows and a warm breeze made the curtains flutter. Breena looked around and she tried to sit up but a stabbing pain in her head forced her back onto the pillow again. The door was tall and made of thick wood. There was a latch instead of a door handle and Breena wondered if she was dreaming all this. Again the darkness came.

Someone was lifting her head and putting a cup of water to her lips. Breena took a sip and blinked a few times to clear her sight. There was a woman beside her. The woman was in her mid-thirties with dark brown hair and tanned colored skin. She was dressed in pale colors and Breena tried to recognize the style but it was foreign to her sense of fashion. The woman had on a long shapeless yellow dress with a robe or long thin flowing jacket over top. She wore no hat but a long colorful scarf hung on her shoulders and down her back as if it had fallen from her head.

"Thank you." Breena said, but the woman gave no reply. "The plane crashed. Did you see my brother and father? They were with me. Are they hurt?"

Again, there was no reply. The woman stood and left the room quickly. Breena slowly sat up and rested on her elbow. Another woman came into the room, similar in dress but with colors of green and white, with a long blue scarf covering her head. She was younger, maybe a little younger than Breena. She had dark brown hair and soft brown eyes. She sat at the bottom of the cot. "English?" Her accent was unfamiliar.

Breena nodded. "My father was in the plane. Is he all right?"

The woman looked as if she was struggling for words. "Men all dead."

Breena covered her face with her hands and collapsed back down onto the cot. She had not remembered anything about the crash until then. She cried for a long time and the woman patted her back and said the word 'sadness' over and over again. It took days for Breena to compose herself enough to carry on a conversation.

Finally, some days later, when one of the women brought her food, she had stopped mourning. The sadness was still there but Breena knew she would have to survive on her own. It was time to work at getting back home. Breena pushed thoughts of her father to the back of her mind. With a forced smile, she looked up at the woman.

"Where am I? It was cold. We were in the Arctic and became lost in a storm and now it's summer. Where is this place?"

"Moatsha. This, city of Moatsha. You from land of cold?" The woman said in broken English.

"No, we were on an expedition to the Arctic. I'm from the United States."

The woman nodded. "Like the others."

"There are others? Can I talk to them?"

The woman shook her head. "They all dead, now. They appear in field after a storm, like you, over the years."

"Where is Moatsha? Is that in Russia or on the northern tip of Canada?"

"Moatsha is much east of Chelm."

Breena rubbed her forehead. This was not helping. How could she get back to the States with directions like that? "Where is that in comparison to the United States?"

"I do not know where United States is."

This was crazy. "How do you know English then?"

"Other man, who comes on machine like yours, teaches it to my family."

"Did he die too?"

"Yes. He was in the legion that protected this city before Arbmoat captured it. We are servants of Arbmoat's house now."

"Maybe if I saw a map of this land then I could tell how far from civilization I am, or better yet, do you have a telephone book?"

"I do not understand the word, telephone."

Breena made a gesture that looked like she was talking on the phone but the woman shrugged her shoulders. Breena looked around. There were no pug-ins for electricity nor were there any phone jacks. Wherever this place was, they were certainly behind the times. The woman brought Breena a map and it showed a landscape that she had never seen before. Being the daughter of Alexander Keets, their house was full of maps, and geography books. She had traveled the world and knew of places and people only seen in magazines. She was a bright intelligent young woman, about to enter university way ahead of her peers, but she had never seen a map like this one. There were no visible landmarks that she could recognize. This map resembled the ancient maps of a time before they discovered the earth was round. There was only one large body of land that encompassed their world. The north and south poles were shaded in with no names or markers and the language was nothing she could distinguish as being a derivative of another language. It had vague similarities to Greek or Hebrew in sound but not in writing. After hours of trying to talk to the woman, Breena began to realize this was not just a situation of her being temporally lost but one of her never being found.

In a week, she would be seventeen and her mother had a wonderful party planned for her. Marty Wellington was going to be there. He was her Dad's brightest first-year student at the university. He had expressed a desire to meet her and she thought he was extremely good looking. Now there would be no party and she may never see her mother again. Breena started to cry at the memory of her father.

Later, the woman brought Breena something to eat. It was some kind of cheese and bread and meat. It tasted like the moose meat her father brought home from his hunting trips. There was a vegetable that looked like a very large radish but tasted more like carrots. The woman encouraged Breena to eat. She smiled and announced, "I am Jaymin. It means 'given to help.' What are you called?"

Breena smiled. "I'm called Breena. It doesn't mean anything. My mother got it from a romance novel and it went well with my family name. She's a writer, in spare time, but she's never published anything. I want to thank you for rescuing me. I imagine if I was left out at the crash site, I might have died."

"My father would like to see you. He said another stray dog would not be trouble and he will see you are skinny and do not eat much, but you must be careful and do not break the laws. The others did not keep the laws and they are all dead now."

"Were they killed because they did not keep the laws?"

"Maybe they were but not by us. Many opportunities were given to them to live the laws and to understand them. Sometimes the law punishes them."

"Well, I will try and keep all the laws. It can't be that hard."

"It is not hard at all. Do all females have hair of sunshine where you come from?"

Breena had not realized how different she looked compared to the young woman beside her. "No. Some have red hair and some have different shades of brown and then there are some who have black hair."

"Most of the Adders have black hair. Most of my peoples' hair is of my color."

"Who are the Adders?"

"They lived in this city before Arbmoat conquered it. We were servants of the Adders before. They are a mighty people who have legions upon legions."

"Well, they can't be that great if they lost a whole city."

Jaymin put her finger to her mouth as if to silence Breena. "They were defeated because of their leader's wickedness. One day they will come up into the city again and it will be Kalat once more."

Over the next few days, Breena was brought before Jaymin's father. He was a large man and Breena soon found out that most of the males were large in stature. There were very few under six feet tall and all looked as if they had spent most of their youth in the gym, body building. He looked at Breena and laughed, then told his daughter that Breena was too skinny to use much food and her skin was pale and sickly and that it was obvious that she was a pampered child. Jaymin's father cautioned her that she would have to labor like the others if she were to stay in their care. Jaymin was instructed to counsel Breena about the laws of coming of age in their land and that she should prepare herself for that.

Breena soon learned the history of the people of the city of Moatsha. At first, it was called the city of Kalat and the people of Adder lived there. It was a huge city and boasted of its fine markets and fine arts. The walls of the city still housed many beautiful paintings on the sides of buildings. The rulers of the city were not industrious and lived off the labor of the people but they had a mighty army with many great captains of their legions. The rulers wanted more land and sent the legions off to conquer other cities. While the legions were gone, Arbmoat came, and drove the rulers from the city. Using the captives, they built up huge walls to surround the city to defend it against the legions when they returned. Arbmoat was very knowledgeable and sent small armies out to defeat parts of the legions as they separated to obtain supplies. With the rulers killed, some of the legions separated and defeated, then the city became Moatsha and never again was called Kalat.

Jaymin told Breena of the other stranger with sun colored hair that was found in the field as Breena was. He was brought to the city when it was still Kalat and a mighty captain befriended him. Jaymin's mother and father were servants to the captain's neighbor. This mighty Captain had a beautiful wife who spent hours talking to the stranger and learned his language. It became popular to learn the English of the stranger. Because of the laws of the women, servants had to be with them at all times for it was unlawful that any man should touch even the hand of another man's wife. Over time the stranger became too friendly with the wife of the captain, but instead of having the stranger put to death, the captain sent him into the army, a legion not his own. The captain loved his wife still and so the overseers did not have her put to death for her iniquity. The captain left the city and lived with his army. His wife was captured when the city became Moatsha and she was taken to another city to become a slave of the king. She died a short time later and it was said that the captain did not grieve.

Breena was taught the ways of the women and it was difficult for her as she saw no equality in their system. Girls became women at the age of sixteen. There was usually a party held with only women present. After the age of eight, females were raised separate from their brothers. Little girls were never touched by their fathers. Not even a hug was permitted. After the age of womanhood, the girls were given long scarves of blue that informed the men of the city that these women were now eligible to marry. When a man saw a female he desired to seek after to become his wife, he could talk to her as long as a servant or family member was present. If she were found acceptable, he would offer her marriage in the form of gifts to both her, and her mother. If the mother accepted the gifts, the daughter was married in a simple ceremony and was sent to live in the home of the new husband. Most new husbands were around thirty, with houses of their own. Their careers were already established and the new wife was placed in a furnished home where she would raise a family. The rich had servants and the poor had none. The servants were usually employed as a family. The servants' social life worked in a similar system but on a smaller scale. Women who did not marry before the age of twenty were considered seconds. They were offered for marriage to men whose wives had died or as second wives to those whose wives could not have children. The second wife was sometimes sought out by the first wife and could not marry the man until the first wife permitted it and the overseer gave his approval. In that case, the second wife was treated with similar respect as the first but had a home of her own on a second level of the house. All women worked together to cook, clean and supply the food for the household. It was considered dishonorable for a man to not have a family as all birthrights worked through the family unit.

Breena could not comprehend the role of women in this society. She was used to spending more time around males than her female friends. Breena could bow-hunt as well as her brother. Even with her high academic scores, she spent a great deal of her time involved in sports. Skinny as she looked around the women of this race, she was sure her endurance for running and the like would far surpass them.

Breena was given clothes similar to Jaymin's, only Jaymin felt because of her hair color; she should have dresses in the shades of soft pastel hues. Of course, because of her age, she was given a long blue scarf that she had to cover her hair with whenever she went out in public. Breena had a terrible time trying to learn the language. Hard as she tried, she could not remember many of the words. Often she pretended she was deaf and mute in public; but conversations were intense with Jaymin and Jaymin was becoming very good at English. Jaymin's younger sister was named Boobie and Breena found herself constantly chuckling at her name. Finally, she told Jaymin what it meant in English and soon they were both laughing at their private joke.

Months went by and Breena became good at helping in the kitchen with Jaymin. They would go outside the city to harvest their gardens and plant the new crops. The seasons were odd as there was no fall or winter and Breena still had a difficult time sleeping at night. The sun did not rise or set as she was used to. In fact, it did not seem to set at all, but the nighttime was the time of the rain. The clouds would come quickly and they would darken the skies.

At the house, Breena was constantly being scolded by Jaymin for wearing her scarf around her waist as a belt or tied in her hair as a headband. She was reminded that the laws governing women were just as strict as those governing men. Both were punishable. In the market place, Breena found that she could take advantage of the women's law in bargaining by standing a bit too close or reaching out and grabbing the items rather than waiting to have them placed before her. Merchants would not dicker but would take their first and lower offer rather than chance touching them, even by accident.

At night Breena would study the map and have Jaymin read to her what was on the maps so she would learn of their geography. Jaymin knew their history very well. The society had a strange sense of industrial progress. Their plumbing and irrigation knowledge were far superior to that of what Breena knew. Each housing unit had separate bathrooms for the owners and servants and each had huge baths with constantly warm water that was filtered automatically. Water was easily supplied to the many gardens both within and throughout the city. Like her culture, one day of the week was set aside to spend in their places of worship. Breena seldom went, as that was where the men sought out the women in blue scarves. Jaymin had a male admirer who was too shy to talk to her as of yet. He spent every worship day staring at her and in the evenings of that same day would walk by their home hoping to catch a glimpse of her in the flower garden. The women were very big on growing flowers and the yard around the house was usually full of them. A little portion of the back yard was set aside for herbs.

There was always a big shady tree in the back with a bench under it for someone to sit on.

The only time Breena ever saw the men of the household was during the meal. Men sat on one side and the women on the other. Jaymin's family consisted of two daughters and four sons but two of the sons were married and one was in the army and lived in a house of his own. Their house was beside the one of their employers. Their house was about two thousand square feet and the home they worked in was twice that size at least.

One evening, as Breena sat in the backyard, under the shady tree, Jaymin's mother came up to her with Jaymin. They were both giggling. A man Breena had seen a few times in the worship place was standing at the entrance of the garden and at first Breena thought that it was Jaymin's admirer. Jaymin told Breena that the man's name was Ashermer and he had come to talk to her. Breena was not impressed. Ashermer was tall like all the other men but there was nothing attractive to her about a thirty-year old man. Breena was still dreaming about the guys her own age, back home.

"Did you tell him that I can't speak his language and I'm way too skinny and sickly?"

Jaymin giggled. "He is a carpenter and has a nice house. He does not mind your flaxen hair."

"Oh Jaymin; he is so old and he looks boring."

"His first wife was a beautiful woman from the city of Fosh. She died a year ago."

"I'm to be a second?" Breena put her hands to her mouth in mock outrage. "Great. Not only do you want me to marry an old man but to be a second too? This is outrageous."

Jaymin leaned close as if she was afraid she would be heard, even though only she and her brother Mid, and her father knew English. "You cannot be choosy. You are a stranger and with yellow hair. Many think you are bad luck."

Breena laughed. "If I am to be a second then I'll wait until I am twenty to marry. There is still so much I have to learn and maybe there are things I can teach you."

Jaymin walked over and talked to the man, then returned to Breena again. The man turned and left the garden. "Sherner says he will visit again. He wants children with yellow hair."

Breena shook her head. "He doesn't know much about the gene pool probabilities, does he? With your race's coloring it is doubtful any children I have, will be blond. They might have lighter hair color and maybe a glimpse of blue in their eyes but not much of a chance of any blue-eyed blondes."

Jaymin gave Breena a funny look and Breena knew she did not understand.

Ashermer did return a couple of times but Breena, although polite did not offer him any encouragement. Jaymin would scold her after Ashermer had left as Breena would act asinine and childish, but Breena would laugh and tell Jaymin not to worry. She felt no feelings of inadequately because she was not yet married off.

Suddenly Ashermer's visits stopped and Breena was relieved until Jaymin told her she had found out why the visits stopped. The king of the land where the city of Moatsha was, had heard of Breena. She was a novelty and he was sending a messenger to see her. The messenger was to see if her looks matched the stories he had heard of her. Rumor had spread that the bold female stranger was as pretty as a delicate flower, and that the king desired to have her in his household if the story was true.

Breena had seen a painting of the king, and she knew that she wanted little to do with him. He was tall, fat, and burly. Jaymin said he was evil and many women died in his household. She was worried for Breena and they planned for her to flee Moatsha for the city of Chelm. It belonged to the people of Adder, but at least she would not have to worry about the king there. Chelm had no king, only a set of overseers to run the government. They would not kill a stranger, just because they came from another city.

The night the messenger was to arrive, the city was attacked by a huge legion, and all the women were sent into hiding in their homes. Breena wanted to see this legion in action and persuaded Jaymin to take her to the front walls where they could see the battle off in the distance. Many of the men left to defend the city on the battlefield, including Jaymin's admirer. The girls slipped passed the guards at the huge gate made of logs and up the steps to the top of the wall that circumvented the city.

The strategy of the battle seemed very archaic to Breena. It seemed senseless for two armies to go out and battle one another when the city could be defended with little effort from the vary walls they stood upon. Man against man, with swords and bows and hatchets. These people had not heard of gunpowder, or weapons that did not require face-to-face confrontation. It took Breena's breath away to watch the tragic scene of carnage before her. So many died and the sounds and cries were overwhelming to the soul. Breena kept repeating how stupid these men were, over and over. It went on for days and group after group of men left the city to replenish the troops that fell. Soon, all that remained were the young boys, very old men, and the females of the city. Terror was sweeping through every household as defeat meant death for the males and slavery for the women, which usually ended in death for them, too. It was the Adders and they were a potent force when their legions were together.

Breena could not understand the women's compromising attitude, and she was not about to just lie down and die, nor was she going to stand back and watch the young male children be killed. Breena told Jaymin to gather the women into the front public square just inside the gate. She told her to use whatever influence she had to get them there. Jaymin told everyone that Breena was magical and could save them and with Breena's unusual reputation, many believed.

Breena tied her scarf around her waist to keep it out of her way. She climbed onto the wall. With Jaymin following her, Breena asked her to translate for her. Breena gave a speech to the women that was similar to a talk she had heard at a woman's rally years before, only changing things in the talk to suit the situation. She told them they were the only ones who could control their destiny; they were left to protect their children. It was their time to be mighty and strong. With her inspiration, they joined together and pushed closed the huge gate and locked it with the log size latch. Breena encouraged them, as they pushed the gate closed. She told them they were the strong ones, the enduring ones.

Next; she told them, that in order to defend the walls, they would have to bring all the large vats they could find, to the tops of the walls. They were to fill them with oil of any kind and to supply a heat source under the vats. This the women did and Breena explained that if they saw the soldiers attempting to scale the walls they were to pour buckets full of hot oil upon them. Guards were appointed and a continuous watch was kept. Next, they made baskets from Breena's directions, in the shape of Lacrosse racquets. Softball sized stones were gathered and other women were placed on the walls to use the racquets to propel the rocks at the invading army. Breena had the women find all the weapons that were left in the city and to bring them to the overseer's house that they had turned into a command center. Even Breena was impressed with how well the women worked together and she knew her father would be proud of her effort, even if she had doubts how long they could hold out.

They were a stronghold for weeks and Breena taught somehow to shoot a bow. They weren't very accurate but the sight of the women shooting their arrows sent the warriors scrambling. Not knowing where the arrows would hit was almost as threatening as accurately hitting their targets. The women were becoming excessively confident that they could keep the enemy at bay forever and Breena sat in the overseer house worrying that the end would come quickly with disastrous results. If these men were similar to the Roman legions Breena had studied in school, not only were they repelling them, they were humiliating them tremendously and that was enough to make the legions want to take the city at any cost.

Breena had made a crude model of the city and the surrounding area, to see what options they had in this bizarre battle. As she studied the model, Jaymin came in excited about what she had heard the women saying.

"We are victorious, Breena. They will never take the city."

Breena looked up. She was very tired and the responsibility of the position she was in was starting to show. "I had hoped that there would be help from the other cities in the kingdom by now, Jaymin."

"But why are they needed? We are doing well."

Breena sighed. "Our supply of oil is getting low and we have had to knock down walls of buildings just to keep the supply of rocks going for the racquets."

"We will defeat them. Do not worry."

Breena sat down on the bench that was behind her and rubbed her face with her hands. "Our arrows will be gone in a few days. Do you have any idea what's next? Hand to hand combat. I have done more harm than good, Jaymin."

"Combat? What is that? You have done a good thing."

"Combat is what the men were doing in the field." She looked over the little model again. "I don't have the tools I need to do anymore."

"We will do well. Soon they will go away."

"If they get in, Jaymin, make sure they are told it was my leadership that kept them out there. I'm the only one responsible." She pushed her hair away from her face. "And please stay beside me. I'm lost without you being there to translate."

Jaymin nodded.

CHAPTER TWO

OVER IN THE CAMP of the legion, the captain was discussing the situation with his assistants. Minab was a massive male, bigger than most. He stood well over six and a half feet tall and his shoulders were broad. The biceps on his arms were wide, the girth of them being that of Breena's waist. His hair was raven black, shoulder length, and wavy. It looked as if it was trimmed with a knife. His skin was not dark but rather like someone who had spent a month on vacation in Hawaii. The uniform he wore, although fancier than the soldiers beneath him, was similar to theirs. There was chest armor made of leather and engraved metal, with a wide leather belt and thick leather shoulder straps. The pants were short and ended at the knee. From the knee to the boot were bulky leather protectors. Solid leather guards also garnished his forearms and the back of his hands, giving support as they carried their heavy sword. The helmet was similar to the Roman headgear, except there were no feathers for decoration, just a wide red leather strip that stood up in the middle and ran from the front to the back of the helmet. The sword he carried was solid polished steel. Its sheath was brilliantly carved brass. The captain was the Adder's most respected commander. He was sent to recapture his home township and was outraged when news from his operatives came back that mere females were holding them back.

One of his spies was Kabay, friend, and closest trustee. He offered to enter the city and kill the leader of the rebels. He found that the weakest point of the city was on the Westside, near the back. Although the back walls could not be scaled, the weak area he had found, could, and without detection. Once the leader fell, the others would surrender. Minab agreed with the plan but said he and two others would accompany Kabay. While he and Kabay slew the leader, the others would open the city gates to their legion. They would do this during the evening rain when they could not be seen as well.

As the rain began to fall, the legion drew quietly closer to the city, and Minab and the other three climbed the wall on the side near the back. It had been the custom over the past three weeks for the legion to rest during the rain and Breena figured this evening would be no different. The lookouts relaxed at their post while the rest of the city rested. Breena and Jaymin slept on cots, in the main area in their headquarters at the overseer's house.

Minab and Kabay burst into the room with their swords drawn. Jaymin screamed and sunk onto the floor. Breena was startled, but she grabbed one of the smaller swords to defend herself. Even though it was a small sword, it was still extremely heavy and as she swung it around it almost pulled her off her feet. With all her might, she held it up and waited.

Kabay and Minab, dripping wet from the rain outside, lowered their weapons at the sight of Breena struggling to keep the sword in the air. They were not accustomed to such a sight and Kabay laughed. Minab, dead serious, shouted for her to drop her weapon on the floor. Breena did not comprehend his words and stood her ground. Minab shouted again and this time Jaymin cried out what the words meant. Breena lowered her sword quickly and it sparked as the metal hit the stone floor tiles, but she did not release her grip. She kept her gaze on Minab and wondered if anyone else could hear her heart pounding.

"Tell them I am the one who organized the women, Jaymin." Breena said slowly.

Jaymin told them and this time Minab smirked. He yelled again for her to drop her weapon. Breena remained steadfast. With one unconstrained swing, Minab hit the blade of Breena's sword, knocking it out of her hand and across the room. Breena grabbed the palm of her hand as the handle ripped out of her grip. It left a small cut that bled considerably. Jaymin started to cry and even Breena began to tremble at her inevitable fate. She didn't know what to do, so she just stood there, her eyes fastened on Minab's every move. Minab walked over to Breena and took a small portion of her hair in his hand. He looked at it and then he sheathed his sword. Slowly he took out his knife and cut a small lock of her hair off. Breena looked down, afraid to look into his fierce glare. She hoped he did not notice that she was shaking. What would he cut next?

Kabay asked Minab if they were going to kill them. Jaymin started to cry even harder and Breena knew good things were not being spoken.

"Tell them we were only protecting our loved ones, Jaymin." Breena said quietly and Jaymin shouted it out so quickly Breena wondered if they understood.

Minab looked at Jaymin and then back at Breena. He took his knife and with a sudden jerk to her waist, cut the blue scarf from around Breena's mid-section. He told Kabay that such an execution should be public to be effective. Casually, he placed the scarf across Breena's wounded hand.

Breena wrapped the scarf around her hand and looked up at Minab. "Are you the captain?" She turned to Jaymin who was still huddled on the floor. "He has to be the leader, right Jaymin?" Her voice almost stuttered the words.

Jaymin stopped crying and looked at Breena. "Yes Breena. It is Minab. I remember him from when he lived here before. He is their greatest captain."

"Was he the one who lost this city before?"

"No, he was not here then. Breena, please be silent. He is going to kill us."

Breena had sized him up already, and had gained courage from logic. "No, I don't think so. We held them back for almost four weeks. It would look cowardly to sneak in here and kill us. We're just measly females. Where is the honor in that? Ask him if there is honor in killing women who have not even lived long enough to be married."

"Minab is mighty and very embittered. I am afraid and cannot say that to him."

"Tell him I want to know about his honor, not you."

Minab walked over to Kabay and whispered something to him. Kabay slowly shook his head. Jaymin told Minab what Breena requested to know, making it perfectly clear that it was Breena, not she, that had asked. Jaymin was very frightened.

Minab walked over to Breena. He came so close Breena fell backwards as she tried to keep away from him. He shouted a few sentences at her then stormed out of the room. Kabay followed him. Breena got up off the floor and sat down on the cot she had been previously sleeping on.

"I don't suppose they've left the city. What did he yell at me?"

Jaymin shook her head. "Minab said that there would be as much honor in your death as there is when a Zibo is killed."

"What's a Zibo?"

"It is a really ugly bug that has legs of a spider and wings like a fly. It is a freak of nature, found in our forest. It eats leaves and although it is not harmful to people, it likes to fly around them and buzz in their ears." She walked over to Breena and sat down beside her. "We are going to die, Breena. I am sure of it." They gave each other hugs.

Breena could possibly accept her fate. Her father was dead and she would never see her mother or home again. Maybe it was that life here wasn't worth a fight anymore, or maybe nothing seemed real anyway. But poor Jaymin; her father and brothers were also dead, now. They were in the army sent to defend the city. It was real to Jaymin, and she knew the horrors of being a captive of war. This must have been terrifying to her. "I'm sorry, Jaymin."

Jaymin started to cry again.

There was a guard placed outside the room that Breena and Jaymin were in, and sounds of the military, moving through the city could be heard through the windows from the streets below. Breena heard no screams or crying from the women and she hoped that meant no one was being hurt. Kabay came back into the room and asked Jaymin if she knew where the overseer's wife was. He wanted her to retrieve her personal belongings from the house Breena had set up as a command point. Minab had claimed the house for his own use.

Guards took Breena and Jaymin to the master bedroom of the house and soon another officer arrived. He told Jaymin who he was and she explained to Breena that he was a physician, sent to minister to her hand. Physicians were the only males allowed physical contact with females who were not their own wives, for obvious reasons, but after months of little exchange with men, Breena felt uneasy. He placed certain herb powders on her cut and wrapped it in a clean bandage.

Minab and Kabay were in the adjoining room discussing the situation.

"It would not be wise to execute them. It would make them martyrs." Minab said as they sat looking over the small model Breena had made. "Look at this." He pointed at the back of the city in the model. "They knew all the weak spots in the city except the one we came over. They are not ordinary females."

"The yellow-haired one is not ordinary and she is a stranger, much like Miller." Kabay watched for Minab's reaction.

"I know. It is difficult to look at her. It brings out the rage I still have towards Miller's kind." Someone brought them food and they began to eat slowly. They had their helmets off but had not removed their swords. "We cannot let them live. It would be said, I gave into pity because they are women. If the yellow hair lived, she would surely organize a rebellion."

"If they took a pledge and we made them slaves to the Adders?"

"It would be dangerous to put someone like her in with suppressed people. She must be watched very closely. She must be humiliated into submission; otherwise the women will believe her to be eminent."

Kabay thought for a moment, and then grinned. "There is a way to do that and it would conclude your retribution upon her kind."

"How?"

"If you were to make her your second, she would have to be submissive to your will and your honor over Miller would be vindicated."

"You talk foolishness! I could not espouse such a Zibo."

"She would become your underling and the women would know she is no different than any other wife. Think of it, Minab. She is ingenious and a warrior in her soul. She would give you warrior sons."

"She is too skinny and pale to produce sons of any kind."

"If she was to die in childbirth, it would not be your fault and then you may choose another. You are a captain and have no posterity. If she was to have an Adder male child, it would compensate for Miller's betrayal."

Minab thought silently for a few moments then he looked at Kabay again. "How could I force a strong disposition like that to submit to such a marriage? She would die rather than live such a life. I can see it in her eyes."

"She is a fighter, but still a female. She will not sanction others to be hurt for her sake. Women are very sacrificial. If she will not agree then we will tell her we will kill the children of the city. A yellow hair will not allow that."

Minab and Kabay came back into the room where the two women were. Minab ordered Kabay to force Breena into a kneeling position. Kabay pushed Breena down onto her knees and carefully moved her hair to the side of her neck. The fact that he touched her showed he held no regard for them as female. He told Jaymin to tell Breena to prepare to die. Jaymin told Breena and then began to beg for mercy. Breena lowered her head and took a deep breath. She was sure the end was impending. Still, it frightened her and she wondered if there would be great pain. Should she close her eyes or leave them open? Would she actually see death? Breena started to tremble again and she bit her lip to prevent herself from crying out as Jaymin had.

Kabay drew his sword out and Jaymin fell to the floor shrieking.

Minab waited until the sword was in the air before he put forth his hand and stopped Kabay. He told Jaymin to be silent and he would tell her how the yellow-haired could receive mercy. Jaymin listened intensely.

"Tell the Zibo that I will spare her if she will become my second. I am in need of a lineage." Minab tone was of indifference.

Jaymin told Breena exactly what Minab said and Breena's eyes widened. "Is he crazy? Why would I marry some unwieldy mass of an anthropoid mercenary? I maybe a Zibo, but he's not going to get his steroid-filled primate hands on me. I'd rather die." She may have been young but she wasn't an infant. Having him touch her was more appalling than the prospect of death.

Jaymin shook her head and begged Breena to reconsider. Minab grabbed the sword from Kabay and raised it in one hand while pushing Breena's head down with the other. "Tell her after her demise, we will slay all the children in the city."

Jaymin translated and Breena immediately held out her hands and asked them to wait. She could not have the deaths of the children on her conscience. "Jaymin; tell him, tell him I will agree if he does not harm any of the children, not even the males."

Jaymin interpreted Breena's words and Minab pushed Breena's head down further. "You have no bargaining strength, Zibo."

Jaymin told Breena what he said but Breena was not willing to except it. "Telling him I will also talk to the women. I will tell them we were wrong in defending the city against them; that Adder rule will be much better than that of Moatsha."

Minab released his grip on Breena's neck as Jaymin imparted Breena's offer. The two men nodded then left the room immediately.

Jaymin hugged Breena and Breena collapsed on the floor with relief. "This is such a nightmare! I used to be happy, Jaymin. I was going to a foremost university and dating gorgeous, but normal guys. My life was all mapped out for success and tranquility. Now, I am walking in hell!" Breena started to cry. "I don't want to marry anyone, especially some colossal behemoth, who thinks I'm just a Zibo."

"Minab is the captain who befriended the other yellow-haired stranger I told you about. You will be payment for the other's betrayal with his first wife. Minab hates your kind. I told you he is very bitter."

The information only made Breena cry harder. She wept for almost an hour until there seemed to be no tears left. Breena wiped her eyes and went into the bathroom to wash her face.

The two men returned with another who was dressed differently. He had no armor on. Minab made Breena kneel again and Breena was quivering as Minab knelt beside her and took her hand in his. She immediately pulled away. Minab became angry and grabbed her hand tightly. The man, without the armor, spoke to them for almost five minutes and Breena did not understand what was being said. Jaymin opened her mouth to translate but Breena shook her head. "It doesn't matter. I have an idea what this is and I really don't want to know the details." Breena whispered to Jaymin.

After it was over and the man in soft clothes had placed a hand on Minab and Breena's head, they stood up. "Jaymin, ask them what is to become of you. It is not fair that you be punished for what I did. Besides; what more could they inflict upon me that could be any worse than this?"

Jaymin asked and Kabay gave her a quick smile. He told her she would be kept around to interpret to the Zibo. He looked at Jaymin in a manner that made her blush and turn away from his gaze. Then he told her he wanted to keep an eye on her personally, to make sure she was obedient to the new laws of the city. Kabay was younger than Minab and had been looking for a wife for some time. Jaymin's boldness and fortitude made her very desirable to him. He too, wanted strong courageous sons. The men left the room again.

Jaymin explained that because Minab's first wife was dead, the ceremony was necessary. If she had been alive, Minab would have the right to make her his second just by bringing her into his household, with the first wife's permission. Hours passed and they returned. This time they took Jaymin and Breena to the courtyard near the gate. All the others in the city had been assembled and soldiers surrounded them. Minab told Jaymin to tell Breena to speak and to keep her promise or there would be instant reprisal. Breena, with Jaymin translating, told the women they had protected their loved ones and that was good but now it was time to surrender to the Adder's rule. She told them they would be safe and the lives of their children were promised to be spared. She hesitated but finally told them she had submitted to Minab's will and would do her best to obey the new rulers. The speech was short and to the point with no capricious sentences said to make the Adder's look overly good.

They separated Breena from Jaymin and she was taken back to the room in the overseer's house where she had previously been. She tried to look out the window but the shutters were locked and she could not open them. It was the first time since she crashed in that land that she was separated from Jaymin and she felt very alone. Hours went by and finally the door opened to the room but it was Minab that entered. Breena backed up into a corner as far away from him as she could. Minab gave no notice of her. He walked over to the big bed and started to undo the buckles on the side of his chest armor that held the back and front together. He took it off and placed it on a chair near the bed. Next he carefully took off his large waist belt with the sheathe that held his sword. Finally, he took off his leg and arm protectors and placed them on the chair. Breena sat down in the corner, fearing that he would want to come near her. Minab walked into the washing room and after a few moments Breena could hear him bathing in the tub. When he came out, he was wearing a long shirt that came down to his ankles and had an open neck. He lay on the bed and covered himself with the thin blanket. Breena sat motionless and could hear his breathing become relaxed and she knew he was a sleep. It had been the most stressful day of her life, even worse than the day she crashed. Exhaustion quickly convinced her to sleep, and she lay in the corner all night.

When she woke the next day, she was alone in the room. The door was locked. She was lonely and hungry and hours passed before Jaymin entered the room with some food.

"You are well?" Jaymin asked as she placed the tray of food on the table by the chair.

"Yes. I slept on the floor, in the corner, all night." Breena started to eat as soon as she sat down. She hadn't eaten at all the day before, and she was hungry.

"He did nothing?" Jaymin was surprised.

Breena swallowed what was in her mouth. "He slept there, and I slept in the corner." She said pointing to the bed. "So, Minab is the one whose wife fooled around with the other strange like me?"

"Fooled around?"

"Did unlawful touching, you know."

"He is the same one I told you about."

"What was this stranger's name?"

Jaymin thought for a long while. "Miller I think. It did not mean anything either or maybe he said his ancestors made bread."

"And your family was the servants?"

"Neighbors to the servants. It was a great game to learn the English."

"So he can't be a violent man if he didn't kill this Miller guy or his wife, right?"

Jaymin shook her head. "He did not become the Adder's greatest commander by being passive." Jaymin had brought Breena a change of clothes. There was another pale blue dress but she had brought her a multi-colored scarf with it. She held it out to her.

"I never thought I'd miss that stupid blue scarf." Breena finished her meal and then bathed before she dressed in the clean clothes. She twisted the scarf and put it on her head as a headband to keep her hair out of her face. Jaymin had also brought brushes, one for the hair and another for the teeth.

"They are setting up rule in the city. Minab found out you were fancied by the king and he is pleased that he has denied him of that desire."

Breena looked in the tin mirror and fixed her scarf headband. "I maybe an ugly little Zibo but, at least, I'm a clean one."

"My mother grieves over my father and brothers. They have allowed me to see her. I must go." She collected the empty plate and cup.

"Oh, yes. You must. Tell your mother I'm sorry."

Jaymin hugged Breena and left. Again, Breena was alone. The physician came into the room and checked Breena's hand. Without Jaymin, there could be no conversation. Breena just gave him a thankful smile. He kept looking at her headband as if it was an odd sight. Then he left.

It started to rain and Breena knew it was night. Minab entered the room and again Breena backed up into a corner. This time he looked at her, and when he noticed her scarf had been twisted around her hair, he approached her. Roughly, he pulled it off and threw it on the floor to show his disapproval. Breena decided right then, she would always wear it improperly, no matter how much he disapproved. It would be her emblem of rebellion. It might be the only thing she could do to feel like an individual character, in this crazy world.

Again, Minab quietly removed his armor and bathed. This time when he returned, he walked immediately over to Breena and grabbed her by the arm. She resisted the best she could, but it was like resisting a bulldozer. Breena squirmed, kicked, and hit at Minab, but he plopped her on the bed with no effort at all. He was constantly yelling at her but Breena did not understand. As he tried to kiss her, she burst into tears. She cried all night long as she unsuccessfully fought against his impervious strength and determination.

Minab left early in the morning and Breena spent hours in the bath, washing Minab's touch from her skin. Jaymin did not return for two days, and by then Breena was despondent from Minab's abuse.

Jaymin came in and was shocked to find Breena's condition but she did not discuss her circumstance. "We can go to the market if you'd like. I have asked, and you are allowed to go. The women have taken up the market in place of their husbands. Come, see how Adder rules. It is not as bad as we thought it would be."

Breena reluctantly agreed. Before she left she put her hair in a ponytail using the scarf as a bow.

"Breena don't wear the scarf like that. You will cause trouble."

"I don't care." Her voice was hollow.

"Please, Breena."

Breena shook her head. "You do not understand, Jaymin. He can't do anything more to me. I just don't care."

They left for the market place and Breena was surprised to see that things were running smoothly. Someone was operating a puppet show and for a few minutes, Breena momentarily lost herself in the fun of watching the silly little play. A small group of the soldiers came through the market flirting with the women and enjoying themselves, by eating some of the local foods prepared there. They stopped in front of Breena and Jaymin, and Breena looked down. She was not ready to look any male in the face. One of the soldiers boldly started talking to Jaymin and she reluctantly answered his questions. He wanted to know if the yellow-haired one belonged to anyone or was that the new way widows wore their scarves. He touched the scarf and Breena cringed. Jaymin quickly started to explain who they were when Kabay came rushing up, followed by an enraged Minab. Minab pushed the young soldier and drew his sword. The soldier pleaded with Minab to hear him out and Breena was terrified what would happen. She begged Minab to listen, that it was a harmless gesture but Minab paid no attention to her English, and ordered the young soldier to draw his sword. Breena began to cry and she hugged Minab's feet, trying to prevent him from hurting the young man. Minab picked her up by one arm and pushed her away, sending the other men fleeing to keep out of her way. Kabay told Jaymin to hold Breena back. The fight was over instantly and as Minab thrust the sword into the soldier, Breena fainted. Minab wiped clean his sword and sheathed it. He looked at Kabay, then casually walked over to Breena, picked her up in his arms, and carried her home.

Breena regained consciousness just as they entered the bedroom. Being in Minab's arms sent her into a panic and she tried to escape. Minab held on to her tightly and ordering Jaymin to tell her to calm down. Jaymin had to hurry just to keep up with them and she was a little out of breath.

"Do not struggle Breena. Minab has just brought you home. You were faint."

Minab put her down on the bed and roughly pulled the scarf from her hair. Breena backed away, but still remained on the bed.

"Tell him to go away. He is a murderer!" She held out her hands, palms facing him, but she knew it was no defense.

Jaymin eyes widened. She did not dare translate.

Minab seemed to explode in angry. He came within inches of Breena's face. "What did she say?" He shouted at Jaymin.

No answer.

"I can take my sword out again, and this time I will cut off your useless ears. What did she say?" Minab directed his question at Jaymin.

She started to cry. "She said for you to go away. That you were a... murderer."

Minab paused, and then in a much calmer tone he told Jaymin to tell Breena that he would not allow anyone to touch his wife. He was the commander of a great army and what was his, belonged to no one else.

"I am not your wife. I am your Zibo. That poor man did not even touch me. He touched my scarf." Breena answered Jaymin and Jaymin relayed Breena's reply back to Minab.

Minab laughed. He had thought of her as just that. "The young soldier will not live long enough to see old age if he continues to be so bold. I did not kill anyone. He may lose the use of his arm though." Minab sat up and moved to the end of the bed. "I am an accomplished swordsman. I meant to hurt him, not kill him. Tell her that and then leave us."

Jaymin did so and left. Breena looked away. She did not want to see Minab's eyes staring at her. Minab rose from the bed and left the room. He returned later with a plateful of cheeses and vegetables and a jug of some kind of drink. He offered Breena some and she refused to look at him. During his absence, Breena had moved to her spot in the corner where he had pulled her from, again and again. Minab looked at her and shrugged his shoulders, and then he ate the food on the plate. Later that evening, he continued his routine of bathing and showing no kindness towards Breena before he fell asleep.

The next day Minab offer Breena food at lunchtime. She had not eaten since the morning, the day before, but she refused the food and again he ate it all himself. The following morning Minab retrieved more food and did not offer Breena any. He ate the entire plateful himself. Jaymin had not been permitted to visit Breena. Loneliness and boredom filled her day. Breena watched as Minab ate the food. She was so hungry she could imagine how it tasted and the smell of the meat on the plate made her mouth water.

That evening when Minab brought food in to the room Breena watched every move he made. He spoke to her, telling her all that was on the plate but he knew she did not understand. He held out a piece of fruit that looked like a peeled banana. Breena licked her lips. He walked over to her corner and sat down on the floor, crossed legged. He was closer now but she would still have to move to reach the food.

Minab waited, with his hand stretched out to her, for a while. Never had he seen such tenacity, even in a man, let alone a woman. Minab placed the fruit back down on the plate and folded his arms. He could watch her for as long as she could watch him. He moved back and rested against the bed.

Soon Minab closed his eyes for a second and then he drifted off into a light sleep. Breena watched as his head leaned slightly to the left and she knew he was snoozing. Slowly, she inched her way towards the food. Just as she picked up the banana-like fruit, Minab's eyes opened and he grabbed her wrist. Breena dropped the food. Why was this, an amusing game to him? Did he not see she was hungry? She put her head down and refused to look up as he talked to her.

"You are so stubborn." Minab said in his own language as he saw her drop the food. He picked it up and offered it to her. She would have to take from his hand if she really wanted it.

Breena was too hungry to fight anymore. She tried to take the fruit but Minab did not release his hold. Was this another game of his?

Breena looked up at him and he shook his head. She lowered her hand and almost cried out with frustration. He offered her the fruit again, this time putting it up to her lips. Breena bit her lower lip to prevent herself from crying. He wanted to feed her. She collapsed on the floor and covered her head with her arms. This time the frustration spilled out in tears. Minab put the food down on the plate and while Breena continued to sob, he left the room, leaving her alone with the food.

Later that evening, Minab came back and found the plate empty and Breena sleeping in the corner on the floor. He picked her up and carried her to the bed. Maybe, thought Minab, she was not as ugly as the Zibo and her hair, though different, was soft and lustrous.

CHAPTER THREE

OVER THE NEXT MONTH, Minab organized the governing of the city. It was now the city of Kalat, again, and certain governing bodies had to be in place before the Adder overseers sent the officials in to rule. Minab's permanent residence was in Chelm, two weeks of travel away, and he could not return until things were set up and in order. Kabay would stay with the majority of the legion and transfer the rule of the city to the new overseer. Minab wanted everything ready so he could return earlier but even with all the preparations needed to be made, it would take another two months before he could leave.

Breena had spent a great deal of time confined to the house. They still had their battles over her scarf. Minab was determined not to allow Breena out in public without the proper apparel, but the scarf continued to be a headband or sometimes even a belt.

Kabay was now properly courting Jaymin, visiting her family, and then sending gifts to her mother, who up until now had refused them and sent them back. She did not want her daughter marrying Adder. Finally, Kabay visited Jaymin's mother and told her if her daughter wed him she would never be a servant again but if it was not permitted, he would not allow her to wed anyone and she would become a second. He offered Jaymin's mother a gift of a small string of gold beads. It was the most valuable piece of jewelry she had ever seen. She accepted it and thus accepted the marriage proposal for her daughter.

Breena was just finishing her morning bath. Sometimes she would scrub herself almost raw as she tried to get the feel of Minab's touch from her skin. Minab had come home late after Breena had fallen asleep on the floor in the corner, and had quickly left in the morning, so Breena did not spend as much time in the huge bath as she usually did. As she combed out her hair, Jaymin came in to see her. She almost bounced into the room.

"Why do you look so unhappy?" Breena asked sarcastically.

Jaymin looked perplexed. "I am not unhappy. Do I not smile?"

Breena shook her head when she realized sarcasm was lost on Jaymin. "You look happy Jaymin. What has happened?"

"My family has accepted Kabay's proposal. We will wed."

Breena tried to smile. In a way, she was envious. Kabay actually seemed to care for Jaymin. At least he made her smile and could even make her blush with just a wink of his eye, in the right manner. Nevertheless, he was too similar to Minab for Breena to like him. With all the time they spent together, they had to have same attitude towards women.

"Can you go out to the market?"

Breena shook her head. She had worn her scarf as a belt yesterday. It was very warm and putting the scarf over her head was too hot for her. Minab had been so upset at her defiance; he raised his hand to her. He didn't hit her, but instead, stormed out of the room, knocking over the table and candle sticks as he left.

"Please wear the scarf properly, Breena. I want you at my ceremony next week. Kabay says I will live here in the overseer's house when we are wed, while he organizes things for the new overseer."

"What new overseer? I thought Minab was the overseer."

"Only for a little while; until the government in the city is fully organized. Minab lives in Chelm."

"Do you think he'll go home and leave me here with your people?" Breena was worried she would be isolated from Jaymin forever. She didn't know anyone else who could speak her language and the silence was torture.

Jaymin knew that was unlikely but she did not want to upset Breena. "Maybe, he did not live with his first wife."

"Only after the Miller thing." Breena was not going to let it get her down. "But after the Miller thing she became a Zibo to him and I'm already one so maybe he'll leave me behind."

Over the next few days Breena wore her scarf correctly, except it would slip off her head and she would leave it down. The day of the ceremony Breena watched as Minab dressed in his armor. Servants had polished it until it gleamed in the sunlight. Breena sat in the corner of the room with her scarf upon her head. She didn't know how to ask to go and it was beginning to look as if Minab would ignore her completely. He finally put on his wide belt that held his sword, which was the last thing he always put on. He left the room without even acknowledging Breena's presence.

Breena sighed and pulled off her scarf. "Sorry, Jaymin," she said to herself. It was going to be another boring day of being imprisoned in her room. She sat for an hour singing to herself. Minab came back into the room and said something to her. She stood up even though she didn't understand. He walked over to her, picked up her scarf, and handed it to her. She placed it on her head. Normally, she was determined not to ever be that cooperative but she was doing it for Jaymin. He gripped her forearm and led her out of the room, down the stairs and out of the house. They walked to Jaymin's house and Breena had a difficult time keeping pace with Minab. When they entered the house Jaymin's mother hugged Breena and showed her where to sit. Breena couldn't talk to anyone so she sat quietly. Every time she looked about, she felt as if the people there were staring at her, judging her. Maybe they all knew she was wed to a man who openly detested her. If they only knew the reason, she chose marriage instead of death.

Jaymin came into the room dressed in a brilliant red. Her scarf was white and Breena thought she looked very beautiful. They knelt as Breena, Minab had, and the same man in soft clothes spoke words over them. He placed his hand on both their heads and then it was over. Everyone gathered around and started to eat the food that was served.

As Breena hugged Jaymin, her scarf fell down and Breena made no attempt to put it back over her head. Minab walked over to her and placed the scarf upon her head, himself. Breena couldn't take it any longer. She pulled the scarf off her head and threw it to the floor in front of Minab's feet, and then she turned and ran. She ran outside and through street after street, heading for the city's gate. If she could only get out of the city before Minab caught up with her. Even if he dragged her back, in her heart she would have won that battle. She could see the gate and it seemed to be so close.

Breena was too afraid to turn around and see if Minab was following her. There the gate was, right in front of her. She lifted the hem of her dress up higher so she could run faster. She was strong and young and all her track running was finally paying off. At a full run, she was out the gate and she wasn't slowing down. Her new goal was the trees in the distance but she could hear something behind her. She gave a quick glance behind her and screamed when she saw Minab on his horse, closing in fast. It seemed in less than an instant he was in front of her and off his horse. She turned to avoid him but he grabbed her and pulled her down. She hit his arm with a thud that almost knocked out what little wind she had left in her.

"I won't. You'll never make me. I will never ever wear that scarf properly, no matter how long I'm imprisoned in that room! Throw me into the deepest, darkest dungeon you have. I still won't." Breena screamed at him, and then she began to sob loudly. "I hate this place. I want' a go home. I want my Mom!" She put her head on his arm and wept.

Minab didn't hit her like Breena thought he would. He just held her tight in his arms, while she wept. When Breena calmed down, Minab picked her up and placed her on his horse. She was too exhausted to run anymore and she knew Minab would catch her before she got very far anyway. As he led them back through the city gate, one of Minab's men shouted something to him. Minab looked back at the horse and at Breena, and shook his head. Then he shouted something back and some of the guards laughed.

Breena didn't need a psychology degree to know they were laughing at her. Her high IQ, and expectations for being the youngest graduate of her father's university, did little for her now. She was no more than an experiment herself. Breena closed her eyes, hung her head, and wished them all away. Minab lifted her down from the horse and Breena resented that even the horses were enormous, like the old workhorses she remembered from her grandparent's farm. Breena ran up to the bedroom and flung herself onto the bed. Nothing was accomplished and she probably ruined Jaymin's wedding.

Jaymin was moved into the same house as Minab and Kabay were in, the old overseer's house. Breena was sure Jaymin was angry with her, as she had not seen her in the three days that past since her wedding. Finally, a week and a half after the wedding, and hours after Minab had left the room, Jaymin knocked and entered Breena's bedroom. She found Breena in the tiny room where the toilet was. Breena was vomiting and little beads of sweat decorated her forehead.

Jaymin dampened a cloth and gave it to Breena so she could wipe her face. "I will get the physician for you."

"No." Breena shouted frantically.

"But you are not well."

"I know what I am." Breena wiped her face and then the tears of frustration that were filling her eyes. "I'm trapped here, forever."

"I do not understand. You know that your land is lost, beyond the cold."

"I had a little hope in the back of mind, that one day I would escape and get out of here. My father knew about lands, and people, and mountains, and I knew something about them too. I figured, one day, I could find my way out of this place."

"And that hope is gone?"

"I could have had a chance on my own but not with another person with me. I am sealed to this place forever, now."

"Who would go with you? I cannot. My place is here with my husband."

"I've been throwing up for the last few days, every morning. I hoped the other symptoms were just stress. I should've known better than to try and excuse the obvious." Breena got up and walked over to the bed. She sat down and hugged one of the pillows.

Jaymin followed her and sat in silence for a few seconds, and then she understood and became very excited. "You are with child? Breena, this is good news! Minab has never had offspring and he will be extremely pleased."

"I don't want to please Minab! I don't want anyone to know. You must promise me, you will tell no one, not anyone." Breena was starting to tremble from the desperation she was beginning to feel.

"Why?" Jaymin was confused at Breena's reaction. This was good news and a time for celebration.

"Promise me." Breena grabbed Jaymin's shoulders.

"I promise, but it is not a good secret."

Breena released her and took a deep breath. She had a few friends in high school that became pregnant and had morning sickness, but it was never like this. Breena felt as if her body was fighting against her. The nausea was finally leaving her and she knew she would be feeling better again, until tomorrow morning. "I'm sorry about what I did on your wedding day."

"It did not interfere with my wedding. You have a strong disposition and Kabay says it will take time for it to be broken and for you to surrender to Minab's will."

"He said that, did he? Well, it's going to take more time than Minab has. Do you realize how uncivilized your culture is? I'm not a horse that has to have its wildness shattered so it can be ridden. I'm not the wild one here. I don't go out and hack people to death over possession of land or a city." Breena groaned.

"Breena; did Minab tell you that he's leaving for Chelm tomorrow?"

Breena's mouth dropped open. "Tomorrow? Is he taking me? I

thought he wasn't going for another month. Jaymin, what am I going to do without you?"

Jaymin hugged Breena and cried. She told her she would miss her too and many hearts would grieve. She also told her that Minab had Breena's processions that were collected long ago from the crash, taken to be loaded on the pack animals. Minab had heard of the possessions and thought it would help Breena adjust to her new home in Chelm.

CHAPTER FOUR

THE NEXT MORNING MINAB left the room early and did not return until Breena had finished her bout of nausea. She was thankful he did not find out. It wasn't as bad as before and Breena thought that maybe it would stop. Minab wanted Breena to ride with him on his horse but Breena pushed him away and started to walk beside the pack animals. Minab tried again but when Breena pushed him away again, he decided it wasn't worth a battle at that time. He allowed her to walk.

They traveled over twenty miles that day and Breena was exhausted by the time they set up camp for the night. She pulled the fur cover off Minab's horse and placed it on the ground so she could sleep on it. Minab brought her food, which she ate without a fight, but only because Minab handed her the plate and did not try to feed it to her. Later, Minab carried her into his tent. She had fallen asleep after eating, and soon the rain would start.

The following morning Breena thought things would go well. She did not feel sick and thought that maybe the fresh air was helping. She sat down on an old log to eat her breakfast but she could smell the meat cooking and she dashed into the trees to vomit. She had not eaten much the day before and it was more of the dry heaves than anything else. Her whole body ached. Minab had watched as Breena ran into the trees. He had brought a physician with him on the trip, so he ordered the physician to go to her aid. The last thing Breena wanted was to have him around, so when he came close she yelled at him to go away and then started to throw sticks and small stones at him. Minab came to see what the matter was. Breena knew she had to do something to confuse them and keep them from thinking about her being sick. She ran behind Minab and continued to yell and throw sticks at the doctor. Minab tried to explain to Breena that the physician was allowed to touch her but Breena wasn't listening, even if she could have understood what he was saying. Minab became frustrated and brought Breena back over to the campsite. Soon they were traveling again and the incident was forgotten. Breena again refused to ride with Minab and the whole day turned out to be a repeat of the day before.

By early evening Breena was feeling famished and Minab watched in astonishment as Breena finished off the plateful of food way before he finished his. He gave her more and she ate that too. It was the first time in a long while she enjoyed every morsel and every different taste of the food. Soon, she became as tired as she used to be on thanksgiving, after a huge meal of turkey with all the trimmings. It wasn't turkey or even a feast but it filled her empty stomach perfectly.

Again, in the early morning, Breena's nausea woke her up and this time Minab followed her into the trees. He called the physician over and Breena was determined he would not get a chance to check her close enough to find out what was wrong. The physician touched her cheek and checked her tongue and eyes, while Breena told him he was a stupid prehistoric ape and that he knew nothing about doctoring. She told him, knowing full well that he could not understand a word she said, that even an imbecile could guess she was pregnant. Minab stared at her as if he understood what she said and Breena stopped talking, worried that he had picked up a word or two from being around her so much. They looked at each other for a few seconds then Minab told the physician to go back to camp.

Minab handed Breena his water bag and Breena took a sip. He said a few things to her and Breena wondered why he wasted his time talking, when she understood nothing of what he said. She handed back his water bag and he smiled at her. "Don't think you've won just because I took a drink from your canteen. You have what you wanted, all right, but I have no intention of letting you know it. I'm a person too and until you realize we're equal in this life, it's always going to be war. You think you can use my body like a toy for your pleasure and a carrier for your off spring, well; we shall see. One of these days, I'll wipe that stupid grin right off your face, myself." She said as she wiped the remains of the water from her lips with the back of her hand, then she turned and walked back to camp.

As Breena walked along that day, she stumbled a few times. The sun was warmer than usual or she was not handling the walking very well, she wasn't sure. Minab offered her a ride on his horse and she shook her head and continued to walk. After she tripped again, Minab rode up beside her. With little effort, he leaned over and with one arm, pulled her up on top of the horse in front of him, onto the saddle. Breena was thirsty and trembling with fatigue. He handed her his water bag again and after she took a drink, he put his arms around her and pulled her close. It was a comforting position and safe from any further advances, so Breena didn't fight against him. Instead, she closed her eyes and fell asleep.

The attack came shortly after the rain stopped that evening. It was a small group of Arbmoat's men, out to revenge Minab's insult to their king. Minab was up and out of the tent before Breena could even fully awaken. She crawled out in time to see Minab in battle with two other warriors. It made Breena's heart pound with fear as sword smashed against sword. The sounds of battle surrounded her and she crawled to the outside corner of the tent. If they got too close, she would run into the woods and hide. Minab looked back at Breena. He was sliced on the side of his left biceps for the distraction. Soon, the protector on his forearm was covered in blood. Someone came rushing towards Breena and Minab placed himself between the attacker and her. He slashed at one of the men, and then sent his sword deep into the side of his other assailant. Breena watched as Minab fought with all his strength.

She understood why he was considered mighty. Another man fell and Minab turned his full attention to the attacker who came after Breena. They fought forcefully and at times only Minab's armor kept him from defeat. The other man slipped on the blood on the ground and Minab drove his sword into the space beneath the chest armor and the belt as he fell. Breena put her hands to her mouth as the man dropped less than three feet in front of her. Minab quickly put his arm around Breena's waist and picked her up. He carried her deep into the woods, away from camp.

When they could no longer hear the sounds of combat, he carefully put her down. They were beside a stream and the sound of the rippling water was a striking contrast to that of clashing swords. Breena was shaking with fear over what had just happened. She stood looking at Minab, realizing he had protected her with his whole being. For some reason he valued her enough to risk his own life. She didn't understand. She thought she was just a Zibo to him. Breena undid her scarf from around her waist and dipped it in the brook, then proceeded to clean Minab's wound. She ripped the hem of her nightgown and wrapped it around his arm as a bandage. He did not flinch when the water touched the open laceration. He just kept his eyes on Breena as she gently administered to his injury. His expression was one of surprise that she knew how to doctor a wound. When it was wrapped and had stopped bleeding, Breena looked up into Minab's face and tried to think of some way to say thank you that he would understand, but Minab did something that shocked Breena. He placed his large hand on Breena's abdomen and in plain English said the word *'baby'*. She didn't know what to do or say. He knew. She didn't know if he knew English or if it was just that one word, but he knew. Slowly she bowed her head and nodded. He had earned the right to know the truth. Breena backed away and sat down on the ground with her back to him. Maybe he was a mighty warrior because he won, in everything. She wasn't ready for this responsibility, especially when it was from a union with someone she hated. No, she didn't hate him but it was nothing like what she had ever wanted.

Someone approached them and Minab drew his sword. He called out and one of his own men answered. Breena followed them as they walked back to camp. He was ignoring her again and it was as if she was expected to follow. Minab joined his army and they started yelling and cheering their victory. As everyone was getting ready to move on Minab called them all to gather. Breena was just coming back from another episode of morning sickness. The events of the early morning had upset her so much she couldn't hold anything down, not even water. As she put another scarf on her head, tying it at the back, instead of draping it over her shoulders, Minab pulled her into the center of camp, where all the men had gathered. He held her by one hand, his grip around her whole biceps. The other hand he placed firmly on her abdomen so everyone could see. With a short speech, Breena knew without understanding the words, that he was telling everyone what he had accomplished. A roar of cheers came from all the men and Breena felt her face redden with humiliation. She pushed Minab's hand away and pulled free from his grip. She walked over to his horse and leaned her head against its belly and cried.

Minab's body cast a shadow against her and she could feel the coolness from the lack of direct sun. She turned around to see him standing there with his arms folded, apparently, proud of his achievement. She started walking even before he had a chance to offer her a ride. It more than annoyed her when he kept riding alongside her, stopping her every so often by positioning his horse in her pathway. Breena would stop then walk around the horse and continue on her way.

It didn't take long for Minab to become annoyed at her stubbornness. Finally, he dismounted and stood in her way. She almost bumped into him. He moved were so quick. In silence, she stood there, not looking up at him, staring at the bottom of his chest plate. He folded his arms as if to tell her this was a standoff. That was fine. She was ready. They stood like that for almost ten minutes, until the convoy had all stopped to look at them. Breena knew that this was just a small thing, but significant in the battle of wills. Things were climacteric and she knew she would have to do something drastic if she were to prove her point. Minab said something to her, loud and clear and Breena knew he had told her to get on the horse. She couldn't even if she wanted too. The horse stood so tall she would need Minab's help to get on. Seeing no reaction, Minab reached out to grab her but Breena quickly snatched Minab's knife from his wide belt. A look of puzzlement spread across Minab's face, then a smile. Surely, she wouldn't try to use that on him. He was a great soldier and she could not harm him with that knife. Breena looked up at him and slowly extended her left arm outward. With the palm of her hand up, she took the knife and cut a three-inch gash into her forearm. It hurt beyond belief, but Breena was not about to show pain. Minab's smile vanished. She dropped the knife by his feet and walked around him.

He was a warrior and this was in a language he understood. She had shown him she felt no pain, or maybe that she was beyond pain; numb. She hoped it worked because it worked, kind of, in the movie she had seen years earlier. The movie was about a female captive in an Indian camp. Breena wondered what he would do next. The blood was dripping down her arm and it stung worse than she ever thought it would. Sometimes her own stupidity surprised her.

Minab watched Breena walk away as he slowly picked up his knife. He wasn't sure what to do. This female was crazy. He mounted his horse and followed her. The others continued in silence. Finally, he came up behind her and scooped her into his arms as he had done before. He took her scarf off her head and wrapped it around her arm. Breena looked up at him for a few moments and he looked down into her eyes. They rode on in silence.

The rest of the trip was difficult for Breena. She was lonely and depressed and it didn't help that no one spoke her language. About five days out of Chelm, Breena wandered away from camp, on purpose. Her belly constantly ached and she knew the stress was becoming too much for her. She had to do some thinking and do it alone, before things got so bad she developed an ulcer. Breena knew they wouldn't have proper medicine for that. Everyone else seemed to have the constitution of a rock. Her father used to council her that if the pressures of school became too demanding, she was just to sit and ponder everything. Solutions were always just a thought, and fifteen minutes away, he would say. As Breena sat on an old log, she shook her head. If he only knew the pressures she was under now. It made school, entrance exams, dating and everything else, look like a picnic. She watched a little mouse scamper through dead leaves, and she rubbed the temples of her forehead. Minab would probably be upset that his prize was missing but she didn't care. How could people like him actually exist? He seemed, to her, to have no compassion in him. She put her head in her hands and slowly started to cry. Her father used to also tell her when she became upset over curfews and credit card limits, that she would grow up soon enough, and to just enjoy her adolescence. What she would give for a simple problem now, such as her mother harping on her for coming home after midnight.

She heard a slight noise behind her and turned around to see what it was. Just as she did so, Minab lunged at a large cat as it was in mid-leap towards Breena. Minab sunk his knife deep into the wild cat before it could scratch him more than once. Breena stood there with her mouth open. She had no idea there were wild vicious animals out in the woods. Minab wiped his blood soaked knife on the dead animal's fur and Breena thought the sight was going to make her vomit. She closed her eyes for a second and swallowed hard, forcing herself to calm down. Minab started to yell at Breena and she knew he was upset that she left the protected area of the campsite. He took out a long thin leather cord and grabbed her hands.

Breena began to panic as Minab started to bind her hands. She frantically shook her head. "Oh, please don't tie my hands. Please. I won't go wandering off again." She struggled to get free even though she knew struggling had always been useless against him, unless he wanted her to escape. "I just came out here to think. You don't know what this is like for me. I've never been pregnant before." She looked up at him but he seemed to be unmoved, even by the tears that were slowly trickling down Breena's cheeks. "You've probably never been worried or hurt or scared to death about anything, but this is overwhelming for me. Please don't tie my hands." Breena started to sob as he tied the knot in the binding on her hands. "I wish I would have died with my father. I wish you had killed me at Moatsha with your sword. At least it would be all over. It would be all over with." Minab tugged at the cord and started pulling Breena back to the camp. "What's the use? Even if you could understand, you wouldn't understand, because you're nothing but a big unfeeling rock."

Minab stopped and for a second Breena wondered if she had managed to get through to him, but he lifted her up and threw her over his shoulder like a sack. The only thing Breena thought she had gotten through to him now was that she wasn't moving fast enough. When they got back to camp, Breena spent the time while waiting for the horses to be packed up; trying to undo the cord with her teeth, but it was futile. Once they began walking Minab made it clear the binding would come off if she rode with him. Breena's stubbornness kept her from volunteering to ride with him, so if Minab wanted Breena riding with him, he would just ride up beside her and pick her up. Breena was afraid of falling off the tall horse so she never put up a struggle. Rather than go through another scene like the one with the knife, Minab decided it was easier not to ask her to do things. She had a warrior's soul and was now going to bare his child, and that was pleasing to him.

Breena continued having morning sickness and was getting tired of it. She received no sympathy; Minab just seemed annoyed that she would have to run into the trees every morning. Soon Breena discovered it was easier on her stomach if she skipped breakfast altogether. That seemed to bother Minab more than her short little trips to the trees. Breena didn't care; she would just flop down on a blanket and hid her face during breakfast. The rest of the trip passed quickly.

As they approached the city of Chelm, people came out to greet them. Not until then had Breena realized how loved Minab was among his people. Women threw flowers in his path and men cheered. Breena could hear the chatter of the women as they noticed her riding with Minab. It was the only time she kept her scarf on her head during the entire trip. It hadn't dawned on her that she was doing it to show people she was Minab's wife, until she reached his home. It was a beautifully big dwelling, as big as the overseer's house in Moatsha, but made from large white colored bricks. Servants came out to greet Minab and he nodded to each one. Minab helped Breena off the horse and she followed him into the house where there was an older woman, wearing a black scarf, waiting for them. Minab introduced her by a simple name, Shirin. Breena shyly nodded and noticed Minab did not tell Shirin her name in return. He talked to Shirin for almost an hour and Breena stood in the background, feeling silly and out of place. She wandered into the garden and sat on one of the benches. Later, Shirin came out to the garden, alone. She stood before Breena and smiled.

"My master says you speak the English of the stranger." Shirin said to Breena.

Breena was so startled she almost fell off the bench. "You speak English too?"

"I was taught by Miller." She looked as if she was struggling to remember words.

"I'm not like Miller." Breena looked down. She was tired of being grouped with this Miller fellow.

"He had yellow hair."

Breena looked passed Shirin for Minab. "Did the bigger than life, Minab, leave?" She asked sarcastically.

"He must visit the chief overseer."

Breena had to know if her suspicions about Minab were right. "Minab doesn't understand English, does he?"

"Much better than I."

Breena's heart sank. Everything she had said to him, about him, he understood. She rubbed her face and groaned.

"You are tired?"

"No. No. Not really." She wondered how she was going to deal with Minab now. She had underestimated him badly. "He told you that this marriage isn't ... normal, right?"

"Minab said you are his rightful reward for Miller's deceit." Shirin wasn't sure reward was the right word.

"Reward, booby prize, whatever. Well, maybe that's what I am to him, but I'm a person, too. I'm Breena Keets and even though I'm not like you people, I'm still a person." Breena almost started to cry. Did no one value people in this demented place?

Shirin gave Breena a smile then told her she would show her to Minab's room on the top floor. Breena followed Shirin up the flight of stairs and into the huge room on the top floor. It was simple in furnishings but the drapes were of a very elegant looking fabric and the bed was huge, to accommodate Minab's large frame, she assumed. The washing room had a bath that was immense and a small washtub in the corner of it, and there was a separate toilet room. The large windows opened to a balcony that over looked the garden. Shirin told Breena to rest, and then she left her alone.

Breena pulled off her scarf and threw it on the floor. Slowly she sat down on one of the chairs and looked around. If she had to spend a good deal of time in this room, at least it had a nice view.

Hours passed and finally Breena checked the door. Minab kept it locked at Moatsha. Surprisingly it opened and she wandered down stairs. Two young women were busy sweeping the front entrance and out onto the front steps which were wide and almost royal looking. Breena smiled at them when they looked up at her. One girl giggled and the other hurried her sweeping onto the steps, away from Breena. They all wore black scarves. Breena strolled into the kitchen where Shirin was instructing others in preparation of the evening meal. She looked at Breena in a funny manner and Breena knew she was wondering where her scarf was. She had not worn it down stairs. Breena casually flipped her hair from where it fell over her shoulders in the front, to the back. Her hair was not as long as any of the other women's and she remembered Jaymin being fascinated at how Breena would braid it from time to time.

"Minab will be present for the meal." Shirin touched her own scarf as if it was a clue for Breena to notice she was missing hers.

Breena noticed they had cups made out of glass. She had not seen them in Moatsha. She walked over and picked one up. "I took an art class in glass blowing. I made a wine glass."

"Glass?"

"This cup is made of glass."

Shirin nodded that she understood.

Minab walked into the house and everyone turned their attention to him. Someone handed him a large metal mug of something and as he sat down at the table, a young girl hurried over and undid the laces of his high boots. He acted as if this was normal behavior and expected. Breena watched partly in awe, at the respect they showed him, and somewhat in disbelief that they could esteem him that way, after knowing he could be a ruthless warrior.

Shirin hurried to put the food on the table where Minab sat, in the great room, which centered the house. Minab motioned for Breena to sit at the table, and then he said something in his own language, to Shirin that made her stop and sit at the table. He told her that his wife ate less than a bird at first and now that she had his child in her, she ate like a growing filly. Then he told Shirin that his wife was more stubborn than any animal he had ever seen. It was probably a characteristic of her race. Minab had told Shirin to sit and watch how stubborn his new wife really was.

He placed a plate in front of Breena and she moved to pick up a piece of fruit that was on it. Minab moved it over by his plate and then he picked up the fruit. He held it out to her. Breena stifled a groan within her. She was hungry and did not want to play games but she would not eat out of his hand. She sat back on her seat and stared at Minab. He was obviously trying to show who was dominant, and rightly so, as it was his house. Breena almost gave in but then she remembered her conversation with Jaymin. Minab wanted her strong will broken. Breena folded her arms. Minab shook his head and laughed. "Then, you will starve." He said in English. They sat staring at each other for a few moments. Breena was surprised at how well he pronounced her language. It was a strange sound to hear coming from his lips.

"Then we will starve." Breena corrected him. She placed her hand on her abdomen and looked down.

Minab moved the plate back in front of her. Breena looked at the plate and then back at Minab. Suddenly, she lost control of her temper. He understood English and he had tricked her. He thought of her as a Zibo. It was not her choice to give this man such a precious gift as a child. One meal missed would not hurt either of them. Breena smacked the plate of food off the table and onto the floor. She jumped to her feet.

"My will is my own, you ... you barbarian! I am not a toy to play your stupid games with," she yelled, then ran up the stairs to the bedroom.

At first, Breena stood over in the far corner of the room away from the door. She was worried Minab would follow her but a half an hour past and he did not come in after her.

The rain started to fall and Minab strolled into the room, disregarding Breena as she sat at the balcony windows, watching the rain. He took off his armor. It would be good to sleep without all his equipment on. In the wilderness it was essential but he was home now. He rubbed his shoulders and then walked into the washing room. After he had bathed and changed into his night robe, he walked over to where Breena was sitting. He closed the shuttered to the balcony. Breena had not looked at him at all and it bothered him greatly. He would not be ignored by her. He picked her up in his arms and Breena fought to get away. She hated that he was so big and strong and could easily manhandle her.

When Minab woke, he was surprised to find Breena snuggled up next to him. She usually slept on the floor away from him. He had a very good sleep, in his own bed and in his own home. He was to report to the church overseer that day and present his wife to him. With Breena carrying his child, it was important to Minab to get the church overseer's blessing on their union. Minab watched Breena sleep. He wondered how a race could last with women who were so delicate looking. Her feet were the size of a child. She was not strong like his people but her will was probably equal to his and Minab wondered how such a massive disposition could fit inside such a small frame.

Breena woke slowly. Soon as she realized she was cuddled up to Minab, she moved away as if she was electrified by his touch. Her body was off the bed and hitting the floor faster than lightening. Minab watched in disappointment to her reaction. Breena sat staring at Minab for only a second, then the morning sickness overcame her, and she ran to the toilet room. Minab was gone by the time she returned.

After Breena bathed and dressed, she came down stairs to find something to eat. Shirin greeted her and offered her cheese and some kind of salted meat. Breena did not like the salty taste but her stomach was empty and she was starting to get the shakes from not eating.

"You must make yourself very beautiful and wear your scarf, as soon as you are finished your meal. Minab will take you to see the church overseer today."

"Why?"

"He will offer a blessing on your union so your first child will be a male."

"That's important to Minab?"

"Yes."

"I hope it's a girl." Breena slowly licked the salt from a small piece of meat.

Shirin looked worried. "You must not speak that way. It would be very sad."

Breena's mind drifted back to the other cultures she had studied that seemed obsessed with male children. "What will happen if it is a girl?"

"Minab may have it killed. It is very bad to have a female child first. Only slaves do not care if their first child is a female. All birthrights go through the male child and with a female, Minab still has no heir."

Breena sat back onto her chair and pondered what Shirin had just said. Would Minab really kill a baby? It made her sick to contemplate how females were valued. "Would he really kill a tiny baby? Does he have to?"

Shirin slowly shook her head. "It is not a law, just a custom. Some let them live, but the mother must have another child quickly, to show she did not deliberately have a female child first."

"Like it was her fault? The female has nothing to do with that. Any educated person knows that." Breena realized the futility of the statement even as she spoke. "If I went to this blessing thing willingly, would that show Minab I wasn't trying to have a girl first?" She stressed the word - trying.

Shirin nodded. "You must wear your scarf to it."

"Yeah, yeah; the stupid scarf again." Breena went upstairs. She decided that since it looked as if she wasn't getting out of this place for the moment then maybe she could change things. She dressed in a dress that was almost teal in color and put on a long open robe that was white, over top. It was one that Jaymin's mother had given her. Breena brushed her hair and braided it in a French braid down the back, tying it with an elastic she found in the trunk that contained her old clothes. She then put on her scarf and tied it in the back. "You have your choice here, Minab. Either I wear it loose and it falls off or I tie it in the back and it stays on. I have no idea why my hair seems to make it slide off. Everyone else's scarf stays put. Besides, it's so hot it makes me want to puke," she said to herself as she looked into the big tin mirror that was on the wall. She jumped when she spotted Minab's reflection behind her.

He was dressed in his armor, it was polished, and gleaming like it was on Jaymin's wedding day. It was truly an impressive sight and he looked almost invincible. Breena almost told him he looked mighty, but her memory shot back to their conflict of wills and she looked away. He had the power to kill the baby she would have and she was defenseless to stop it, except by persuasion.

"Come," was all he said.

They entered a building that Breena assumed was a church. It was tiered in the shape of a pyramid, on the outside, but not as big and not with more than three tiers. The great room inside was huge with rows of benches. At the front was some kind of symbol. Breena did not recognize it. It was similar to neither Egyptian nor early Arabic, yet it was, odd. There were ten fine cloths or banners of brilliant colors on the walls, and ten gold goblets on a table. Every time she stopped to look at the spectacular décor, Minab gently pushed her closer and closer to the front. Once at the front he placed his hand on her shoulder and compelled her to kneel. Breena was tired of the aching feelings of anxiety she was having in her stomach. Everything was so different and everything always seemed to depend on her behavior. How could she submit to a culture that seemed to go against everything inside her? A man in soft clothes came out and Minab went to talk to him. The man didn't look very holy, Breena thought. He wore no fancy robes or anything special. His clothes were an off white. His outer robe or jacket was orange. The only difference was his cape like garment that he wore over top of everything else. Minab and the man talked for a long time and Breena sat down on her legs. Her knees were starting to hurt. Finally, the man and Minab walked over to Breena and she reluctantly rose onto her knees again. If she cooperated, she thought, maybe Minab would not even think of harming the baby if it did turn out to be a female. The man spoke to her for a while and Minab did not translate. Minab knelt beside her and the man continued to talk. Breena's attention wandered and she slowly began to look around.

Suddenly Minab pulled her dress up and the man tried to place his hand on Breena's abdomen. Breena tried to push him away but Minab grabbed her wrists. "He will bless the child." Minab said sternly. Breena stopped struggling but she didn't like the other man's touch any more than she liked Minab's touch.

"Will you kill him for touching me?"

"No."

The war of the wills arose again and Breena looked up at Minab. "It won't make any difference. Whatever it is won't change because of this blessing." She smiled. "Male or female, this little warrior is mine." She knew that would upset Minab. He thought of Breena as just a temporary caretaker.

The blessing was finished and Minab roughly pulled Breena to her feet. Her mind was moving fast to come up with something that would ensure the life of her baby, no matter what sex it was. "Female warriors of my tribe are honored. Not only can they fight but they can use their brains too and, to top it all off, they give birth to even more intelligent children with each generation. You even think about harming them when they are children and your whole family will be cursed for generations to come." Breena pointed to the soft clothed man. "Ask him. He'll tell you. You don't ever bring a curse upon a family on purpose. That's just downright stupid."

Minab said something to the holy man then hauled Breena out of the building so roughly she thought he would pull her arm off. "Your stories are not true. Your race is too weak to have warriors." He said angrily.

"I kept that pathetic army of yours out of Moatsha for almost four weeks! You'd still be out there if you hadn't gotten sneaky and crawled into the city like a rat. Your strength only helps when you're close enough to do hand to hand battle." Breena continued to tell him as he literally dragged her home with his grip on her upper arm. "Male or female, this kid is a better warrior than either of us, because he comes from both of us."

Minab stopped. "He will be Adder!"

"If it is a female, will you kill her?"

Minab did not answer and when they returned to the house Breena ran upstairs and slammed the door shut.

Shirin brought food up to Breena. She was sleeping in the far corner on the floor, her scarf thrown over by the balcony. Shirin woke her as she picked up the scarf and placed it gently on the bed. "You are married to a warrior who is Adder. The scarf should be worn with pride."

"I am definitely not proud of this marriage." Breena had taken one of the large pillows from the bed over to the corner to sleep on. The floor was cold to her body. She took a deep breath and decided to change the subject. "Why do you and the other servants wear black scarves?"

"We are not paid servants. I was the widow of an overseer in a city

Minab captured. He should have killed my entire household. Instead, he made us slaves and gave us our lives back."

"How generous. Not much of a trade, if you ask me."

"Minab is a benevolent man and a strong master."

"What was the first wife like?"

Shirin smiled and sat on the bed as Breena ate the food she brought her. "Annek was very beautiful. She wanted to be Minab's wife since she was just a girl, and used to watch him march back into Kalat with his legion. He was the youngest captain in the army, very valiant, much honored. She would watch him at the church on the holy day and Minab was flattered that she would risk her mother's wrath for smiling at him. He chose her and they were married.

Annek was a proper mistress of the house and very popular at the parties they attended. Minab was disappointed when they had been married for two years and she bore him no off spring."

"So did Miller just touch Minab's wife or worse?"

Shirin looked down in shame. "What Minab knows and what we, who were there, know, are two different stories. He suspected. It was a great disgrace for such an honorable warrior. He had grown to love Miller. His heart was greatly wounded. A great friendship was lost."

Breena took a deep breath. "Well I'm not Miller and he has no right to treat me like a whipping boy."

"He whips you?" Shirin asked in shock, putting her hand up to her lips.

"No. That's just a way of saying; he treats me like I'm a Zibo."

"You do not treat your husband with the respect you should."

"He's no better than me."

"He treats you as a wife."

"Yeah, well you don't have to be with him at night. My people treat their women differently. We aren't objects, toys, or carrying cases for their off spring. We aren't picked or paid for with cheap trinkets. We choose each other. I had no say in this union! Not in anything!" Breena's frustration filled her and she began to cry. Her brave front was, for the moment, collapsing.

"Minab said that your people have female warriors. Who is left to love the children?"

Breena thought about her mother. She was the one who loved the children. She was always there making sure life was better for her. Dad provided the entertainment and drive in her life but her mother always had a hug and a kiss to give away. She fed the strays and was the entire caretaker for their neighborhood. Breena's mom was the one all the children on the block went to when their parents weren't home. Breena's heart ached for her mother's worried voice asking her if she had brought enough underwear. She sniffed back a tear. "The women are just warriors in their souls and they fight for their loved one, for a better life for their babies." It bothered Breena that she could see the similarity in their cultures and that back home in her country, families were falling apart faster than anything.

It was late when Minab came into the room. It had been raining for a while and Minab had a thick cape on over his armor. It was sopping wet and he draped it over one of the chairs. He took off his wide belt with his sword and sat down on another chair.

"Will you kill our baby if it is a girl?" The voice came out of the silence of the night.

Minab turned around to look at the corner of the room where Breena was. He was surprised she was not asleep. "It will be Adder too. Pray for a male, but I will not harm it, if it is not."

Breena nodded then she walked over to Minab and knelt down in front of him. She slowly undid his laces and Minab, amazed, sat up straight, to watch her. Breena would not meet his eyes and when she had removed his shoes she hurried back to her pillow in the corner.

CHAPTER FIVE

OVER THE NEXT FEW weeks, Breena began to modernize the kitchen in the house. She told Minab her plans and he was not interested but told her to have Shirin obey her instruction and to have someone restore the fireplace to how Breena wanted it. With Breena's drawings as directions, the fireplace was redone so that it had two shelves on the side that would be used as ovens, with thick wooden doors. She had a metal-smith make her a grater and fix the rods on the fireplace so they swung out making it easier to cook. Everyone thought Breena was so clever but Breena made sure everyone knew it was how it was done in her country. She just didn't tell them it was done over a hundred years ago. A grill was installed in the fireplace as well as other simple time and labor saving devices. Over all, Breena was quite pleased with the changes and told Shirin to allow others to copy her efforts.

Over the next month, Breena's abdomen swelled and she avoided Minab as much as possible. When he was home, he would constantly be looking at her belly. The child inside her began to move and at times Breena thought there might be a war of wills going on in there too. She should have paid more attention to the sex education classes at school. Was she supposed to get this big, this fast? Her friend, who was pregnant during the last year of school, never even showed until her sixth month. Breena was in her fifth month and already she felt stuffed.

There were rituals Breena had to endure to show Minab she was trying to produce a male child. Breena laughed at the strong thick roots Shirin tied to their bedposts and cringed at the cold jelly stuff that Shirin poured over her belly. It seemed ridiculous to her but Minab believed in it all and Breena knew she was only trying to placate his temperament. Minab brought her a drink that was to be consumed on the morning of a worship day. It was green and smelled like grass and she was sure that besides herbs, there must have been millet, peas, or spinach in it too. It tasted awful and Breena spent the entire time in church trying to stay still so she wouldn't throw it all up.

Minab also brought her a small clay container of some other herbs that he was told, if placed on the tip of the tongue early every morning, would stop the morning sickness. It worked and Breena was very thankful, but she didn't say anything to Minab.

As Breena experimented in the kitchen with various foods on the new cooking elements, she would ask Shirin questions on the subject of having babies. Shirin had bore seven children and her first child was male. She had four miscarriages or 'too early births' as Shirin called them. Breena figured she would be as close to an expert as she could find in this strange place. The bonus was she could explain things to Breena in her own language.

Breena began to worry about her size and approached Shirin carefully on the subject. She didn't want Shirin to get suspicious and end up telling Minab anything.

"In some cultures, not mine, but in some, they are very upset if twins are born. Does your culture think that way, I mean, if more than one child is born at once?"

"Two babies would be a great gift to the husband. It would be a cause for much celebration."

The subject was dropped and Breena would approach it later. Minab had returned from a week away training his soldiers. He told Shirin to prepare a special meal for a friend who would arrive later. He was disappointed Breena did not come and undo his laces, which would have been the custom upon the return of the husband from a trip of any length over four days. Shirin scolded Breena for her disregard. Breena only saw it as meaning he would be in the bedroom that night, and she wouldn't have the bed to herself, which meant she'd be sleeping on the floor that night, or at least trying.

Just before the big meal of the day, another big man, in the uniform of a warrior, arrived at the house entrance. Minab and the other man embraced and laughed with each other. Breena thought it was odd to see Minab act that way with another male. He was never that friendly with other friends, although Breena thought he was always belligerent. Now there would be two jingoistic chauvinists around the house talking about their war stories. Breena hid from them in the corner of the kitchen. There was a spot there that had an opening, like a small window, that she could observe them, yet stay out of their view.

Breena was shocked when she heard them speaking English. The other man was called Zorban and both he and Minab had known each other from childhood, Shirin told her.

Zorban was surprised at the changes in Minab's life. "The stranger I heard about was a female? Moreover, you took her to wife. What is a female stranger like?"

In their language Minab replied, "She is obstinate and contentious. She is not like Miller." Minab knew Breena was listening and that was the reason he used the foreign language of English for only certain things that were spoken.

Shirin put the plates of food on a tray. "Breena, it is customary for you to serve your husband when he has guests."

"He can get his own food." Breena relied. "Last time I looked, he had a heartbeat and a pair of legs."

Shirin walked over to Breena and smacked her on the back of the head. "You will have respect for my master."

Breena was shocked by the slap. It didn't hurt but it showed Shirin was upset by Breena's disrespectful attitude.

"Minab would fight to the death for you." Shirin told Breena. "You are the wife of a mighty captain and could enjoy many privileges if you would but pay homage to him."

Breena remembered the fight she witnessed in the wilderness on the trip to Chelm and nodded. "Fine; I'll take him and his guest their food but don't expect me to stay and eat with them."

"You must stay until you are told to leave."

Breena picked up the tray and carried it in to the great room where they were.

Zorban looked at Breena as if she was his prey. "You have picked well. She is as beautiful as she is exotic." He said in his own language.

Breena was immediately uncomfortable around him. She knew the change of language must mean they were saying things she wasn't suppose to hear. They were probably talking about all the things that were wrong with her. She put the tray down and Zorban notice she was pregnant.

"You have given her a child to bear already? Minab you have indeed been diligent." The statement was in English.

Minab switched back to his language. "Look at her face. She is annoyed at our conversation. She thinks it an insult that I touch her. She knows nothing of being a woman."

Breena was tired, and the thought of what Minab was going to want in the night was distressing her. He was rough and crude and knew no gentleness.

"Do you enjoy being a wife of a mighty captain?" Zorban asked her in English.

"There is not much honor in winning a battle against a victim my size. Maybe Minab is mighty because he only fights Zibos."

Minab shifted on his chair. The statement angered him.

Zorban laughed. "She must be an amusement for you during the rain, Minab. Such an exotic garden for your seed to grow in."

Breena couldn't stand it any longer. She dropped the plate of food that she was going to give Minab back onto the tray. "You're a pig! You may be dressed in shinny armor but you're still a full-grown hog. Is that all you barbarians think about?"

Minab rose to his feet. Breena had not only insulted a guest in his house, but using the term 'pig' was a transgression not quickly forgiven. A pig was considered one of the lowest and filthiest of animals, usually infested with worms or sores. The meat could not be preserved and only the lowest of the classes ever ate it. He grabbed Breena by the wrists. Breena cringed. She was sure he would hit her this time.

"They are an arrogant breed, Minab. She may be reparation for Miller but you will have to work at her understanding of our ways." Zorban was defusing the situation. "You must have known there would be a price for her splendor."

Minab eased his hold and pulled Breena onto his lap as he sat back down. Breena struggled to get free to no avail. Minab put his arm around her and placed his free hand firmly across her belly. "Inside here is a warrior that will be a great conqueror. If she is strong enough to birth this one, I will have a whole army full before I am finished with her." He held Breena's chin in his fingers. "You will ask for Zorban's forgiveness; now."

Breena looked over at Zorban. She was silent for a few moments and Minab tightened his hold on her. Breena knew she would not win anything in this battle. "I am unacquainted to your protocol. In my world, the men do not treat the women with such disregard. Considering women risk their lives to bare their husband's children, it is a slight to them that their husbands show them that they are of no worth. It is not weak to care for your wife. The men in my world are valiant champions who can kill many with one blow. Yet, they respect their women. I am sorry you lean in a different direction."

Minab looked at Zorban and both wondered if what she had said was in the way of an apology. Minab released Breena. "Leave us."

Breena went back into the kitchen. Shirin asked if they had finished their food and if they wanted more. Breena told her she didn't know that Minab sent her out of the room because she was not a very good hostess.

That evening, Breena was pulled over to the bed by an angry Minab who ordered her not sleep on the floor from now on. He would not tolerate her behavior as much as he did before. Breena woke early the next morning next to Minab. It had been hot the night before and Minab had left his nightshirt off. Breena noticed new wounds and the scars he had from previous battles. She took a bit of the herbs from the clay container that stopped her morning sickness, and placed it on her tongue. She sat waiting for her nausea to calm down as the herbs took effect. Cautiously, she looked closer at Minab's scars. He had a large scar under his right rib and she touched it lightly. Minab stirred and Breena pulled back. He did not wake. Leaning closer again, she examined the new scars, one was tiny, and another was a long straight laceration. Minab opened his eyes but Breena did not notice. He reached up and placed his hand behind her head, and then he pulled her close and kissed her. It was a gentle undemanding kiss and Breena did not resist. Breena had not had kisses from many men before she had gone on the expedition with her father, but Minab's kiss was like the first she ever received. It was soft and was not meant to coerce her. Minab, impressed with her reaction, kissed her again in the same manner. Breena became frightened by what might come next and she pulled away. They sat in silence staring at each other and Minab knew that Breena had been intimidated.

"How could you get hurt teaching your own troops?" Breena blurted out as she tried to calm the anxiety she was feeling.

Minab looked at the new wounds. "It does not hurt. They are minor scratches caused by impassioned recruits." He stated matter-of-factly.

"You've been in many battles. That scar looks bad. It must have hurt a great deal." Breena pointed to the long one under his right side of his ribcage.

Minab sat up. "It was not from battle. It was inflicted by my father when I was just beginning to discipline myself as a warrior."

The thought of a father hurting his son like that made Breena feel sick. She pulled up her nightgown all the way up to her thigh. "I got this from a bull on my grandfather's farm." It wasn't really from the bull but from some barbwire as she had crawled under it to get away from the bull.

Minab laughed. It wasn't very big and nothing to boast about. He lowered Breena back onto her pillow and kissed her gently again. She did not rebuff him and Minab decided he would try a new method to get what he wanted from her. Maybe tenderness would conquer her strong willpower. Maybe too much strength would destroy a delicate flower like her. He arose and dressed immediately, then left the house.

Later, Breena came down from her room in a better mood than she had been in since Minab brought her to Chelm. She found Shirin and asked her a few questions, in a manner she had previously planned.

"Shirin, I need to ask you something but I can't have you talking to Minab about it."

"I will not be disloyal to my master."

"I understand completely but this will not be disloyal. You can tell him, but not for at least two months."

Shirin thought about it for a few minutes then nodded.

Breena made her verbally promise not to tell for two whole months. "How do you tell if you are going to have more than one baby?"

Shirin's mouth fell open, and then she squealed with delight.

"Now, I just suspect it. It wouldn't be fair to get excited if it turned out to not be true, right?"

Shirin composed herself. "We will ask the physician."

"But Minab will find out and I don't want him to know until I can tell him properly."

"We will go to my physician. He does not associate with the freemen. You must wear a black scarf and we must bring something for payment. Minab has silver coins in his room. We will take one. He will not miss one."

That afternoon Breena and Shirin went to her physician. It was a forty-minute walk and Breena was tired by the time they got there. They went into an old building. Shirin had Breena hold a funny little stone doll while the physician pushed on her belly and tried to feel for the baby's form. He constantly talked to Shirin and Breena knew her suspicions were accurate when he got excited and held up two fingers. Shirin told Breena he could feel two little shapes, and although very tiny, there were indeed two babies. By the time, they returned home Breena was ill. She was tired from the walk and her abdomen ached from the pushing it endured. Breena went up stairs and vomited. She laid down to rest and soon fell asleep. Shirin brought her up some food but Breena ate very little. When Minab returned to the house Shirin told him his wife was not feeling well. Minab immediately went to see his wife. Breena knew Shirin was excited about the news and she hoped that nothing had been said to Minab. The next day Minab left to go train with his legion again. He was gone for another week.

This time when Minab returned Breena sat at his feet and undid his shoes. She figured if Shirin saw her trying to do what was customary, she would keep her promise and not tell Minab about the twins.

That worship day was a special festival when the men would give thanks for their blessings by giving coins to the ecclesiastic at the church. Minab went alone, as women were not usually taken on that day. Shirin came running upstairs to tell Breena what her son had seen at church. Minab had given fifteen coins of thanksgiving. It was customary to give ten at the most and only if you had an extremely good year.

When Minab came to bed, he gave Breena a dainty necklace of pearls. They were small but whiter than any she had seen in any jewelry shop back home. Breena didn't know what to say. It was the first time Minab had given her a gift. Minab spent the rest of the evening being as gentle with Breena as he had been when he kissed her and she had not resisted. Breena was completely bewildered by his behavior but she had no desire to have a conflict over wills as long as he was treating her like that. Breena knew he had won again, but only by default. She had relinquished the battle, for the moment.

CHAPTER SIX

$\int$HIRIN TOOK BREENA INTO the market the next day to buy fabric for new clothes. Shirin was constantly putting Breena's scarf back up whenever it fell down because she knew Breena would not. It was another warm day and the scarf began to make Breena feel smothered. She began walking ahead of Shirin so the scarf would remain down for longer periods of time. Shirin picked out beautiful material of deep blue and gold and some white material that was soft and light. Breena snuck off over to a food stand where they had fruits coated with thick firm syrup on a stick. She found out how much it was using her hands to sign out the amount. Breena bought one and as she stood a little out of every one's way, she enjoyed the treat.

"You should wear the scarf up. The shimmer in the sun from your gold hair is almost too much pleasure for a man to bear." The voice came from behind her and although she did not recognize it, it had a tone of familiarity.

Breena turned around to find Zorban standing too close to her for her own comfort. She backed slowly away. Zorban was big like Minab but his hair was longer and he had a small goatee and mustache. He smiled and gave her a slow nod of his head as a greeting.

"It is so hot that if I wore the scarf, I think I would faint." Breena finished the last bite of her treat and licked the tip of her index finger and thumb. "Shirin will find me soon enough and make me put it back up."

"Come; sit in the shade by the well here. It is much cooler with the breeze that blows down the back street." Zorban said pointing to the well behind him.

Breena wasn't sure what the etiquette should be. She had seldom talked to another man in the past ten months. Reluctantly, she walked over to the edge of the well and sat down. It did seem cooler there. She kept her distance from Zorban.

"Do not be afraid. I will stay a respectable distance." Zorban said with a chuckled.

"Do you have a wife?"

"Yes. I also have one magnificent son and four daughters."

Breena relaxed. Somehow, that made her feel a little safer. "You must be very happy that your wife gave you so many children."

Zorban frowned. "She bore me only one son and now she is fat and there has not been any children in two years."

Breena's safe zone dwindled. "Maybe she is just tired."

"Maybe I should get a second, to help her."

"I better go." Breena stood up.

"You are offended. It is our way and is not said to offend you. After all, I am just a pig. Is that not right?" Zorban was smiling and teasing Breena.

Breena blushed as she looked away. He was very clever in his conversation, but there was something that Breena did not trust about him.

"Minab is very lucky to have such a prize. Have you been busy making him a son with blue eyes like yours?"

Breena shrugged her shoulders. "Already made; it's just growing now, but I doubt it will have blue eyes."

"Why not?"

"There are too many generations of black hair and brown eyes to fight against."

Zorban smiled again. "But you are a fighter aren't you? And that would make it possible."

Breena did not answer. She knew he would not understand the scientific reasoning behind her logic. "I better go."

Zorban stood up also and walked a couple of steps closer. "Do you know what happens to a widow if her husband has no brothers, like Minab?"

Breena shook her head.

"They become the seconds to the husband's best friend."

Breena looked at Zorban and decided she did not like the way the conversation was going. "Are you threatening my husband?"

Zorban gave her a phony look, as if he was pretending to be shocked at her accusation. "No. I was just saying that if something was to happen, I would make sure Minab had his army of sons. Only, they'd all look like me." Zorban folded his arms and Breena quickly turned and ran to find Shirin.

Shirin was disappointed that Breena wanted to go home.

When Minab came home, he seemed agitated and did not go see Breena right away. She was in the garden in the back picking vegetables for a salad. He called for Shirin, and Breena took notice that his voice was full of rage. She hurried to the kitchen just in time to see Minab slap Shirin across the face. She ran to stand between them.

"Minab; what has happened that has made you so angry?" She yelled.

Shirin had moved back against the far wall and was crying.

"She took you to see her priest. I will not have you near those wicked men."

"We only went to the market today, Minab."

"It was not today. You went with her to her side of the city where the idol worshipers dwell."

Breena knew he was talking about the trip to the physician they had made. She looked back at Shirin.

"Master, it was to help you get a male child." Shirin cried out.

"I will not have idols in my household!" He opened the palm of his hand to reveal a little stone figure, and then he threw it against the wall. It smashed against the brick, breaking in half and shattering clay pots and dishes in every direction. Then he grabbed Breena by the shoulders. "There is but one God and he is not the size of my hand and carved out of stone." He continued to yell.

"I didn't know it would upset you. I'm sorry."

Minab let go of Breena. "We must go to the worship place and ask for forgiveness for this insult and any other insult you may have committed."

"I have done nothing else wrong, that I am aware of. Except not wearing that stupid scarf like I should."

Minab still looked angry. "I have been told you are too big."

Breena understood Minab did not have the command of her language as she did. "What do you mean? What are you trying to tell me?"

Minab seemed almost in a rage and he would not be reasoned with. "It was posed that maybe you were with child before I wed you. You must be in your seventh or eighth month and not as it should be, if it was mine."

Breena's temperature flared and she could feel her anger zoom straight to a boil. Without forethought she slapped Minab across the face, as hard as she could, which dumbfounded him. A woman never struck her husband in his culture. "How dare you question my virtue! All my life I waited for that one special person. My mother used to tell me my wedding night would be the most memorable night of my life and I ended up spending it with you! Don't you dare question me on that when everything that has happened to me has been by force."

Breena was so upset she grabbed the flat pan; Shirin fried food on, and took a swing at Minab. He grabbed it from her hands and threw it down. They faced each other and Minab called her a name that even without translation, Breena knew, it meant that she was a whore.

Immediately Breena grabbed the broom handle and stomped it down on the top of Minab's foot. She knew it was a weak spot in his armor. Minab grabbed the toe of his boot and gowned.

"You ever call me that again and I will kill you as you sleep." Breena shouted. "I'm as big as I am, because there are two warriors inside and I hope they are both girls!" She ran passed Minab and up the stairs, slamming the bedroom door behind her. The situation left her exhausted and shaking. She plopped down on the bed and cried herself to sleep.

Minab stood in stunned silence as Breena ran upstairs.

Shirin started to pick up the pieces of clay pots and dishes in the kitchen. "Never have I seen such a sight as that. She is so different." Shirin rambled on in her own language.

"Is what she said true?" Minab demanded to know.

Shirin hid the little broken idol from Minab's view. "Yes, yes. Your wife asked me not to tell you but I told her I would not keep secrets. I would have said something before but she asked me to let her be the one to say. She is so peculiar."

Minab walked towards the stairway then turned to Shirin. "I must go to the Holy Place. If I find anymore of your idols in this household I will take back that gift I gave you many years ago." Minab left the house quickly.

Shirin took out the little broken idol and placed it with the rest of the garbage, and then she cried in fear over Minab's violent threat.

When Breena woke, she had a terrible headache. Minab was asleep next to her. She got up, bathed, and dressed then she went down to the kitchen. She had missed the final meal of the day and she was hungry. She found some salted meat and fruit to eat. She fell asleep at the table in the kitchen and Shirin woke her when she started to prepare the morning meal.

"Did my master beat you last night?" Shirin asked Breena.

"No, Shirin, he didn't. Is Zorban a mighty warrior too?"

"Yes, he is a captain and ruthless also. Zorban and Minab used to fight side by side when they were younger. I saw you talking to Zorban yesterday. He is to be watched. He acts like he loves Minab but then his eyes tell a different story."

"I know what you mean." Breena was surprised that others saw what she saw in Zorban. "I plan on staying far away from him."

Minab entered the room, to let them know he was up and wanted his meal. Breena stood up and they exchanged looks but no words. Minab walked into the great room and Shirin hurried to bring him his meal.

After Minab left the house, Breena went out into the garden and sat on the bench. Shirin wanted to start on the new dresses for Breena that day but Breena was busy trying to figure out what she would do next in her relationship with the man who was her husband. Breena was resigned to the fact that men, obviously, never said sorry in this culture.

"Such a pretty bird, trapped in her own garden. One so beautiful should be free to fly." The voice came from the back gate and Breena knew immediately, it was Zorban.

"You should not be here. Guests come through our front entrance, not the back gate." Breena was not in the mood to listen to his prattle.

Zorban opened the gate and walked into the garden. "You are very bold for a female."

"You want something that's devoted and timid, get a pet." Maybe rudeness would turn him off and he'd go away.

Zorban laughed. "It would be dangerous to have a pet that is as wild as a lioness."

"Yes, especially one who is looking out for her litter. What do you want Zorban?"

"I was concerned for you. Minab seemed very angry after we finished our talk."

"You're the one who told him all those lies and got him upset? You're even lower than a pig. You're a pig's ass." Breena stood up and faced him. "I don't know what you were trying to accomplish but it didn't work. I went to see Shirin's physician, not her priest."

Zorban looked angry about being called a pig's ass but he kept his tone of voice civil. "You cannot be too careful with Shirin's kind. They are pagans."

Breena walked towards the house. "Oh, and as for my size. I'm giving Minab two big beautiful warrior sons, so you go home to your wife and daughters. Oh, and go home to your one little male child too. Minab is even happier with me now than he ever was." Breena walked into the house and closed the door. Whatever Zorban's ambition was in making Breena's life even more miserable than it already was, she was not about to let him accomplish his goals.

When Minab came home it was evening and Breena was sleeping already. She was becoming tired early in the evening lately. Minab walked into the room and Breena opened her eyes. He took off his armor and noticed she was not sleeping. He sat down on the side of the bed and took something from a pouch. It was another necklace. This one was a gold chain with a beautiful red stone attached at the end. He tried to hand it to Breena but she put her hands under the covers and did not take the gift. "The mother of my children should have precious things." His face showed the disappointment he was feeling that she did not accept his gift.

"I would rather have something else."

Minab raised his eyebrows. "This stone was taken from the mines of Kilabrow. It is very precious. What else could you want?"

"If you were actually sorry that hurt me; that would be much more valuable to me."

"I did not strike you."

"You made me feel even more worthless than a Zibo. You hurt my, my soul."

"I was misinformed."

"You were lied to by that rat. He professes to be your friend but he has other ambitions."

"Zorban told me he came by to see me today, but I was not home. So he talked to you. He said you blamed him."

"He covers his tracks pretty well."

"Will you accept this offering?" He put the necklace on the bed sheet beside Breena.

Breena picked it up and placed it back in Minab's hand. "I want something else."

"I will bring you a ring to match tomorrow."

"I don't want a ring or any other trinket. If you want to offer me something that's tangible, then offer me a sword of my own and teach me how to use it."

"That is ridiculous."

"It is what I want. I am a wife of a mighty warrior and I am to have warrior sons. I want my own sword. One that isn't too heavy for me to swing."

"You do not have the physical strength to use it on anyone. Besides, I will protect you."

Breena sat back and folded her arms. "Then take your gifts back. You are self-serving when you bring me bobbles. They are beautiful and very useless, just like you think of me."

Minab took the necklace and put it back into the pouch. "I will get you a knife and I will teach you how to throw it accurately. If a knife is used properly, it can be as deadly as a sword. Will that satisfy your warrior soul?"

Breena smiled. She was happy that Minab granted her request. "Yes and I went to see Shirin's physician, not her priest."

Minab gave her a doubtful look.

"Do I look like the type who'd believe a stone carving could do anything? It's just an ugly little rock."

The next evening Minab brought Breena a knife. It had a six-inch blade and an exquisitely carved handle with a ruby at the end. It was a thin handle therefore; it would be easier for Breena to hold. There was also a case of thick leather to carry it in. Breena was happy that he kept his word about the knife and she thanked him with a hug. Minab laughed and picked her up in his arms. Maybe, he thought, with such gratitude as that, he should have brought her a sword after all.

Minab took Breena out to where he trained his troops, to teach her how to throw the knife. Breena liked being out of the city and away from Zorban's surprise visits, which were becoming too frequent. Minab liked showing off his unique wife. He knew his men were watching as he stood behind Breena and guided her hand with each throw. Breena loved learning new things and she would get excited each time the knife hit inside the target. Minab would also show Breena how skilled he was at throwing the knife. Breena's attentiveness to Minab's display, pleased him and Breena knew it, but with all that he was skilled at, she was not about to tell him exactly how impressive he really was.

Breena learned technique quickly but her accuracy wasn't very good. She told Minab she was a quick learner and with practice she would become very good. As Breena became better at her new hobby, and that was how Minab thought of it, he made her stay home and practice on a target he had made in the garden. Shirin was disgusted by Breena's display of manly skills and she would try to find any excuse to distract her from practicing.

Minab told Breena he would have to go to Kalat in a couple of days to escort Kabay back to Chelm. His legion had returned a month ago and with Arbmoat's king still angered by Minab's takeover and marriage to the flaxen stranger, the chief overseer did not want Kabay's band to return alone.

The next morning, Breena accompanied Shirin to the market place. She had learned to sew from Shirin and wanted to buy fabric to make Minab a new nightshirt. Breena wanted to show Minab that she was thankful to him for teaching her a skill no other man would ever teach his wife in this culture. As she looked over the fabric, Zorban walked over to her and offered her a sugared fruit treat. Breena looked at Shirin and she nodded that it was acceptable to take the treat. Zorban handed it to Shirin, who in turn, handed it to Breena. Breena walked over to the well she had once sat at and Shirin followed.

"Leave us, female." Zorban sternly ordered Shirin.

Shirin looked at Breena and she nodded. "You can stand over there by the fruit table and watch us, if you like, Shirin."

After Shirin left, Zorban leaned towards Breena, but still kept his distance. "You cannot be too sure of her kind. They like to cause trouble by lying about what actually happens."

Breena took a small bite of the treat. "Thank you for the candied fruit. I was out where Minab trains his men. I didn't see you there. Are your men so good that they don't need training?"

Zorban touched the handle of his sword. "I train my men in a more difficult spot. There, they learn the skills needed for actual combat."

"Minab says he has quite a few new recruits. Maybe they need to know the basics before they get into the more difficult stuff."

"Maybe they are not very good and Minab doesn't want to lose them all in the first portion of their training. Do you like watching your husband show his skill as a swordsman?"

Breena took another bite of the treat and nodded. "When he was bringing me here from Moatsha, we were attacked. Minab protected me against three assailants at once. Minab saved me from certain death. He was very impressive."

"If he values you so much, why does he not decorate you with gold and silver and precious stones? If you were my woman, I would make sure you were rewarded for the gifts you carry within you."

Breena stood up. The conversation was headed in the wrong direction. "Maybe my husband has given me gifts and they are at home." She told him.

"Why would you leave them at home?"

"I'm the solitary member of my tribe in this whole land. I am one of a kind. Why would I want to be decorated with things that you can buy anywhere?" Breena nodded to Zorban and then walked back to Shirin. She asked her to help pick out the nicest and coolest material there, so they could purchase it and return home quickly.

Breena worried about Zorban's friendliness all day. With Minab going back to Kalat, could Zorban be planning to hurt him? What could be the reason for someone to eliminate a lifelong friend? Even if Zorban's talk was real and he was hinting that Breena would become his, upon Minab's death, the widow should have a say. Breena sat thinking about it for the rest of the day and Shirin was disappointed in the amount of progress she had made on the nightshirt she was sewing.

"Shirin, when your husband died, did you become part of your brother-in-law's household?"

"My husband died in the takeover of our city. I belonged to the captures."

"What would have happened if your husband had died working at everyday stuff?"

"Then, I would become part of my husband's oldest remaining brother's house. He would care for me."

"What if he didn't have a brother?"

"Then a close friend of my husband's could claim me as his second. That way, I would be cared for and my children would not be without a father."

"Do you have the right to say no?"

"Yes; but you would be without income, so your children could be taken away, if you owed any money. It would be a terrible thing to be a widow, without belonging to a household."

"Women don't seem to have many choices in this society." Breena said disappointedly.

Minab entered the house with Zorban, and Shirin hurried to organize the meal for them. Breena watched them as they sat in the great room and talked. A young slave girl came hurrying by Breena to undo her master's laces but Breena stopped her. "Shirin, please tell little Topel here, I will attend to Minab's laces." She said as she gently gripped the girl's arm. Shirin did so and Breena walked into the great room. She knelt in front of Minab and undid his laces, ignoring Zorban. Minab was a little surprised at Breena's actions but sat back watching her, as she undid and removed his footwear.

"Minab, when you go to Kalat, could I come with you? I want to see Jaymin, Kabay's wife." She asked in a soft tone.

"Kabay's wife will be returning with him to Chelm. You can see her then."

Breena sat up on her knees and rested her tummy against Minab's legs. She usually didn't get that close to him on her own accord. Minab took notice and was a little unsettled by her. "Please, let me come with you. I won't cause you any problems." She asked again.

With Breena's actions, Minab was beginning to find it difficult to maintain his uncompromising disposition with her. "It is a fourteen day journey there and a fourteen day journey back. You will not be comfortable."

"I can handle it."

Zorban leaned forward, towards Minab. "I have heard that those who carry two children usually shorten their day of delivery."

Minab looked at Breena again. She had placed her hands on his knees. "I would not chance that you should deliver in the wilderness. You will stay here."

"I feel fine, Minab. I still have two months to go. Please, otherwise I will be lonely here, by myself." Breena gave him the look she would use on her father to get him to change his decision on something. With her countenance looking disappointed, and her head slightly tilted down and her eyes steadfastly beholding him as if he was all that existed, she asked again if she could go.

Minab knew he had to change her approach or he might give in. He stood up and lifted Breena to her feet. "You have Shirin for company. It would not be good for you to accompany me on such a rugged journey." He leaned close to her and whispered. "Besides, I will not be here to disturb you at night. You will sleep well, during my absence."

Breena was not going to give up that easily but she knew it was useless to continue at that point. "Things are different now and I will miss you. I will not feel safe." She glanced quickly in Zorban's direction then back at Minab.

Minab gave Breena a gentle kiss on the cheek. She smiled back at him and left to bring them something to eat from the kitchen.

"What have you done to tame your wildcat?" Zorban asked Minab in their language.

Minab smiled. "She has come to know that I am captain of my household and will not tolerate her rebellious attitude any longer. I am equitable and she has not been harmed in my care. Her breed must be handled with gentleness, from time to time. They are not able to endure constant restrictions upon the freedom of their soul."

"She continues to wear her cover off of her head."

"It is her emancipation and it is not of great importance over all. I will allow it in my household, for the time being, and as long as she remains companionable."

"You are too indulgent upon her. She has turned you into her puppy." Zorban was baiting him.

"My wife is not like other women. She is not Adder. My methods obtain obedience, and, I am not her puppy." Minab was becoming angry.

Breena brought in the food and as she served Minab first, she asked once more if she could go with him. He had suddenly became apathetic and told her to listen to his words and not to ask again. With his change in demeanor, Breena knew Zorban must have said something to him.

When they were in bed, and the rain could be heard, Breena thought she better calm the waves Zorban had made. "Since you forbid me to go with you, will you do something for me?"

"It is good that you have accepted my decision. You contend with me, too much. What do you want me to do? Do you want me to bring you back a gift?"

"Yes."

"I will. What do you want? And do not ask for a sword."

"I want you to bring me back... you, in one piece with no cuts or wounds."

Minab gave her a baffled look.

"I had a bad dream about you. Someone is out to hurt you and I'm afraid." Breena knew from what Shirin had told her that Adder tradition was to pay attention to dreams.

"You are not Adder. Your dreams are caused by eating too many treats."

"Be careful anyway. I don't want my warrior children raised by someone else."

Minab pulled Breena close and kissed her. "You are a strange woman. I am always careful and on my guard while I am traveling, but I will take only my best soldiers and leave the newcomers here. Will that make you not so afraid?"

"Yes." Breena knew she would have to pay for her attentiveness to Minab, for now he thought she wanted him close to her on his last night home.

Minab left the following day and the trip to Kalat was uneventful. Breena however, received a summons just a week after he left. She was afraid of encountering Zorban so Breena stayed in the house, not even venturing into the garden. The summons came to the door in the form of a letter and Shirin brought it up to Breena immediately. It was naturally, not in the English language, so Shirin translated. Shirin told Breena that it was from Karisha, second to the Chief overseer and widow of Minab's father. Minab's mother had become her husband's brother's second. The Chief overseer's first wife died years ago, and Karisha was now his consort in life. Breena did not even know Minab's mother was still alive. He had not mentioned her. She had asked to have Breena brought to the house of the Chief overseer so she may see her. Breena was very nervous. Shirin told her that Karisha was as influential as a woman could get. Although she had no authority herself, she had the ear and heart of the Chief overseer, and that was all the power any woman could ever hope for.

Breena was dressed in her sapphire colored dress. Shirin said it made her hair glow and her eyes sparkle even more than they already did. Breena entered the house and she and Shirin were seated in the great room. It was huge with many chairs, a few sofas, and tables, in the room. There were a few odd looking musical instruments in the corner on stands, and the walls were decorated with paintings of people. There was a painting of Minab in his best armor standing with his sword drawn and his shield in his hand. He looked very muscular, stalwart, and unconquerable. Breena stood mesmerized in front of Minab's life size portrait as the woman came in the room. Shirin stood and nodded her respect. She was four inches taller than Breena's height of five feet four. Her hair was black with wisps of gray. She was still attractive but more mature in her face, yet she still stood with dignity.

Karisha said something and Breena turned around quickly.

"Oh. Excuse me. I didn't notice you. This picture is excellent. It looks just like him." Breena apologized and Shirin translated.

Karisha sat in a chair and pointed to one beside her for Breena to sit in. Breena carefully sat down. She was much bigger now and not looking clumsy was becoming a chore. Shirin translated everything to both parties.

"You are very right. The picture portrays my son very well."

"Minab never told me about you. Our marriage didn't start very well. He probably thought I'd embarrass him in front of you if we were to meet."

"I had asked to meet you as soon as I heard he had taken a second. He did not want to talk about you. He said you were just a second and there was no need to meet until he had some lineage."

Breena knew Minab did not love her, but it was still a little disappointing to hear. "Oh."

"You are not what I expected. They said you were a stranger but I did not expect you to look so exotic, so lovely."

Breena blushed. She wondered if Minab thought of her that way. "Minab told you about the babies, didn't he?"

"No. He did not even mention you were with child. Sometimes the wife or child does not survive the first delivery. It would be normal for a man to not show excitement to his mother until the child was delivered."

Breena cringed. "It kind of, makes it sound like breeding a horse or some kind of pet."

Karisha laughed. "A good wife will bare her husband strong children and it is then, that she is honored. You are to deliver soon?"

Breena shook her head and held up two fingers. "I'm having twins. Two."

Karisha smiled. "That is something worthy of honor. Are you a good wife? I have heard dreadful stories."

Breena looked down. "No. I guess I'm not a very good wife. This is very hard for me. I don't even know how I came to be in your land. This culture is very difficult for me to understand. I'm the stranger here, but you are all just as strange to me."

Karisha looked astonished. "Why are we so difficult to understand? We lead simple lives."

Breena shook her head. "Women usually don't marry even once until they are twenty years old, where I come from. We are equals in society and do many things the men do. We go to great schools and choose our own mates. We are not just so the men can have a lineage."

Karisha looked even more shocked. "This land you came from is very strange indeed."

"Before I came here, I was planning on going to school and to become a scholar in the study of how people think. I've been many places and done many things. No one told me what to do and I was not even planning on getting married for years. To be forced into a marriage without love, and to be constantly forced to do other things, is horrifying to my soul. Can you understand?"

Karisha smiled and nodded. "You will have my son's children soon and you will be like unto Adder. Eventually; you will become accustomed to it."

"I don't know if my heart will allow me to become accustomed to it."

"Tell Minab, when the babies are born that I would like to meet them. I am sorry that you grieve for your old ways but my son will not allow you to disgrace him. If you continue to resist his authority, he will punish you severely. It is his right."

Karisha stood and without another word, departed from the room. Breena felt like she had been cut off in mid-stride. Men treated women badly in this land because women allowed it. If she were to stay for the rest of her life here, she would not accept that and her only wish would be to change things.

CHAPTER SEVEN

WHEN MINAB REACHED KALAT, Kabay greeted him at the gates. Once back at Chelm, with Kabay and his men there, his legion would be whole again. Another captain, Volcar, now resided in Kalat and his legion would be the city's protectors. Kabay welcomed Minab into his home for food and lodging. Jaymin hurried to serve them and Minab told her she was greatly missed by his wife. Jaymin, still keeping Breena's secret asked if Breena liked Chelm, hoping he would tell her she was with child. Surely, he must know by now. He said she did not say if she liked Chelm or not.

"Have you broken that strong will yet?" Kabay was amused at the thought of how bizarre their marriage must be.

"There are things she still fights against, but she is not strong enough to fight my will forever."

Jaymin left the room and Minab asked if Kabay was to have hopes for a lineage soon. Kabay nodded and said it was early but that Jaymin was with child. Minab laughed and slapped Kabay on the shoulder then he told him his wife too was with child and soon their sons would play together.

* * *

Breena had no desire to bump into Zorban but she was beginning to feel trapped inside the house. She brought a blanket outside and spread it out under the tree. The sun was warm and soon she had fallen asleep. What woke her were tiny little pebbles falling on her. She opened her eyes and sat up. Zorban was sitting on the bench just a few feet away; his hand full of tiny little stones.

Breena looked around, worried that Shirin would see him and misunderstand, or worse, ignore him and leave her to his mercy. "You put me in a very compromising position when you show up here like this. My husband is not in the city and I am not chaperoned."

Zorban shook his head. "If Minab was to walk out here and see us, he would think nothing of it. I am his lifelong friend. I used to come and talked with Annek all the time. She was his first wife."

"Minab may not be as trusting of any man, after Miller."

"Minab knows I hated Miller as much as he. It was my legion Miller was sent to."

"He died fighting beside your men? However, you knew he would not have been a very good warrior in hand-to-hand combat. The men of my race are not as big as your people."

"He did not die with any of my men. I took him into the wilderness and slew him."

Breena's eyes widened.

"Do not look surprised. He had humiliated my friend, one of my own. Minab was too benevolent. I could not allow Miller to go unpunished. It was making us all look weak." Zorban sat up in a less casual position. "He died like an animal. He was less than that, anyway."

Breena bit her lower lip and glanced towards the house for a moment.

"You are frightened by my story?"

"You talk of killing as if it is of no significance."

"His was not an honorable death, and an honorable death is very important. Annek died alone."

"Did you hate her too?"

"No. I loved her. She was my friend."

"You loved Minab's wife?"

"We knew each other long before Minab took her to wife. She was my neighbor's child and as she grew, I knew she would be beautiful. But, she wanted Minab, and they wed while I was in a distant place. She should have been mine. Minab left her alone for months, before Arbmoat took Kalat. He did not even grieve when told she was dead. He recently had their marriage officially dissolved by the church, so she died without a mate."

"But she was with Miller and she shouldn't have been."

"I do not understand why she would do that. Miller was nothing. He was weak and unmanly. Maybe, it was because she had no children to care for and Miller needed friends."

"Minab did not have her killed."

"I was grateful for that. It was why I took care of Miller personally. But now Minab has you, with your enchanting hair and beguiling eyes, and your magical body that gives him two sons."

"Do you hate Minab?"

"Sometimes." Zorban stood up. "When he is no longer around, I will have you and I will miss him."

Breena stood up and ran into the house. She could not bear Zorban's intensity any longer.

*   *   *

The caravan back to Chelm was loaded at night just before the rain. They would leave first thing after the rain. Minab had noticed a change in Kabay. He was too relaxed for a warrior. Minab told Kabay marriage was making him soft and once back in Chelm he would have to fortify himself. He would train the new ones for a while.

The trip back to Chelm was also uneventful until during the rain on the eighth day out. A large group of men attacked the procession, catching some asleep in their tent. Minab was one of the first to hear the shouts from the guards and was out of his tent and into the rain immediately. Kabay came out of his tent soon after, but was not fully armored which angered Minab.

Minab jumped in front of Kabay and deflected a slash of a sword that would surely have hit Kabay on his unprotected arm. "Kabay, get your wife and flee into the woods." Minab shouted. Kabay scooped up Jaymin and carried her into the thick bush.

The fight was vicious and Minab would have been defeated, had he not brought his best men along with him. These warriors, that they fought, were well trained, and as it rained their deceit were revealed. At first, Minab thought they were Arbmoat's king's men because they wore no helmets and had brown hair, but the rain soon washed out the clay they had put in their hair. As Minab looked over the campsite after the battle, he found that the attackers had hair that was as black as a raven's feathers, unmistakably Adder. He thought they were much too skilled to be king's men. Arbmoat never had warriors as skilled as Adder.

Kabay returned and Minab faced him angrily. "You enjoy the company of your wife more than staying alive?" Minab shouted furiously as he hit Kabay, knocking him to the ground.

Kabay knew he had acted inappropriately. Warriors slept in full armor as they traveled. It was a critical rule of survival. He got up off the ground and Minab hit him again.

"You, who fought at Carouge and Tobarra. You; who was victoriously by my side at Hammond. I do not need an incompetent such as yourself; as a leader in my legion." Minab shouted as Kabay stood once more, and again was knocked to the ground. Jaymin watched in horror and cried for her husband.

Minab grabbed a hold of Kabay's broad shoulders and pulled him to his feet. "If I lose you, I will lose you honorably, to a battle where we are outnumbered twenty to one. I will not have you die because you enjoy your wife's company too much." Minab threw him back down onto the ground. "I will not lose a good friend because he has become careless." He said in a softer tone, and then he turned, and walked away.

Minab was troubled over the attack of unknown men who were Adder. They wore plain armor and tried to appear as king's men, but Adder never fought against Adder. Minab had their bodies lined up on the ground and asked his men if any recognized the faces of the dead. Dashand, a good soldier and excellent bowman of Minab's legion said he thought he had seen a few in Chelm, weeks ago. They were with others that could have been some of the other dead men that now lay upon the ground. Minab was furious at the manner of deception. Someone was out to kill him and his men. One of his own; was trying to murder a brother.

Minab had his men who died in battle, buried. He had not lost many but their deaths upset him greatly. Each of his men, this elite company he called his best, were like brothers to him.

As Minab and his men discussed the possibilities of who was behind the attack, his mind was filled with many names. He had enemies but they were not Adder; yet these enemies whose lifeless forms lay on the ground before them, were from Chelm. Even to him, their faces held familiarity. These well-trained soldiers were fine products of a skilled teacher. Their style, he had seen before, but his mind refused to remember with whom the expertise laid.

Minab figured whoever was behind the raid would think him dead. If he arrived back in Chelm ahead of schedule, maybe he could find who seemed to mourn him before his death had been announced.

He mounted his horse and rode steady, arriving through the city's back entrance three days prior to their expected time of arrival.

CHAPTER EIGHT

BREENA HAD MADE A batch of cookies. Shirin called them funny little sweet cakes. The kitchen was hot from the fireplace, so while it cooled, Breena went out to the garden to fan herself with her homemade fan. Zorban came walking through the back gate, looking very self-assured.

"I don't want you coming here when Minab is not home." Breena stated. "If you keep showing up without announcing yourself, I will tell Minab everything you have said to me."

Zorban laughed. "You belong to my household already and know it not. Soon I will visit you every evening during the rain."

Breena was avoiding his face until then, but his statement made Breena's heart race. "What have you done?"

"I have done nothing, but my men are very loyal. My secret band has already finished the job I sent them to do, by now."

Breena was stunned and she began to tremble. Tears filled her eyes as she thought about what could have happened to Minab.

"Why the tears? You did not like Minab's touch or his methods of producing an heir."

Breena's tears spilled over on to her cheeks and she spoke the name of Minab over and over. "You're wrong. We... Minab was starting to like me. He liked me. I wasn't just an incubator or a Zibo to him anymore."

Breena was having trouble controlling her tears. She was surprised at the feelings for Minab that whirled around her thoughts. "I'll never become your second. I'll die first."

Zorban shook his head and smiled. "Of course you will. You wouldn't want death to over take your babies too, would you?"

Breena had been previously practicing her knife throwing earlier that day, and had left it under the bench. She slowly reached down and scratched her ankle, and then she picked up the knife and hid it behind her back.

Zorban moved closer to her and Breena took out the knife. "Stay away from me or I will kill you."

Zorban laughed when he saw the small knife. "You are just postponing what will come to pass. I want to touch your hair. I want to take a kiss from you." He stepped closer still.

Breena threw the knife and it penetrated Zorban's arm, just beside the thick shoulder strap that held the armor together. Zorban looked surprised, then annoyed. He pulled the knife out and roughly grabbed Breena by the wrists.

"Don't touch me!" Breena screamed, then her attention changed and she looked beyond Zorban. As Zorban tried to force Breena's face closer to his, Minab slammed open the back gate with such force it shook leaves from the trees and the brushes. Zorban turned to look over his shoulder and immediately released Breena. She fell to the ground hard but managed to crawl away.

Minab's sword was already drawn and the look on his face was intense. "Your men were loyal, but they weren't very good swordsmen. Maybe you should have spent more time teaching them and less time trying to procure my wife."

Zorban smiled. "I was just comforting her. We thought you were dead."

"Why would you think that, Zorban?"

Zorban knew his explanation revealed too much. How much had Minab heard of their conversation? "You have misunderstood, Minab."

"I understand you sent those men to kill me so you could have my wife as your second. I understand by the look in her eyes she loathes your touch even more than she does mine."

Zorban drew his sword. "She is just a yellow hair stranger. She is just your second, a Zibo. Is she worth our friendship?"

Minab looked over at Breena as she sat huddled against the back door to the house. "I would die for her."

"Then I will grant you your desire." Zorban nodded politely.

They had been speaking English and Breena looked up as she heard Minab speak about her. She blinked her vision clear. Zorban and Minab were evenly matched. Breena groaned as a shape pain traveled through her abdomen, around to the back.

The two men faced each other and came together with a thunderous clash of metal. Each sound of a blow tore through Breena's soul. Minab again, was her protector. The sun reflected off the steel of their swords. Each time they were raised and swung, it looked like flashes of lightening. Minab would plunge and Zorban would deflect, then Zorban would thrust and Minab would bring his sword down and smash them both into the ground. With each swing, Breena trembled at the possible outcome. Their swords collided together, resisting each other as blade slid along blade. They came chest to chest and Minab pushed Zorban back against the bench, which toppled over. Zorban pulled out a knife from his belt and slashed at Minab, putting a long gash down his triceps. Minab smashed his sword against the knife, sending it into the bushes. Breena seeing Minab's blood, screamed out for Minab, but she did not distract him. He hit waist high, trying to knock Zorban's sword from his hand, but caught him at the wrist. Zorban relinquished his grip immediately and his heavy sword fell to the ground.

Zorban looked at his almost severed hand, and then he slowly returned his gaze upon Minab. "Finish this Minab. I cannot survive as a warrior with only one hand."

Minab lowered his sword. He shook his head and slowly spoke Zorban's name.

Zorban smiled. His body was starting to go numb from the loss of blood from his hand. Blood gushed from the wound. "If you allow me to live, my friend, I will become as a snake and during a night when you are away, I will kill your posterity and take your wife, leaving her used."

Minab yelled violently out of frustration and grief. It was almost a roar, and as he did so, he gripped his sword in both his hands, and swinging in a half circle, aimed at Zorban.

As Minab's blow struck Zorban's neck, Breena went into hysterics. She backed up against the door as tightly as she could and covered her face with her hands. Minab looked at his friend for only a second. It was over. He sheathed his sword and walked over to Breena.

Breena felt his approach and desperately tried to retreat even further. Another pain etched its way through her body. She looked up at Minab and with tears streaming down her face, she shook her head. "I'm sorry I didn't tell you. I didn't think you'd believe me. I didn't think Zorban would actually try and harm you."

"I would not have believed it if I had not heard him speak the words." Minab squatted down beside Breena. She was holding her belly as she rocked back and forth. "Are you in pain?"

Breena nodded and Minab picked her up in his arms. Breena put her arms around him and buried her face in his neck, as she held on to him tight. Minab brought her into the kitchen. He did not have to shout for Shirin. She had been cowering in the kitchen listening to the battle.

"Shirin, she is in pain. I think it must be her time."

Shirin guided Minab to a back bedroom that had been prepared earlier, for the birth. The bed was without a mattress but had a thick blanket over its wooden base. Minab placed Breena on the blanket. "I must speak with the Chief overseer and the Holy man. They must be told a great captain has died."

Breena started to sob and Minab leaned over and kissed her. "I know you do not understand. It is our way and it could not have ended any differently. You are my wife and I will protect you. I will provide for you. It is time for you to concentrate on what is your way. My son wants life." Minab left the room and Shirin followed him.

"Do you want Zorban's body sent home?"

"No. Leave him. I will tell his men to come and collect their shame. See that my wife is cared for at this time. You do it. You are knowledgeable in these things."

Minab left and went to see the chief overseer. He told him what had happened and Takmana, the chief overseer summoned Zorban's men. He ordered that they bring Zorban back to his own household to be prepared for burial. Takmana then counseled Minab to visit the Holy man and then to visit Zorban's widow. Zorban's brother, Frosth, would care for her but Minab knew Zorban's window had a right to know who had killed her husband, but he would soften the reason why.

When Minab returned to his home, it was beginning to rain. Zorban's body had been taken away and the activity in the household was centered on the back bedroom. Minab found Shirin talking with a young female servant from another household. The young woman had just given birth the day before to a little female child that did not live through the day. Yathsa had agreed to be a wet nurse to the babies should they both live. Shirin figured Breena too weak to handle the feeding of both babies at the same time. Minab waved off those who hurried to serve him.

"My wife?" Minab asked Shirin.

"It has been eight hours and your wife is still struggling. It is difficult for her and she is very tired. I worry for her."

Minab walked into the back bedroom and found Breena on her knees and elbows. Her legs were spread and she was resting her head on the pillow that was between her arms. Her face was very pink and her hair was wet from perspiration. She looked exhausted. She had changed from her clothes into a nightshirt.

Minab pulled a chair over to the bed and sat down. "Wife, how is my son?"

Breena opened her eyes and looked at Minab. "Stuck." She started to laugh but the jiggling hurt her. "Minab, I have been your wife for almost nine months now and not once have you ever called me by my name. My name is Breena. I'd be Breena Elizabeth Keets whatever your last name is, except you people don't have a last name. So, if you can't call me by my name, get the hell out! I'm not in the mood to put up with your troglodyte behavior at this moment..." She trailed off as she gripped the pillow to brace for another contraction. She moaned and then started to cry.

Minab reached out and moved the hair that had fallen over Breena's face. "Wife, if you are not a warrior and cannot deliver my son, I will leave. It is what I expected, from a Zibo."

Breena looked back up at him. She didn't need her emotional pain to match her physical pain, right then. "Get out, you stupid oversized..." Breena began to call Minab every disheartening name she could think of. She picked up the pillow and threw it. It smacked him on the side of his head. "These are my babies and I'll give birth when I damn well please! The only part of these babies that belongs to you is their stubbornness."

Minab picked up the pillow and placed it beside Breena. "That part definitely belongs to their mother." He stood, and then left the room.

Breena started to cry again. More than anything she wanted Minab beside her. Shirin came in and wiped Breena's face with a cool wet cloth. "Shirin, what if he's right? What if I'm nothing but a stupid little Zibo and can't do it?"

Shirin leaned close. "When Minab's father died, I saw Minab cry. He was a full-grown man, a powerful and ruthless warrior, yet he cried for an hour. I never ever want to see that again. You will deliver, and you and the babies will be fine." Shirin ordered Breena to lie on her back so she could check her.

It was the start of a new day when Shirin came out into the kitchen. She washed her hands and started to give orders to the kitchen girls with their cooking duties before she noticed Minab. He was sitting on the floor, leaning against the wall, in a corner. His eyes were closed and he was deep in sleep. The clatter of pots woke him. He looked up at Shirin and then started to get upon his feet.

"Soon." Shirin nodded.

Minab hesitated, and then walked into the back bedroom. Breena was on her back and she looked worse than before. She slowly looked over at Minab. "I thought I wasn't fast enough for you. You know nothing about giving life."

"Teach me." Minab sat down on the chair beside the bed and took Breena's hand in his.

Breena became agitated and yelled for Shirin.

Shirin came running back in. "Do not hold her hand, Master."

Breena thumped on the bed with her foot and screamed. One of the kitchen girls came running in with a couple of small blankets. She was so excited she just stood behind Shirin and bounced on her toes as she clutched the blankets in her arms. Breena got up on her elbows and held her breath, then her face turned red and she cried out. Minab had not let go of her hand, and he was shocked at the force with which Breena clamped down onto his. She hurt him. Breena took another quick breath and bore down. Minab let go of her hand this time. She lay back and held onto the bedpost. Breena pulled on the bedpost so hard, it cracked. Shirin quickly turned the baby and Breena gave a small push and then started to laugh. Shirin turned the baby upside down and cleared its mouth. The baby let out a loud cry and Shirin grabbed one of the small blankets and wrapped the baby. Minab sat captivated by the sight. Shirin placed the baby on Breena's upper abdomen and tied the cord, then cut it.

"Welcome your son, master." Shirin opened the blanket so Minab could behold his son. The baby was crying loudly and Minab leaned over and touched his tiny hand. Minab grinned and looked back at Breena. She was watching the tiny infant's every move. She closed her eyes, gave another small push, and relaxed. Shirin took the infant and wrapped him tightly in his blanket, and then she placed him in a smooth wooden box on a table in the corner.

"Oh, oh Shirin; it's starting again." Breena shouted nervously, and she began to grip the bedpost again.

Minab stood up and walked over to where Shirin stood. Breena took another breath and Shirin turned the baby's head. The body was gently eased out and Minab's smiles never vanished. Shirin did the same thing with the new baby as she had with the other. Breena looked at this baby and touched its tiny fingers.

"You win again, Minab. You always win; two sons." Breena wasn't really disappointed. She was extremely pleased that she had finally delivered, that she wasn't weak.

Minab walked over to the chair again and sat down. He folded his arms and looked at Breena. In all his existence, he had never felt so pleased with life. "Thank you wi... thank-you Breena. You have done well. You have given me more than I had hoped for."

Breena smiled back at Minab. Her eyes filled with tears. She didn't mind that she had given him what he desired, not now. "Shirin, could I see them again? Could you bring them close so I may touch them?"

Shirin picked up the first. Both were tiny but not weak. The first had hair that was as black as his father's was. "Feed this one and then we will bath him."

Breena just stared at the baby Shirin had placed in her arms. "Shirin." She wanted to tell Shirin she didn't know how. She had never even seen a baby being nursed before, except for one time in the city of Kalat when it was Moatsha.

Shirin walked over to Breena and undid the top of her nightshirt. "Lift the baby up to you."

The baby didn't need any encouragement once he was placed close enough to nurse. Breena smiled. She was doing it. She was providing nourishment for her babies. It only nursed for a few minutes, and then fell asleep. Shirin took him, gave him to the young girl, and instructed her to bathe him carefully in the small tub of water on the table and to wrap him in a clean blanket after. Then Shirin picked up the second baby and handed him to Breena. The second baby had hair that was definitely light brown, with streaks of blond hair among it. Breena nursed him and as she did, she touched his hair. "It's light colored. That's amazing."

Minab touched the baby's hair also. "My first son shall be called

Sheb. It means, strong willed. The second shall be called Tian. It means, like unto the first."

"Do I not get a say in what they are called?"

"No, but if we have daughters, I will let you choose their names."

Breena shook her head. "It's a good thing I like those names or I'd just call them whatever I wanted."

Minab shook his head and smiled. He was glad she liked the names, too.

Shirin took the other baby from Breena. "Breena must rest. We will clean her up now and give her food." It was Shirin's way of telling her master to leave without telling him.

Minab stood up. He leaned over to Breena and kissed her. "I did well in my choice for wife." He turned and left the room.

Breena closed her eyes. She was very tired. "Thank you for helping me Shirin. I would not have made it without you."

Shirin wiped Breena's face with a warm moist cloth. "It has been interesting since you were brought to Chelm. Not many men witness their son's birth. You have gone against the custom but I think my master is grateful for the experience."

Breena kept her eyes closed. "If you could change a custom Shirin, what would it be?"

Shirin was silent for a moment then she smiled. "I would wish a hug from my sons. When they turn eight they no longer touch their mothers."

Breena opened her eyes. "What do you say about changing a whole bunch of stupid customs?"

"If it were possible I would have joy."

"I thought giving birth to two sons was going to be impossible. It just means the other things are going to be easy. You watch. Life is not over yet. You'll get your hugs one day, I promise."

"Sleep now, my master's wife. You have done much and deserve the rest."

Minab went to visit his mother and was surprised to find out she had met with Breena. Karisha was delighted to learn that Minab had been given two sons. She counseled Minab to watch over his wife, that she must have been sent here, just to magnify her husband and to reward him for his duty to his God and his people.

Kabay arrived at the city's entrance and Minab was there to greet him. They embraced and Minab told him all that had happened. Jaymin was ecstatic over the news of Breena's delivery of twins. She begged her husband to take her to her friend. Kabay became angry and scolded Jaymin for her persistence but Minab invited them to stay at his abode while their home was made ready. Jaymin was thankful for Minab's intervention. Breena's influence over Jaymin's behavior had already put her in trouble with her husband during the few months they had been married. Minab asked Shirin to take Jaymin to Breena when they arrived at the house. Minab and Kabay sat in the great room and talked while Shirin served them.

"I have been given a great gift, Kabay. I witnessed my sons come into this world. My wife labored mightily in her travail. These females are more than they appear. I am grateful to my own mother for the ordeal she endured for my birth."

"It is their duty, Minab."

"You have not witnessed what I have. No wonder they mourn so greatly at their posterity's death. It is more than what we have seen. It is more difficult than if they had to tear a limb off to give life. It is equal to when we die to protect them."

"All this was felt by witnessing a birth?"

"And more; you must see for yourself when Jaymin delivers."

"It is not the custom."

"Is it against the custom to ascertain something not learned even by the scholars? It is not only nourishment for the spirit, but it will change things in your heart."

"Has Minab become a philosopher?"

Minab laughed. "I have not only become a philosopher, I have become a man. For no male can be that, until he has seen the birth of the soul of his soul and flesh of his flesh."

Jaymin cried when she saw Breena sleeping on the bed in the back room. The bed had been changed and cleaned up. Beside Breena, on the floor, were the two little wooden boxes. Inside the open boxes were the babies. Jaymin bent down beside Breena.

"Breena, my friend who is more of a sister than my sister, awake and show me your wondrous accomplishments."

Breena opened her eyes and reached out for Jaymin. "Jaymin? Oh Jaymin, I've missed you terribly. I am so glad you are here."

"Minab boasts of your achievement. I have never seen such a serious warrior so jubilant. It is as if he has conquered the greatest of legions."

"Well I didn't do such a bad job, myself." Breena pointed to the babies. "Jaymin; it took forever and hurt so much. It's hard to believe women go through this every day."

Jaymin looked at the babies. "One is like the father, and the other similar to the mother. I pray they get along better than you and Minab."

Breena blushed. "Things are a little better than they were when we left Kalat. Minab was even beside me when the babies were born. He thanked me and said I did well. I guess I'm not a Zibo anymore."

*   *   *

Twelve days after the birth, Breena's sons were introduced at a feast thrown by Minab. They were circumcised, their names were presented to the church, and they were blessed. Breena sat in a chair beside Minab. Jaymin translated for her, as Minab would not perform such a lowly duty. Minab knew many would be whispering about the scarf not being on Breena's head, but he did not want to fight with her on such a special day. It was a joyful event with many friends and relatives around. Breena met Minab's sisters and his uncle, the chief overseer. Breena held the little infant boys in her arms and Minab was surprised when she handed Sheb to him. Men never held their children.

"You must take him. I have things to do." Minab told her.

"You put this little guy in me to hold for nine months. Now it's your turn, and don't give me that garbage about touching. He's your son and you're going to touch and hold him and show your love to him."

"Do not counsel your husband, wife."

"Fine; I think I'll call him mommy's little cherub instead of Sheb and for the next eight years I'm teach him how to cook and sew. By the time you start teaching him how to be a warrior, he'll be a fine little girl."

Minab looked at her, trying to wonder if she was serious. "You cannot take the fight out of a warrior."

"Sure I can. It works on the same principle as what happens to a duck when it's raised by a chicken." Breena held out her son and Minab took him.

Kabay looked at Minab and chuckled. "You have become a wet nurse now?"

Sheb let out a vociferous cry and Minab laughed. "I am teaching my son the art of the war cry."

Breena traded sons with Minab. "I think it actually means he wet his diaper."

CHAPTER NINE

L IFE OVER THE NEXT few weeks was quiet. Breena was busy learning to mother and Minab was always watching. Breena, according to tradition, slept in the back bedroom with the two babies. Her days of separation from her husband were to be sixty. Minab came home one day and told Breena he had to take his legion to the land south of Kalat, to help defend a city called Tobarra. Karoute, ruler of the Naphtas had come up against the city to take it from the Adders. They were under siege and Minab's legion was to depart right away. Minab looked at his sons once more, and then he took Breena into his arms. "When I return, you will be my wife once more." He kissed Breena roughly and left. Breena stood at the door and watched him ride away. A sudden pain filled her heart as she realized that in war, even the invincible were sometimes, slain.

Minab traveled with his legion to the south towards Tobarra. They traveled fast, with only six hours of sleep a night. Time was important as Karoute was a tyrant and took no prisoners, not even female. By the time they reach their destination the battle was waning. Karoute had killed the forces sent out from the city and he was now heading for the gate. Minab sent Kabay and his men around to the other side of the city. They would attack from the west. Hasteal and his men would move south and attack from there. Minab and his men would attack from the east. Karoute would be boxed in. Only their speedy entry into the city would save them from Minab's legion. So far, the city had barricaded itself well. The battle was bloody. Karoute's men were skilled but their numbers had declined from their previous battle with the people of Tabarra. They were outnumbered by five thousand. But, before they could be defeated, Karoute took flight with five hundred of his best men. He had been humiliated. He sent a messenger to Minab, telling him that vengeance would find him soon, and that he should sleep with one eye open. Minab was not intimidated. He had heard these threats before. They secured the city for the people of Tobarra and celebrated, then headed home.

Breena had placed her babies down for the night. They were sleeping through the night now and growing well. With Yathsa helping Breena nourish the babies, they lacked in nothing. Minab had been gone for over two weeks. He would be surprised to see how his sons had grown. Breena was coming into the kitchen when two men came through the back gate and entered the house. They were dressed in dark rain gear and held little knives in their hands. Young Topel saw them first and screamed. One put a knife to her throat and she was silenced. Shirin gasped at the sight but did not cry out. Breena stood frozen to the floor. Her concern was for her sons.

"What do they want? Ask them Shirin, quickly."

Shirin did so and they asked where Minab's female was. Shirin told Breena they had come to kill her.

"Ask if I am to be told why."

They told Shirin it was to revenge a humiliation that had occurred to their superior.

"Once death has occurred there is no chance to go any further. Tell them that, Shirin. Tell them; even death will not change the fables that will be made about the humiliation."

They asked who the strange yellow hair was who talked like an overseer and they were told she was the wife of Minab. The two men conferred, and then they threw a black sack over Breena's head. They told Shirin to tell Minab that they would trade his wife for him. That they would be in a camp near Basherda, a small village near the river Teruta and he was to come alone. One threw Breena over his shoulder and they left as silently as they came.

They traveled for hours and Breena was sick from the jostling of the horse and the dark smelly sack that covered her face. Her hands were tied behind her and a small cord secured the sack around her neck. They stopped, took her off the horse, and threw her in a tent. An older man came in to the tent and undid the sack. When he took it off Breena's head, he spoke to her but she could not understand anything that was being said. She told him she could not speak their language and he in turn, shook his head indicating he did not understand her. Over the period of many hours, many men came to take a peek at Breena. She was beginning to feel like a monkey at the zoo. They had never seen yellow hair before. Breena's breasts ached to feed her babies. They brought her food and Karoute himself came to see the yellow hair, Minab's unusual wife.

A few hours later, Breena was brought out into the middle of camp. There in the midst was Minab, alone and without a weapon. He looked at Breena and nodded. "They will take you back. They have what they want."

"No. They will kill you. This isn't honorable. Where is the honor of an execution?" Breena feared for Minab.

"It is our way. Go, they have promised your safety. Kabay will care for you in his household. Breena, know that I love you."

Breena began to cry. One of the men gave her a shove towards the horses and Breena turned around and slugged him in the face, sending him to the ground. Karoute laughed and said something to Minab.

"Wait! Wait! Please Minab, let me say something to their leader. Translate for me." Breena could not go and leave Minab behind. Breena would not go and leave Minab behind.

Minab nodded and waved his hand for her to speak. She took a deep breath. "I have been in this land for over a year and I have seen honor. I have met and loved honorable people. Where is your honor?

Is yours a tribe without standards and values? Is this what you call honor?"

Minab translated and Karoute asked how they could show honor to this strange female. Breena walked up to Karoute and without fear or doubt, she told him that her husband could beat any man Karoute had there, in a one to one battle. She told him her husband was not only a good swordsman, but was a warrior even with just his hands. Honor was settling a humiliation either as army to army or one to one. There was no veneration in an execution. All it showed was that with enough rats, if grouped, even a bull could be brought down.

Karoute did not like the similitude of his army to that of a group of rats. He looked at Breena and then nodded. He said he would pick out one man to fight Minab. If Minab won, they would be set free, but if he lost both Minab and Breena would die.

Breena looked at Minab. "Will he keep his word?"

Minab asked and Karoute yelled angrily that his word is law. Minab was satisfied. They brought out a soldier that towered over Minab by six inches. Breena thought Minab was the most powerful man she had ever seen until then. Minab looked back at Breena. "If I fail, my wife, I take consolation in knowing you are mine, forever, but my soul will pain at knowing, they will hurt you." He touched Breena's cheek tenderly with his hand.

They took Breena over to stand by Karoute and the two warriors confronted each other. Minab's armor was removed and strapped to a horse. Should he be defeated, it would be sent back to his men. Minab looked just as big without his armor but not as indestructible. Breena stood with her hands to her mouth. Had she done the right thing? As the men began to fight it was heart wrenching for Breena. She was a woman who could barely watch a football game back home. Boxing and wrestling used to be sports she had no comprehension of and no desire to observe. Now, she was in a world that glorified it, embraced it, and made it an intricate part of life.

They fought with fists and force. Minab could box and wrestle well but the other man had pure strength and threw Minab around like a toy. Minab knew he had to keep from getting close enough to be picked up or the giant would defeat him just by that one maneuver. The giant's strangulation grip was another thing Minab knew he had to avoid. His arms were like a vice.

The giant came at Minab and Minab hit him in the face. No reaction. Minab was becoming worried. This giant was not a man who could feel pain. The giant grabbed Minab by the neck. Minab clenched his fists and boxed him in the ears. The giant let go. He felt that blow and with his hands over his ears twirled around as if he was dizzy. Minab kicked him in the knee and the monstrous man went down. Minab was on top of him in a second and he began to hit him with one blow after another. As blood began to gush, Breena looked away. She could not handle the sight. Minab was winning but Breena couldn't stand the thought of anyone being hurt.

Karoute waved his hands and yelled. The fight was over. Breena ran to Minab and hugged him. His face was starting to swell from the blows he had received and he didn't look much different from the unconscious giant that lay upon the ground. Minab pushed Breena behind him and started to back out of the camp. He had ample doubt that Karoute would keep his word. They moved over by the horse that had Minab's amour tied on to its back. Karoutes men stood watching, their weapons slowly being raised. Suddenly with a roar, Minab's men attacked from all sides. As they ran passed Minab, towards Karoute's men, Minab quickly placed Breena on the horse and got up behind her.

"Karoute is out-numbered and will be defeated. I will take you home. There is no need for you to see this slaughter."

Breena leaned back against Minab. Just hours before, she thought she would never see her babies again and now both she and Minab would soon be home with them. It wasn't until they reached the city and their house that Breena realized how hurt Minab was. He kept swaying behind her and as they approached their threshold, he gave out a small groan and fell off the horse. Breena screamed and Shirin came running out. The male servants brought Minab into the house and up to his bed. Minab was bleeding from his lower back. Breena had not seen the giant pull a small knife from his boot and he push it into Minab's back. Minab had not fully felt its affects until then. The physician was called, and he ministered to Minab. He told Shirin to tell Breena that Minab must stay in bed for a week to give the wound time to heal. The blade of the knife came very close to piercing an organ that could have killed him.

Breena fed her babies and then slept on the floor beside Minab's bed. Minab woke early, just after the rain ended. He leaned over and tried to pick Breena up from the floor, but the strain sent a sharp pain into his back.

"Minab, you must rest. What are you trying to do, kill yourself? You need to be careful."

"I want my wife beside me."

"You are not well, Minab. You're supposed to rest and give your wounds time to heal."

"I am a warrior. I do not have time for self pity."

Breena sat beside him on the bed. "This is serious Minab. The physician said you could have died." Then Breena slapped him on the shoulder. "You could have died while you were taking me home. You never said anything. You said you'd protect me. That means you're not going to die on me. Now stay in bed or I'll..."

Minab smiled. "You will what? You do not even have a hope of keeping me here if I do not want to stay."

"You get out of bed and you will never get the chance to have another son by me. I'll sleep in the back bedroom forever."

Minab laughed. "You think I would miss you?"

Breena leaned forward and kissed Minab passionately. Minab was so surprised he didn't move. Breena had hugged him before but never had she kissed him. He started to put his arms around her but she slipped out of his hands and stood up.

"You'd miss me. I don't have to think it. I know it." Breena headed for the door. "I'll bring you some food. I even have some of those tiny sweet cakes you like."

After Breena brought Minab something to eat, she told him she was going out to the market with Shirin. Minab told Breena to wear her scarf. She was not only a married woman but also a mother now and outside of their house she was to wear the proper clothing or she could not go.

Kabay had arrived just as they were leaving and Breena told Shirin to tell Kabay to make sure Minab stayed in bed while he was there. Kabay told her through Shirin, that it was not a woman's place to tell a warrior anything. Breena put her hands on her hips and walked up to Kabay, so close, they almost touched. Kabay backed away.

"This is my house, Kabay and if you want to enter it and see Minab, you'll do as I ask. Otherwise, you may leave."

Kabay's face reddened with anger as Shirin translated but he remained silent. Breena gave him a smile, put her scarf on her head and left.

As they were in the market place, looking at fabric, Breena noticed a man that looked like Minab, from the back. He was even wearing armor. Before Shirin could stop Breena, she walked up to him. "This is really dumb, Minab. Is it worth risking your health just to check up on me and see if I'm wearing this stupid scarf?"

The man turned around and Breena stepped back. He did indeed look like Minab, only younger, but it wasn't Minab. He looked at her intensely, as if he was shocked at her manners.

"I'm sorry. I thought you were Minab." Breena felt terribly embarrassed. Shirin ran up to her and started to scold her.

"You speak the English of a stranger and you know Minab?" The man asked.

Breena ignored Shirin and replied in surprise. "And you also speak English!"

The man smiled and it made him look even more like Minab. "I also know Minab. How is it that you know him so intimately?"

Breena started to stutter. "I. We… in Kalat we were…who are you?" She asked.

"Minab is my brother."

"No. Minab has no brother. Zorban said so."

"Ah, Zorban. How is he these days?"

"Dead."

The man's smile vanished. "He was a good warrior. Minab must grieve the loss of his close friend."

"You must not talk with this man, Breena. Minab would not permit it." Shirin told Breena as she tried to pull her away.

"Why?" Breena stood her ground and looked back at the warrior.

The man took a step towards her. "Minab disowned me as a brother. He used to tell people I was dead, now, I never existed, according to what you have been told. Alas, Shirin is right. You should not be talking to me." The man looked at Breena's scarf and his eyes widened. "How do you know my brother?" He asked slowly, anticipating the answer.

"I am his wife."

The man shook his head. "My brother took a stranger to wife? But, he hates the strangers."

Shirin gave Breena a hard pull and it almost knocked her off her feet. Her scarf fell to the ground. "Minab has been hurt in battle. You must visit him." Breena took the opportunity to speak as Shirin hurried to put Breena's scarf back on.

"He would not welcome me, I assure you."

"I will talk to him." Breena managed to say as Shirin roughly put Breena's scarf on her and then pushed her away from the man.

Breena was full of questions but Shirin refused to talk about it. She just told Breena he was a wicked man. As soon as Breena got home, she asked Shirin to bring the babies up to see Minab then she hurried up the stairs to see him. Kabay was still there. He was in a chair beside the bed, talking to Minab. Breena bounced onto the bed and Kabay stood up. Such an intimate sight was nothing like he had ever seen before.

"Wife, it is improper to display affection like this in front of others, especially men."

"What affection?" Breena looked at Kabay's face and giggled. "You mean me being on the bed with you is being affectionate?" She was excited about the news of Minab's brother but this new twist had side tracked her thoughts.

"This is something private between a husband and wife."

Breena started to laugh, and then she moved closer to Minab. "Is this embarrassing to Kabay?"

"Yes, greatly."

"So you and Kabay can talk about all sorts of things like making babies and how we act but this is too embarrassing?"

"It is our way, wife."

"There you go again, calling me wife. I have a name." Breena crawled up close to Minab and stood upon her knees. She touched his hair and Minab gave her a stern look. "Well, you should hear what we say about you men." Side tracked again, but this time only temporarily. "I never realized your hair was so soft."

Minab said something to Kabay in their language and he answered. Minab turned back to Breena. "What things do you talk about, concerning us?" Minab asked her.

"Tell Kabay I could really make him blush if I wanted to exaggerate, but," she sighed, "...I just heard he was a great kisser."

Minab became angry. "That should not be of interest to you."

Breena laughed at his angry expression. "Fine, if you're going to get all upset I won't tell you anymore." She moved away but stayed on the bed.

Shirin brought the babies into the room and apologized to Minab, saying Breena asked for them to be brought to the bedroom. Breena put them down on the bed beside her.

"These babies should not be here. Take them back." Minab said loudly.

Breena picked them up in her arms. "That's your choice but, they go, I go. See you in the morning, husband. I'll be down stairs and into the back bedroom." She headed for the door.

"Wife."

Breena continued to walk away.

"Breena."

She turned around and faced Minab.

"It is our custom that children do not spend long periods of time with the father. It is our custom that the mother raises the sons until they are eight, then they can spend time with their father."

"My sons will not be spending time with someone they don't know. Your custom breeds fear, not love, and respect. My sons will be fearless of their father."

"We will talk later."

"Not without the babies. And, you can quote customs all you want. It doesn't make it right."

"They will not respect me if they are too familiar."

"Garbage! I loved and respected my father more than any man and he was one of my best friends."

"It is unthinkable for a father to befriend his daughter. She will one day belong to some other man."

"Well, where is a woman supposed to find friendship? It certainly isn't from her husband." Breena stormed out of the room with the babies and did not come back even though Minab called after her.

Later as the rain fell, the door of the back bedroom where Breena and the babies slept opened. Minab, dressed in his nightshirt, walked slowly in and knelt down beside the bed where Breena slept. Breena woke immediately. "Minab, you shouldn't be walking around."

"Wife, you must stop this attitude. I am your husband and I will be obeyed."

"That would make me your slave, not your wife."

Minab picked Breena up and put her over his shoulder. Breena didn't struggle much. She was afraid she would re-hurt his injury. She didn't yell either. She was afraid she'd wake the babies. Minab carried her up stairs to their room and tossed her on the bed. "Slave or wife, you will obey. In the morning I will tell you how you will raise my sons." Minab got back into the bed and pulled her close. Breena struggled hard this time.

The next morning Breena hurried down to feed the babies before Minab woke. Minab started yelling for her as soon as he awoke and found she was not there. Breena knew she would have to go see him. He would only come and get her if she didn't go. Just before she went upstairs, she took a scarf from the kitchen. Breena walked into the room and sat on a chair. She folded her arms and silently stared at Minab. It didn't take long before Minab became upset. Breena was wearing a black scarf on her head. Pain showed on Minab's face as he got out of the bed and pulled the scarf from Breena's head. He had re-injured his wound the night before, struggling with Breena. He sat back down on the bed and looked at her.

"You will not wear this." He said as he shook the scarf at her. Breena shrugged her shoulders. She didn't answer him. "My sons will be raised in the traditions of their father." Again, Breena said nothing. 'Kabay is very upset. He does not want Jaymin around you anymore."

"Is that everything?"

Minab was unsure of her temperament. "Yes."

Breena stood up and left the room. Hours past and soon Shirin came running up to Minab. "Oh master, what should I do? She is scrubbing the floor and surely, the mistress of the house should not be doing so. It is not good for the babies' milk."

"What are you ranting about, Shirin?"

"Your wife! She is down on her knees scrubbing the floor."

Minab gave out a small sigh of discouragement. He slowly stood up and put on a robe then followed Shirin down stairs. Breena was in the entrance, wearing a black scarf and scrubbing the stone tiled floor with a brush. Minab walked over and stood just in front of her. Breena scrubbed around and in-between, his feet. "Stop this!" Minab pulled the scarf off her once more. Breena did not stop and Minab pulled her up onto her feet. He groaned with pain. His wound was very painful. "Get upstairs or I will carry you up there."

"Go ahead. It will be said by many, that the great Minab died of injuries while fighting with his little slave wife."

Minab picked her up and took her upstairs into the bedroom. "You will stay here until I tell you to leave."

"I ache. Our sons need to be fed." Breena touched her chest.

Minab shouted for Shirin and asked her to bring the babies up to the bedroom, so Breena could feed them. Shirin brought Tian; Yathsa had just fed Sheb. Breena took Tian in her arms and sat down on the bed to feed him. Minab watched Breena then slowly he looked around. Here Breena was, in bed next to him, feeding her child. This was exactly what she wanted the day before and he had now commanded her to do so. Breena smiled as she looked down at Tian. He smiled back and held onto her finger with all his might. Breena quietly began telling Tian a story. It was about his father and how his Minab's legion conquered the city of Moatsha. Minab closed his eyes and pretended not to listen, but he opened them again when Breena told Tian about how tiny females held them at bay, for over three weeks and it was only because Minab and his warriors were too strong, even for the astute females, that they were defeated. Minab looked at Breena when she told Tian that the battle was like a huge old toad attacking a little Zibo, but unlike the real swamps, the Zibos were all female and only the toad's size made him a conqueror.

Minab made Breena spend the next three days in their room. Breena didn't mind. The babies were brought to her to be fed and she always kept them for an hour afterwards, telling Minab it was important that the babies fall asleep in their mother's arms after they nursed. Minab had seen more of his two sons than most men of Adder did during the first year of a child's life. Breena would constantly describe their facial expressions and Minab could not help but look, out of curiosity. She had him watching them sleep by telling Minab what she thought their dreams were about. It was always dreams of the great battles their father fought in.

CHAPTER TEN

INAB WAS SOON FEELING much better and the pain had ceased. Breena wanted to go to the market to buy some supplies to make some treats. Minab liked the unusual sweets she cooked but did not want her away from where he could keep an eye on her. He decided to accompany her and Shirin to the market. As they walked along within the tiny crowd at the market place Breena saw him again. It was the same man who said he was Minab's brother. He stood with his back to them looking at the carved leathers.

"Minab, is that where you bought my knife? Let's go see what other things they have." Breena pointed to the stand where the man was.

"You are still interested in weapons? You can not even look at blood without it causing you to suffer in your heart." Minab was not paying too much attention; He did not like the market place. There were always too many women there.

Breena hastened her walk and Minab reluctantly followed her. Just as Minab reached the booth, the man Breena had met before, turned around. They stood face to face. Minab's expression changed dramatically and instantly. The man opposite Minab started to smile, and then it vanished from his face.

"Minab, he looks just like you? Are you related?" Breena turned to the other man. "Hello." She smiled as if the whole thing was planned.

Minab grabbed Breena roughly by the arm and moved her away. "You are not to talk to that man, ever."

Breena pulled her arm free. "You're hurting me. All I said was hello. You're related aren't you? Is he your brother?"

Minab stormed away and Breena followed him. By the time she caught up beside him, he was walking briskly towards the area of the city where they lived.

"Who is he, Minab? Why have you never told me you had a brother? Man, he looks so much like you, it's incredible. What did he do to make you so angry? It couldn't have been that bad, you're always angry about everything, anyway."

Minab stopped and grabbed Breena by the shoulders. "Woman, keep quiet!" He released her and continued walking. Breena slowed down and Minab, thinking she might go back to the market place, grabbed her arm and moved her along, right up to their house.

Minab was so upset, he pushed the little slave girl away when she came to undo his laces. He stormed into the back garden. Breena gave the little girl a small hug and showed her by expressions that said to not worry about Minab. Then she followed Minab into the garden. She found him pacing. His face showed the tempest in his thoughts. He took out his sword and whipped at a bush of long stemmed roses, sending them flying into the air and onto the ground.

"That's not anger. That is hate. Why?"

Minab turned and glared at Breena and she wished she had remained quiet. Then he sheathed his sword and sat down on the bench. Breena walked over to him and knelt in front of him. "He is responsible for my father's death," he told her. His voice was calm.

"I'm sorry Minab. You loved your father as much as I loved mine."

Minab looked down at Breena. He doubted she understood. Her father was just a little child's hero. Minab's father was Adder's greatest warrior. He lifted Breena up and sat her on the bench beside him. "Wife, do not interfere in this. It is not your concern."

Breena stood up. "Fine; I won't ask. I know what I am to you. You scared the hell out of me in Moatsha. I thought some monster was forcing me to become his wife. Then you..." Breena started to cry. "I was only seventeen, for crying out loud. In my real life, back home, I just became an adult only a month ago. I hate this world of yours. It's too violent and cruel. You don't see me as anything other than a possession." Breena ran into the house and into the back bedroom where her babies were sleeping. She sat in the corner of the room and cried. Memories of her life as the daughter of Alexander Keets came flooding back to her and the sense of loneliness was overwhelming. She looked at her sleeping babies and wondered what life would be like for them. They were to become warriors. There would be no choice, here. In her world, they could be doctors, teachers, or anything they wanted. They would never see life as she had seen it, if they stayed here.

Breena went to Minab's room and searched through the chests that contained her provisions from the plane that was gathered for her. She found her winter clothes, boots, and mitts. She found her father's compass. She found her father's gun. It was a nine millimeter extended twelve shot. It was fully loaded. Breena shoved it to the bottom of the chest. If they ever found out how to make a weapon like that, they'd kill off whole cities, whole tribes. Breena took out a pen and writing pad she found, and began to reconstruct the plane ride that brought her here. Where was here? They were flying perpendicular to the ground using the altimeter, then the storm hit. She should have landed on top of the world but instead, it was as if she landed... Breena threw the pen and pad down then stared at the sketch she had just made. What if this outrageous drawing was more than a theory? What if she had actually made it to the top of the world? What if she was at the top and had gone inside? Breena had once read of a theory such as that. The sun that never set, no stars ever showed. It was a civilization that knew nothing of the rest of the world. Ten banners representing the ten cultures that lived in here. Ten! There was Adder, Naphtas, Dim, Gash, Simms, and Zebs. Those were the six that Breena knew about from stories from Jaymin and Shirin. What if their names had been altered over time? They believed in one God, except Shirin's people. But she had told her they were a mixture of all the ten cultures. Ten tribes! Breena stuffed all the clothes and compass back into the wooden trunk. She needed time to think about this hypothesis. If what she thought was true, then the one and only way to get out was the same way they came in, through the top of the world.

When Minab walked into the room, Breena quickly shut the lid to the trunk. She looked at him as if for the first time. Was this man whose babies she had bore, part of a lost civilization? Before, she had thought he was from some weird little country. Her home was still out there, she just didn't know where. Now, if she was right, things were all different. Choices had to be made. Should she escape with or without her children? They would never survive the cold terrain she would have to travel through. If she got out and could never get back, they would be here forever, without her. Should she seek help from Minab? Would he ever let her go? If he went with her, could he ever survive in her world? He had no education; he could read and write but seldom did so. He could speak English but could not write it, yet these people had the ability to pick up a language rapidly. In her world where computers ran everything, including warfare, would his kind ever fit in? Woman's lib would completely blow his mind! It might take years to figure out how she could leave and survive the journey to civilization after she reached the North Pole on her side. In addition, that was if her theory was true and not just some desperate grasp at anything that might bring her hope.

Minab knelt down beside her and started kissing her. Breena tensed up completely. She didn't need or want anymore ties to this place than she already had. She struggled to free herself from his arms. Minab let her go and she crawled around to the other side of the trunk so something was between them.

Minab figured she was still angry about his refusal to tell her about his brother. He sat down on the floor opposite her. "Tivas is the man you saw. He is my younger brother. He was born third in our family. We have a sister in-between us and many after he was born. My mother had seven other females and then one more female, many rains ago, with my uncle who became her husband after my father died."

Breena didn't really want to know about Minab's life at that moment. She kept thinking it would only make it harder to leave. She didn't want to be his friend. She didn't want to feel anything for him.

Minab continued. "Tivas and I have always fought, over females and praise from our father, over just about everything. Tivas was living in Chelm and was visiting us in Kalat. Miller arrived about that time and things become, complicated. Tivas fell in love with Shirin's daughter, a slave. I would not give her to him and he would not accept my decision. He illicitly gave her a child and when I threw him out, he challenged me. He could not wed an idol worshiper and to touch a female, who is not his, was even worse! I did not want to fight my brother but he had broken our laws. My father intervened in our fight and he was injured accidentally by Tivas. We thought the wound had healed but months later when my father and his great legion battled Gash, he fell off his horse and died. There were no new injuries, just the reddened scar from the one Tivas inflicted."

Breena shook her head. "That doesn't mean it was the wound Tivas inflicted, that killed him. It could have been heart failure, blood clots. He could have died from just about anything. People don't just die from an old wound. If it were blood poisoning or an infection, he would have shown all kinds of signs. You weren't even there when he died. How are you so sure that Tivas killed him?"

"I do not understand all this about infection or blood clots."

"Sometimes people die without wounds. Women die during childbirth sometimes. There is no wound from a sword or knife there."

"Shirin's daughter died in childbirth. It was her time and she could not deliver."

"Did anyone see your father die? Did they tell you what happened? Did he grab his chest or arm first?"

Minab shook his head. "I do not know."

"Is it a disgrace for a warrior to die without a fresh wound?"

Minab looked at Breena as if she had just asked a very odd question. "He died in battle. It was honorable."

"It sounds as if you just blamed Tivas because you wanted to blame someone. Your father died honorably. Maybe Gash killed him, not by the sword but by the strain of another battle. Stress is a very big killer in my world."

"I do not understand how this stress can kill."

Breena stood up and held out her hand. "I'll give you an example." She led him down stairs into the garden. She found a long, flat, thin piece of wood over by the fence and placed it like a bridge between two big rocks. Breena then took a smaller flat rock and placed in on the stick. The stick bent to the weight. "This is one battle after another. Stress." She placed another flat rock on top of the last and it bent even more. When she placed another flat rock on, the stick snapped. "That's stress and the stick is broken, dead."

Minab became angry and stood up. He put his eyes upon other things as he tried to dismiss what he had just learned. "My brother still transgressed our laws."

Breena shook her head. "In this world what do you expect? I don't see a whole lot of love in marriages around here. Maybe he wanted her so bad that he didn't think. Love can make you do stupid things. Do you punish people forever, just because they break one law? Is there nothing he could ever do to fix his mistake? Boy; am I glad you're not God."

"This talk is disrespectful." Minab placed his hand firmly on her shoulder.

"Your lack of forgiveness is disrespectful. In my world, you'd be the pagan."

Minab stormed into the house and Breena went to nurse her babies. After, she carried Sheb around the kitchen and told him all about the process of fixing a meal. She knew he didn't understand but she wanted her babies to know everything. In her mind, she could see herself taking them on field trips all over the city. She'd take them to the blacksmith, the market, and the church, then over to the overseers so they would know how their country is run. Maybe they could be inventors or diplomats.

Minab came down stairs dressed in his finest armor, and left the house without saying good-bye to anyone. Breena slept in the back room with her babies and did not see Minab until morning. When Minab walked into the kitchen to tell Shirin he was up and wanted something to eat, Breena was nursing Tian.

"Are you going to make some of those tiny cakes today?" Minab seemed in a good mood.

"I didn't get the supplies yesterday. We came home from the market early."

"You may take Shirin this morning and go back to the market if you would like."

"Are you coming with us?"

"No. I have to go visit my mother."

"She wanted to see the babies again. Do you want to take them?"

Minab gave Breena a disapproving look, and then smiled. "Some other time we will both go and take them with us."

Breena hurried and bathed the babies so they would sleep while they were gone. Yathsa was always there for the babies anyway.

When Breena arrived at the market, she asked Shirin to buy the supplies while she went for a walk. Breena wanted to find Tivas and talk with him. She spotted him talking with a group of soldiers. She gave him a wave when he finally looked in her direction. He excused himself from the group and walked over to where she was.

"You like dangerous situations, do you not?" He asked her as he looked around to see who could be watching them.

"Minab would not fight you."

Tivas laughed. "I was not thinking of myself. Did Minab not command you not to talk to me?"

"He spews out so many rules and orders; I can't keep half of them straight. We talked yesterday and I think he realized you were not to blame for your father's death."

Breena's bluntness startled Tivas. "But it was my fault. I was doing so many things that were wrong back then. When I wounded my father, I was so disgusted with myself, I just ran. It made me a coward and I am still ashamed."

"That was long ago and you talk as if you have learned from your experiences. You can change things, and your father did not die from your wound. It was just his time. He died during battle so it was very honorable."

Tivas shook his head. "Your talk is very peculiar. Adder women are not bold, as you are. Why do you speak with wisdom when you look so young and appear as a woman? Have you cast a spell over us all?"

Breena smiled. "It's just good old Keet's logic. Tivas, do you want to get back with your brother?" Her scarf slipped off her head and stayed on her shoulders. She left it there.

"That is not possible. Even if he no longer blamed me for father, I have done other wicked things."

"You're talking about Shirin's daughter?"

Tivas nodded. "He told you much. I thought if she was with child, he would have to give her to me, to save the reputation of our family."

"You weren't the only one to blame, Tivas. Shirin's daughter could have said no."

"Tanisha was blameless. She was a slave girl and would do as she was told."

"It seems to me, you need to apologize to Shirin more than Minab. It is her family that was wronged."

"But she is a slave."

"She is a very fine person who would probably stay with Minab even if she wasn't a slave. You can't change the past, but you can fix the future, Tivas."

"Maybe your wisdom is right. You are my brother's wife, and his hate for the strangers was great and now you say he no longer blames me for father. God must smile upon you or you do indeed, case spells."

Breena smiled but in her thoughts, she worried that God didn't know where she was anymore than her own mother did.

Tivas bowed to her. "I will attempt to make amends to Shirin and

I will then ask my brother for forgiveness. It has been many rains since we have talked. It has been many rains since I have gone to visit my mother."

"You're an uncle now too."

"Minab has had a son?"

"I had them but they are his sons."

Tivas laughed. "They? Two? Minab has been truly blessed."

Breena spotted Shirin walking towards her. "I better go, Shirin is heading this way." Breena put her scarf back upon her head and walked towards Shirin.

Shirin looked angry and as she began to scold. Breena gave her a scowl. "Don't start, Shirin. I don't know much about your customs and stuff, but I know people. They are all the same, everywhere." Breena walked on without her and Shirin hurried to catch up.

Breena bought two fruit treats and gave one to Shirin. Someone called out Breena's name. It was Jaymin. Breena's ran and hugged her. "Oh Breena, it is good to see you. I have been forbidden to come to see you at your house."

"I know, but this is the market and you never know who you're going to meet here." Breena patted Jaymin's slightly bulging tummy and laughed. Then she noticed Jaymin was covering her left eye with the scarf. She pulled it back, thinking it was just put on too tight, revealing a blackened eye. "Jaymin, what happened?"

Jaymin looked down and said nothing.

"What happened? Did Kabay hit you?"

"It was my fault."

"Oh bull! Have you not noticed that the men around here are all hulks? They all are huge compared to the women. What could you have done to make this your fault?"

"He was angry. He told me I should be forever grateful that he took me from my servant parents and made me his. I was angry because he had just told me not to see you anymore. I told him the only difference between then and now was I was his personal servant now. I should not have said that." She shook her head timidly.

Breena was livid. Her face turned pale and her lips tightened. "Don't worry Jaymin. I will make sure this never happens again." She hugged Jaymin and ran home, leaving Shirin behind with an armful of supplies.

Breena burst into the house and ran up stairs looking for Minab. He wasn't there. She ran down stairs and asked one of the slaves for Minab. She pointed to the garden.

Minab was out in the garden on the bench. He could tell Breena was upset as soon as he saw her. "Wife, what has happened?"

"He hit her. That ..." She searched for a word Minab could understand. "That scum, low life, pathetic excuse for a man!"

Minab stood up. "Who? What has happened?"

"Kabay hit Jaymin. She is carrying his child, and he hit her."

Minab relaxed and sat down again. "She must have done something terrible to provoke him. A warrior is not easily provoked."

Breena stopped in her tracks and looked at Minab "You're not going to do anything?"

"It is not my place."

"You are his captain."

"It is not my place, wife."

"Fine! If you won't do anything, I will."

"Breena."

"The next time you leave this house, even for a second, I'm going to be over there like a shot, and I'll be in-his-face! I'll be the one provoking him, and once he hits me, you'll have to do something."

"I will have to kill him. Is that what you want?" Minab's voice was casual as if he didn't really believe she would cause that much trouble or maybe he hoped she wouldn't.

"Yes. No. But if he hits her again, I think I'll kill him, myself. Now, is it your place?"

Minab stood up. "I understand. Jaymin is your friend. This would not be my place but as his captain, I should see that my men act honorable. It is not honorable to hit a female unless we are at war with them."

*   *   *

Minab walked into the house, leaving Breena in the garden. He left the house immediately. She was so upset she had trouble nursing her babies. Shirin came home and they made tiny sweet cakes for Minab.

Minab was greeted at the entrance of Kabay's house by a male servant, and then shown to the great room. Kabay's house was much smaller than Minab's house but was comfortable. Kabay had three servants, one male, and two female. Kabay came into the great room and Minab and he clasped hands.

"I have come to invite you and your wife to a party we are going to be having. There will be a few other officers in my legion there with their wives. I am hoping my wife will learn from the other wives about raising warrior sons."

"My wife is yet to have a son. I will gladly come but Jaymin is not well enough these days to socialize." Kabay nodded and slowly turned as Jaymin walked into the house.

"She seems well to me. May I ask her if she feels well enough to pay a visit upon my household?"

Kabay hesitated but then nodded. "Come here, wife."

Jaymin walked slowly over to where they sat. She kept her head carefully covered.

Minab smiled and cautiously scanned her face. He could see that Breena had told the truth. "I see that you are tired. Perhaps, you could join your husband some other time. I apologize to you and your husband." Minab stood up and Jaymin excused herself and left the room. Minab walked towards the front entrance and Kabay followed. "I have been troubled Kabay, about something that my wife has said she would do, concerning you."

"What might that be?"

Minab laughed. "It was silly, a female notion. She said that Jaymin is her closest friend and she values her greatly. My wife had indicated that if Jaymin were to be hurt or injured because of some dishonorable action, on your part, she would confront you, forcefully. I told her that would be a mistake, because then I would find it my place to defend her and we know what the results of that would be." Minab slapped Kabay's shoulder as old friends do. "It would be a great loss over such a minor indiscretion."

Kabay stared at Minab and knew what he meant. He nodded and glanced back at the doorway that Jaymin had exited from. "Perhaps, next week you and your wife would like to visit our home for a meal. Jaymin is like your wife in many ways, and perchance, maybe I could see how you handle her defiance. It has only left me mystified beyond my abilities to control myself, at times."

"It will be well for you to remember that these women of ours are not like the others and that they will produce the elect of warrior sons for us."

Kabay straightened his posture and nodded. "I stand corrected and look forward to standing by your side in battle again one day."

Minab smiled. "I too, look forward to that, Kabay. I am happy that my wife's notion was just a silly thing and did not have to come to pass." Minab left and returned to his home.

When Minab returned home Shirin told him Breena was upstairs in the bath with the babies. Minab was curious as the bath was huge and bathing a child in there would not be like bathing him in a basin. When he looked into the bathing room, Breena was in the tub. She was dressed in only her thin undershirt and underpants. Yathsa was sitting on the floor beside the tub, drying Sheb. Breena had Tian in the water with her. Tian was kicking and slashing in the water as Breena held him and both she and Yathsa were laughing at the baby's excitement.

"You are teaching them to not fear the water. That is good."

Minab's voice startled Breena. She was not expecting him home for a while. Breena handed Tian to Yathsa. The babies were dried and Breena asked Yathsa to take the boys down to their room. In the five short months that Yathsa had been helping Breena feed the babies, she had learned English very well. After Yathsa left, Breena reached for a towel. Minab picked it up and threw it over in the corner. Breena would have to get out of the bath to retrieve it. Breena folded her arms over her chest as she stood in the water that was chest high to her. She stood looking at Minab, trying to evaluate his actions.

"I spoke with Kabay. It was a small misunderstanding and Jaymin need not worry any longer. Kabay would like us both to come to a meal there next week." Minab stood by the tub looking down at her. He could not take his eyes off her.

"Thank you. You think I was interfering, don't you?"

Minab sarcastically shook his head. "Never."

"It's just that you men are so big that you don't realize your own strength. A hit like that, isn't like spanking a child. It leaves more pain than what shows up in bruises."

"I will never hit you."

"You've wanted to."

Minab laughed. "Many times, you are very frustrating."

"I'd like to get out now. Can I have my towel?"

Minab pointed to the towel that he tossed over in the corner. Breena gave Minab a weak smile. She did not want to play this game. Shirin had told her that with the babies starting to eat a bit of solid food now, it was feasible that she could become pregnant again. Breena did not want that. Shirin had told her she had some herbs that would reduce the chances and Breena had only started taking it yesterday. Minab walked into the bedroom and Breena made a dash for the towel. She took off her wet clothes and dried herself quickly. Minab walked back into the bathing room. His armor was off. He looked disappointed at Breena's progress. Breena put the towel around her and as she hurried to get out of the room, Minab wrapped his huge arm around her and pulled her into the tub with him.

Over the next week, things went along smoothly. Minab and Breena went to Kabay's for a meal and Jaymin told Breena she was being treated well and Kabay seemed extra kind to her. In his own way, he had even apologized, bringing her a silver bracelet. Later on in the week, Shirin helped Breena finish the nightshirt they had started sewing before the babies were born. Breena understood the quality of things that were hand-made now. With no sewing machine or massive production lines, clothing was made slowly, with each stitch done by hand, with patience, and hard work. However, Breena wanted Minab to see it was done well so there were many times she had to redo a sleeve over and over again until it was done right. When she was finally finished, Breena placed it in a small box covered in bark. In her culture, the box would have been worth more than the nightshirt, but here it was a common covering for baskets and box frames. She gave it to Minab as he sat eating his morning meal. She told him she was sorry it was so late being done but it was her first attempt at sewing and she had to learn how to do every part of the shirt, right down to the collar. Minab examined it carefully and smiled. It was indeed, made well and he was not expecting to ever receive a gift from Breena. She had given birth to his children and that was a great gift, in itself. Breena found the celebrations difficult in this culture. They did not celebrate Christmas or birthdays, except the males', eighth and fourteenth birthday and the females', sixteenth birthday. There were no seasons other than summer it seemed, and with no moon seen, they dated things by the rains with their center point being, the few days a year that it did not rain at all. Even with their unusual rain calendar, a year in their time was similar to one in the Julian calendar Breena was use to having.

Minab thanked Breena with a gentle kiss and Breena could not understand why it made her feel guilty that she had not done more. It seemed such a simple thing, yet Minab was genuinely pleased.

Someone knocked on the entrance door and Yathsa answered. It was Tivas requesting to speak to Minab. As he stood at the doorway, even Breena could see that he was extremely nervous. Minab stood up but did not go to the doorway. Breena thought he might not allow him in but finally Minab said he could come in. Minab asked everyone to leave them and when Breena did not go with the others, he asked her to leave them also. Breena did not want to cause any trouble so she went to her spot in the kitchen where she could see and hear what was going on. She motioned for Shirin to translate, as they were not talking in English.

"Why have you come?" Minab asked boldly. He was not relaxed and his posture was tense.

Tivas did not look at his eyes. "I have come to make amends to Shirin for the wrong I have caused her family. I have three hundred gold pieces in my pouch."

It was a great deal of money. For Tivas who was a soldier and not a captain, it represented a year's savings. "Do you think you can buy her forgiveness?" Minab asked. His voice was indifferent.

"No. I have come to buy her freedom; if you will allow it."

Shirin gasped as she translated what Tivas was saying, then she started to cry and Breena put her arms around her to comfort her.

"Three hundred gold pieces is not enough for her freedom."

Tivas took a deep breath and placed the pouch on the table that was to his left in the entrance. "Then, I will bring more. I have two hundred more pieces at home."

Shirin covered her mouth to prevent herself from gasping even louder. "Five hundred gold pieces; no slave is worth that." She whispered.

Minab shook his head. "What makes you think I would take coins from you? What makes you think you could buy a slave from me, ever?"

"I am not purchasing Shirin. She will be free to do as she pleases. I only desire to purchase her freedom as a slave."

Shirin was so shocked she had to sit down. "Freedom."

Minab looked at Tivas for a few minutes. "If I was to do this, I would require more."

"I have no more gold to give. What else would you have me do?" Tivas' voice showed concern.

"You will be transferred into my legion. You will serve under me." Minab stated boldly. "You will train with my new-lings."

Tivas closed his eyes for a second. It was a difficult thing Minab was asking of him. In Minab's legion, he would not have a rank as he now had and Minab would work him harder than anyone else would.

"I will do as you request but I need to know if that will be enough to satisfy you?"

"It will be enough for me. I do not know if it will be enough for Shirin." He nodded in her direction.

Minab called Shirin into the great room. Breena followed her in hope that she would not be told to leave again.

Minab told Shirin, her freedom had been purchased and she was free to leave or to stay on, as a servant of his household. Minab knew already what the answer would be. She would choose to stay. Even with the low wage servants were paid, it would be better for her than to be on the streets homeless. Shirin was just happy to have the freedom to choose. She kept putting her hands to her mouth to silence her little squeals of enthusiasm. She nodded and said she would stay. Minab then asked her if she would accept this as Tivas' apology for the wrong that was done to her family.

Shirin became silent. Breena did not understand what had been said to Shirin as nothing was being translated anymore, but Breena could tell by Shirin expression, it was very serious. Shirin looked at Tivas with contempt in her eyes, but she slowly nodded. It would not bring back her daughter but Shirin knew her daughter would be happy to have her mother freed. Breena thought Tivas looked humbled. He must have wanted forgiveness desperately to offer all that he had.

Minab turned again to his brother. In English he said, "You will transfer into my legion tomorrow. They are doing drills for three weeks, at Metcomb, south of Chelm. You will go there." Minab turned and left the room. He went upstairs without saying another word.

Shirin ran into the kitchen to tell the others of her news, leaving Breena and Tivas alone. Tivas handed Breena the pouch. "I will return shortly with the other coins. Could you see that Minab gets them also?" He said to Breena in English. He seemed defeated.

"Minab wanted you in his legion. At least you will be near your brother." Breena tried to cheer Tivas up.

"You do not understand what the transfer will mean. I will be stripped of my rank and he will have me worked very hard. It will not be a pleasant reposition."

"Shirin forgave you."

"Yes. For that, I feel relieved. Even with her freedom granted, she did not have to forgive me. It is a great weight lifted." Tivas took a few steps back. "I will return shortly." He left and Breena went upstairs to find Minab. He was sitting in a chair looking out over the balcony at the garden.

Breena handed him the pouch. "That was a good thing, wasn't it? Will you forgive your brother, now?"

Minab looked at Breena with his eyes but he did not turn his head. He said nothing.

"Your brother says you'll work him very hard. It won't be as bad as he thinks, will it?"

"If he dies in training camp, at least it will be honorable."

"Dies in camp?" Breena began to worry.

"I have allowed him to enter my house and also to purchase Shirin's freedom. Now, it is time for Tivas to earn his forgiveness."

"Why must everything be done with pain and hardship and pushing people beyond their abilities?" Breena walked over to the bed and sat down. She covered her face with her hands and started to cry. She hated all the anguish that seemed to be intertwined in this civilization. Sometimes it was too much to handle.

Minab walked over to Breena, sat down beside her, and took her in her arms. "If forgiveness was just handed to him, he would never believe it was genuine. This way he'll know for sure."

Tivas returned and gave another pouch to Breena, who passed it on to Minab. The next day Minab left for Metcomb for three weeks. Breena spent the three weeks Minab was gone imagining all sorts of terrible things that were happening to Tivas. She felt very guilty. When her husband returned, Breena found it very difficult not to ask about Tivas. She undid his laces and brought him his meal. She even brought him the babies so he could see them, knowing he would complain, but enjoy their company anyway. That evening in bed, during the rains, as Minab held her close, Breena asked.

"How is your brother handling being in your legion?"

"Are you more concerned for my brother than for your own husband?"

"My husband is the captain. No one pushes him, except himself."

"Tivas is in the care of the physician here in Chelm. He became sick after being on guard for a week, at night, in the rain, and during practice, his response was slow. He was slashed in the side by another new recruit."

"Oh no; will he be all right?"

Minab kissed Breena on her temple. "He will survive to fight again."

"Could we go see him?"

Minab gave a small chuckle. "One would think you were his mother. I will take you to see him, tomorrow, but I will not visit. The others would think he was someone special, and he is not."

When Breena walked into the room where the sick and wounded were cared for, she was glad to see it was not full. Tivas and another man were the only ones in a room with row upon row of beds. Breena sat down in a chair beside Tivas' bed. He was sleeping. Breena was pleased to see his color was that healthy looking tan all the people had. Breena leaned over and whispered his name. Tivas opened his eyes. He smiled.

"How are you feeling?"

Tivas nodded. "I will survive." He said and his voice was hoarse and barely above a whisper.

"Oh Tivas, you have an awful cold. Are they giving you anything for it? Are they feeding you well?"

Tivas smiled again. "I am getting better." He moved slightly and his face showed pain.

"Minab said you were wounded. Is that healing too?"

"Those half-witted young recruits are very sporadic. Dueling with them is like chasing after a rabbit. You never know what direction they will go. I was trying not to wound them but I should have been just trying to defend myself."

"Minab didn't want to come because it would look like you were special to him."

Tivas chuckled. "You are very diplomatic, but it was not expected that anyone should come to visit. You make me wish I were married. Women are better medicine than anything the physician could give me. Minab must be greatly pampered."

"I feel guilty that things turned out the way they have. You could have been killed."

"Do not feel guilty. It has turned out well. I have worked hard and I do not think Minab is disappointed in my effort. I would not have my brother back if you and I had not met at the market."

Breena smiled. She felt good. Tivas felt forgiven and Minab was content. Now, if only she could figure out the dilemma she felt within herself between her desire to go home and her love for her children. If she rationalized it all out, she knew the chances of ever getting home were slim and it would take a plane ticket handed to her to consider leaving her children, and only if she was sure she could come back for them.

Minab was waiting for Breena as she came out of the building. He placed her upon his horse and got up behind her. "It is time for you to go home and be with your own sons. Tivas is not a child."

"When you were hurt, I worried about you, and you're not a child either."

"I did not need your worry. Women spend too much time thinking about things they have no power to change." Minab turned his horse and headed for their home.

Breena leaned back against Minab's chest. She wondered for a moment what would have happened if it had been some other warrior, instead of Minab that had captured Moatsha. What would have happened if he had been sadistic and just wanted to torture her? Breena shuttered and Minab put his arm around her, thinking she was chilled.

Tivas healed and returned to duty. Minab went to fight against a group of bandits who were raiding small villages to the east of Chelm. Minab sent his men into the towns to guard them while he, Kabay, and his best spies went seeking the robbers. They used the same tactics the bandits used to rob people. They found their camps and waited until during the rain to attack. They were gone for almost two months.

Sheb and Tian were eight months old when Jaymin went into labor. Breena was visiting and she sent word for Shirin to come and help Jaymin. Jaymin's time of delivery was six hours. Breena was surprised to see how well Jaymin handled it. She didn't seem to be in half the pain Breena had been, during her delivery. Breena marveled at the skill and calmness Shirin showed. She hadn't paid too much attention during her delivery, but now she could see exactly what Shirin did for her. It was a healthy baby boy and Jaymin cried with joy. Breena was excited for her. She knew Minab would not have put a daughter to death if it had been born first because he had given her that promise, but Kabay had not said anything to Jaymin. Breena was sure Kabay would not have been so kind, if Jaymin had delivered a girl.

Minab and Kabay came home five days after the birth. Kabay was already thrilled with the defeat of the bandits, so when he found out he had become a father of a male child; he was exhilarated. When the baby was twelve days old, Kabay threw a feast. All his friends and relatives were present, except for Jaymin's parents, as they would not arrive in time. The baby was circumcised, given the name of Maclesh, which means 'chosen to come', and then he was given a blessing. It was a fine party and Breena was thrilled to see Jaymin so happy.

While Breena sat in the garden of Kabay's house, Minab strolled out. Breena was thinking about the parties her family used to have. With her father's job as a professor, her parents had a big house. Her brother had married and moved out so Breena didn't even have to share the main bathroom with anyone. They had a swimming pool and a Jacuzzi, big screen T.V. and she even had a car of her own. It was a jeep and she loved taking it to the beach on her free weekends. Minab quietly sat down beside Breena. She was staring at a flower she had plucked, twirling it around with her fingers. It wasn't until he spoke that she even became aware of someone else's presence.

"What did you say?" She asked when she realized he had said something to her.

"Why are you out here?"

Breena quickly put her scarf back upon her head. "Too many people speaking a language I don't understand. Besides, it's so hot in there, I figured you wouldn't be too upset if I came out here and took off this dumb scarf. Nobody can see me out here."

"I am not used to having someone else's wife the center of attention anymore." Minab touched Breena's hair.

"Was your first wife the center of attention? I heard she was unbelievably beautiful." Minab looked away and Breena thought that maybe she shouldn't have said anything about her. "I'm sorry; none of my business." She slowly added.

Minab looked confused. "You do not mind talking about her?"

Breena shrugged her shoulders. "Shirin said you loved her very much. Besides, she was your first. I'm just a second."

"They do not marry like that where the strangers live?"

Breena shook her head. "Some not only have second marriages but thirds and fourths. Heck, most don't even bother to marry. They just live together."

"Yet they claim to believe in God? It sounds like a very wicked place. You are wise to be out of there."

"I'd say we weren't as violent as your people, but that would only be true in some cases. You'd hate it there."

"Why do you think that?"

"Women are physicians and lawyers and judges and soldiers and teachers and carpenters. They can be, and are just about anything they want to be."

Minab shook his head. "How can you miss a place like that?"

"It has as many good things in it, as bad. When a baby is born early, I mean really early, we can save it. If your heart or kidney is bad, it can be taken out, and you can replace it with a healthy one. We have wagons that move without horses and machines that can plant a whole field in one day by using just one person."

"You make up stories."

Breena smiled. "That machine they found me beside and the one Miller came in, could fly in the air, like a bird."

"That was what Miller said. It was just a story. Nothing can do that. Miller's wagon was too heavy."

"If I could go back, would you go with me?"

"I would never let you go back. You belong to me. You are my wife." Minab was becoming upset.

"Don't worry. There isn't much of a chance of me ever getting back there, anyway. I'd need a plane, a wagon that flies." Breena stood up. "I'm really tired. Could we go home?"

Minab took Breena home and after she fed the babies, she went upstairs and she fell asleep. Yathsa had stopped helping Breena feed her babies, so Breena was the only one nursing them now. Yathsa found that she was with child and her husband wanted her to stay home and work with him.

Minab did a surprising thing the next day. He invited Tivas over to the house for a meal with them. Breena served them and sat with them during the meal.

Minab seemed to have a reason for inviting Tivas, and as soon as they were finished the meal he began to talk about his reason. "Tivas, you are only a bit younger than I am. You should take a wife and begin your lineage."

Tivas was surprised at Minab's declaration. "I cannot afford a wife at this moment. I am but a foot soldier now."

"Nevertheless, you should be attending the holy days at the worship place and see what is now available."

Breena stood up. "Be sure to bring your shopping list. Excuse me, but I will not sit here and listen to this." She stormed out of the room and went into the kitchen. She wanted to start making some treats for the next day.

"It is a shame she is the only one of her kind. Their race must be entertaining." Tivas said. "They say the oddest things about life."

Minab laughed. "She has become calm, compared to when I first took her from Kalat. Zorban thought her a wildcat."

"What happened with Zorban?"

Minab tensed up. His jaw became stiff. "He tried to procure my wife. He also planned to have me killed."

Tivas nodded. "She is unique. Many would like heirs through her. Variety is more precious than gold or silver."

"You need to maintain our lineage as well."

Tivas looked down. "I have sold my house to pay off my debts. I have nothing to offer a wife."

"Your rank will be returned to you in time, brother. Until then, my house is also yours. It is big enough for two families."

Tivas didn't know what to say. His brother had offered him much. "I cannot accept. I am not deserving of your generosity."

"The past is over. We are brothers, once more. You gave all you had for a slave's freedom. What would you give for your brother?"

"My life." Tivas was serious and controlled in his answer.

"Then it is settled." Minab called for Breena to come out of the kitchen so he could see her.

Breena slowly walked out of the kitchen. Minab turned to his brother and smiled. "You would not want a female with an attitude of a stranger. They are very obstinate." He said to Tivas in their language. He told him to observe her temperament once she understood what they are saying. Minab placed his hand on Breena's abdomen once she was close enough for him to touch her. He began talking in English so she would understand. "It is important to have a wife with good hips and straight posture. They must carry a child well and maybe if they are built as my wife, they will bare you two the first time."

Breena pulled away. "Maybe you would like to hear what the physical qualities of a good husband are? So far, all I've seen are men built like gorillas."

"You will be silent, wife." Minab winked at Tivas.

"Silence yourself. I don't want to hear this trash." Breena pulled away and walked back into the kitchen. Both men laughed which only infuriated Breena even more.

Minab stood up and came into the kitchen. "You are cooking some of your tiny cakes?"

"Maybe, maybe not. Either way, you're not getting any. They'll make you fat. I'm sure no one wants a rolley polley captain, waddling out to the battle field." Breena cracked the eggs, divided them, and roughly threw the yokes in one bowel and the whites in another. She started to beat the egg whites vigorously. Minab came closer and folded his arms.

"You are too easily upset. It is a compliment that I parade you in front of others."

"I am not a prized horse!" Breena slapped the spoon into the bowl with such force; it sent some of the egg whites flying onto Minab's face. "Opps." Breena looked up at Minab and almost laughed. She covered her mouth with her hand.

Minab slowly wiped the egg whites off his face with his hand. Then he casually picked up the bowl of yokes and poured it over Breena's head. Minab grinned with satisfaction.

"Oh, yuck..." Breena let the yokes drip down her hair. She grabbed a handful of flour and threw it at Minab, hitting him on the left side of his face and hair.

Minab nodded sarcastically. Breena could not tell if he was angry or what. Minab snatched the pitcher of milk from the table before Breena could get to it. He threw the milk at her and it drenched her front, completely. Breena gasped from the sensation of the cool milk running down her body. She looked at the small sack of flour on the table. Both reached for the sack and both slipped on the eggs that were smeared across the floor. Minab went down first with Breena on top of him. They had knocked the sack of flour off the table. It hit Breena on the back of the head as it fell, open side up, onto her. For a second, Minab and Breena stared at each other. Breena wondered if Minab was furious, but then they both realized how ridiculous they looked, and they burst out laughing at each other. Minab put his arms around Breena and amidst the flour and eggs and milk, kissed her fervently. Breena enjoyed it and kissed him back.

"Is this how it is to be wed, Minab?" Tivas asked as he stood at the kitchen doorway watching their little food fight. "I do not remember our parents acting like this, ever."

Minab looked up at Tivas and laughed. "It is true, Tivas. A marriage to a stranger is not a normal thing, but it is not dull either."

CHAPTER ELEVEN

IVAS MOVED FROM CAMP into Minab's house and for the following four holy days he attended the worship place with Minab and Breena. Tivas was always whispering to Minab and Breena knew they were discussing the women there. There was one young girl named Trela who was extremely pretty and more delicate looking compared to the others. Tivas found out she was a daughter of a minor overseer and he began courting her properly. Minab would comment on his proceedings to Breena as if he was proud of his brother's progress. Breena was silent about it all. She knew that if Tivas brought a bride home to their house, obedient as she would be, Breena would soon convert her to her way of thinking. Tivas would have his hands full if he thought she would be uninfluenced by Breena's philosophy.

Shirin was enjoying her freedom and her new income. She bought new clothes and changed her scarf color to that of a widow. When she accompanied Breena to the market she was thrilled to be able to purchase a fruit treat for Breena and herself out of her own wages.

Breena was starting to worry about her health. She was constantly tired lately, so she started to eat more vegetables and made less treats to snack on. Minab enjoyed her introduction of new foods. Breena experimented and discovered a recipe similar to pizza and homemade noodles with cheese sauce.

When Breena woke feeling nauseated, she became really frightened and immediately sought Shirin's advice. Shirin asked her if she had missed her time and Breena told her it was all been mixed up since the birth of the twins. Shirin told Breena sometimes the herbs did not prevent her from becoming pregnant and she should stop taking them. Breena was somber. This was not what she wanted to happen. It would only close the coffin on her hopes of ever getting home again. She kept quiet and Shirin agreed to let Breena tell her husband when she thought the time was right.

Tivas wed Trela and brought her home. Trela was a shy girl who had no sisters and only one brother. Breena felt sorry for her and it was difficult for them to communicate, as Trela could not speak English. Trela and Tivas spent four days alone in their section of the house getting to know each other. Shirin said she only saw Trela once; when she came into the kitchen to bring them back some food. Breena was amazed at how obedient Trela was. She would undo Tivas' laces immediately and wait until he approved the meal before she ate. Breena set about teaching her English words. She wanted desperately to communicate with the girl.

A call was sent to Minab and his legion for service. They had to go back to Kalat as Arbmoat had raided the city. The legion there had defended it but many of Arbmoat's men were still hiding in the wilderness and had become thieves of the night, raiding with small groups during the rain. Tivas went with the legion. While they were gone, both Shirin and Breena worked on teaching Trela English. With Minab gone, Breena did not have to work hard to hide her morning sickness. She found it interesting that the one thing that bothered her most about her mother, she had become. She never thought she'd be as good of a mother as her own mom would, and now she would have more children than her mother had. She hoped it would be another boy. How could she ever raise a girl in this world? With her attitudes, she would grow up rebellious and discontent. Would she ever find another man with as much understanding as Minab, for her daughter to marry?

Breena was very confused over her feeling for Minab. Trying to stay objective about him was becoming harder every day. How could she remain impersonal with a man she was so close to, a man who treated her with understanding, in a crazy culture. He was trying harder to become a part of her life, than she ever was trying to become a part of his. Minab had told her he loved her. Breena had yet to even respond to that love, aside from the occasional hug and kiss.

When Minab came home, Breena was glad for his return. His attitude was always very chauvinistic for the first few days he was home but soon, he would mellow in his demeanor and Breena thought, then, she would tell him about her pregnancy. Minab knew it upset Breena that he did not greet his sons more affectionately than he did but it was not the custom. He did, however, ruffle their hair as a greeting. Sheb and Tian were learning to walk and Minab thought their progress funny. Others thought him odd, that he would brag of the achievements of babies, but Minab valued his sons greatly. Tian had light brown hair now, which was unusual. It was not blonde like his mother's but still uncommon. Both Sheb and Tian had dark blue eyes with flecks of brown in them.

As they lay in bed, Breena wondered if she should tell Minab about the baby but Minab started to talk to her about more children before she could say anything.

"My sons are a year old now. It is time for you to give me more." Minab sat up. "Have you been taking herbs from Shirin's physician? You will have my children and shall not try to prevent them. It is your place as wife."

"I'm not your personal baby factory." Breena tried to get up but Minab pulled her down again.

"Yes you are. That is what a woman does."

Breena was terrified of having more children. The last delivery was almost twenty hours long. The babies weren't full term and still they were big for her. Minab had no idea what that fear was like.

"I'm not taking anything. Maybe there is something wrong with me. That's what you get when you marry someone, like you did."

"You will conceive again. It was no problem the first time."

"I'll probably never have twins again."

"It was a sign blessing our union. You were always meant to be mine."

The next day there was talk of a horrific battle brewing in the south. A ruler called Portess was winding his way north towards Chelm. He had many legions and was determined to conquer the cities owned by Adder. Tivas and Kabay met with Minab to discuss what would happen. The chief overseer called a council and all the captains attended.

Breena had never seen such preparation before. They began to fortify the city just in case Portess was successful in getting through to Chelm. If he did, it would mean great devastation had occurred and many would have already died. Portess' hatred for the Adder tribe was deep.

Minab came home and told Breena he would be leaving the next day. He spent the evening in their room with his wife and his sons. Breena knew that this was not a battle like the others. Minab was serious and somber about the future. His warnings were grave.

"If they make it through, take my sons and flee east. You have two horses for just that and I want you to use them. Take food, water, and all the gold coins I have, and do not stop until you have reached Drostom. Once there, find a man named Fetchmos. Tell him you are my wife and they are my sons. Give him the coins and he will keep you safe in the caves of Belmorhsa."

"You're frightening me, Minab." Breena eyes began to fill with tears as she started to realize Minab's warnings said nothing of him. "You'll come back for me. Promise, you'll come back for me."

Minab kissed her gently. "I will come back for you but I cannot leave my men. This is just in case we are slow at defeating Protess' legions. You sound worried for me. Could you care for me, more then you have yet to reveal?"

"I just wouldn't know what to do, if you left me to do all the work. That's all." She hesitated in even saying those callous words.

"What must I do to have you love me?"

Breena looked at Minab and her heart ached. Whatever way this union started out, it was not the same now. This man beside her would have died to protect her, many times. He had done what he could to treat her with love, in the only way he knew how. They had two sons together and soon would be having another child. Breena knew Minab and she were linked forever to each other. If she felt nothing, it was only because she refused to allow herself to feel anything. Breena looked at her two sleeping babies as they lay on a blanket in the corner of the room.

"Do you know that your sons are wonderful?"

"Yes." Minab smiled at her question.

"Will our next child be wonderful, like them?"

Minab put his arms around her and kissed her again. "If we make another child then we will have to continue our future together. I could not die and leave the bond we have."

Breena kissed him back and whispered. "We should make that bond stronger then, shouldn't we? Minab, I am afraid to tell you I love you. I am afraid of losing myself completely."

"That is how it is meant to be. I too have lost myself in you and now we are one in mind and soul."

"I love you, Minab. Please don't ever hurt me."

Minab had heard what he most wanted to hear from her lips. If he were to fight in battle and die, he would feel her love forever. His response to her was in the form of kisses, in the form of love.

*   *   *

The next morning Breena felt a foreboding like she had never felt before. It seemed to thicken the air and everyone around her seemed to sense it, as tones were kept low. Breena searched through her trunks to find her father's wallet. She had seen it in there when she looked through the trunk before. Once she found the wallet, she took the small graduation picture she had given her father. It was a pretty picture with her blond hair in soft waves and a smile that told her father the world was before her. She heard Minab call for her and she ran to gather the boys to say good-bye to their father. Minab knew it was important to Breena so he gave each son a hug and handed them back to Shirin to hold. Then he took Breena in his arms and kissed her, something that would be considered very bold, as emotions were not expressed that way in public. Breena handed him the picture and Minab marveled at the little painting. Breena decided not to tell him it wasn't a painting. She told him she loved him instead and Minab touched her hair and caressed her cheek. He mounted his horse and began to ride away. Breena ran after him.

"Minab, I have to tell you something." Breena said and Minab stopped. He leaned over and picked her up, placing her sideways on the saddle, just in front of him. "Minab, we're going to have another baby. You've given me another child."

Minab grinned. "I know. I could see it in your eyes last night. I hoped you would tell me before I left."

"I'm sorry I kept it from you. I can't promise another boy, but I'll pray for one for you."

Minab leaned his lips close to her and whispered in her ear. "I will be thankful for a female, if she has eyes that dance, like her mother's. We will celebrate when I return." He kissed Breena before he lifted her back down, and then he rode off.

Breena stood and watched the legion ride away. She watched them until none could be seen and then slowly she turned and came back home. Trela and Shirin were busy with the laundry and Breena helped them. It was going to be hard to keep from thinking about what awaited Minab's legion. Time seemed to be motionless, as the days turned into weeks, and then months. Breena found it hard to comprehend how men could fight, day after day for such long periods of time.

The whole city waited for messages from the battlefield but none came. It was as if they had ridden off the edge of the earth. Every worship day the churches were full and soon they began to fill on the day's in-between. Trela cried herself to sleep at night and sometimes Breena would come into her room and talk. Trela did not want to become a widow before her husband could give her a child. Breena almost felt guilty with her belly beginning to grow and Trela yearning for one of her own. They became close friends and Trela learned the English language quickly. Sometimes Jaymin, with her son, and Trela and Shirin and Breena, with her sons, packed a picnic lunch and went just outside the city, to eat down by the riverbed. Sometimes the women spent the day braiding each other's hair, the way Breena had taught them.

Finally, word came that the legion was returning and everyone gathered to greet them. The men marched into the city and Breena, Trela, and Jaymin stood at the entrance of the city waiting for their husbands.

"I see them!" Yelled Jaymin and they all looked.

Tivas ran to Trela and hugged her tight. It had been a terrible battle with many comrades killed and many taken by Portess, to be tortured and killed later. Portess was known for his sadistic treatment. They had won, just barely and it would not be known as a victorious ending. Portess had retreated. Kabay found Jaymin and embraced her. It was good to get back to loved ones. Breena looked beyond them. Minab would be coming home to a wife that loved him too. He knew that. She could still feel his good-bye kiss and the movement within her, reminded her constantly of how much she missed him.

As Breena stood watching Tivas and Kabay hug their wives, she could not understand where Minab was. He was supposed to be in the lead, with his men proudly behind him. She could not even see his magnificent black horse with its decorated saddle. "Tivas, where is Minab? I don't see him anywhere."

Tivas broke from his embrace with Trela. He walked over to Breena and became very somber. "Breena, Minab did not return with us." There were tears in his eyes and his voice was shaky.

"Well, where is he? Is he hurt?" Breena began to worry.

"He did not return from an attack against Portess. Many were taken prisoner."

"Well, go get him. Break him out of the prison. He would have never left you." Breena felt as if she had been thrown into a deep hole. Everything was echoing and nothing seemed real.

"Portess never allows his prisoners to live."

That statement made Breena's mind spin. She had begun to accept the reality of this world and now she hoped it was as unreal as it seemed when she first came here. "You're lying. He said he'd return. Go find him. Bring my husband back." Breena's heart began to pound, and the air seemed thick. It couldn't be. He loved her and she him. He knew that now. He said they'd celebrate when he returned. Breena began to sob as she sank down to the ground.

"It was honorable. He ..."

"Don't you say it!" Breena interrupted him. "He's not dead. I couldn't handle it if he was dead. He's not." She stiffened her countenance and stopped the tears. "I'm not going to cry because he's just simply, not dead. He'll be back. He said he would." Breena stood but her legs became numb and she dropped to the ground again and began to weep uncontrollably. Her heart told her, that reality would not be denied.

Kabay broke the tradition. He motioned towards Breena and Jaymin nodded her consent. He bent down and hugged Breena tight. "I'm sorry. I should have been there for him. I should have been there, captured, instead of him. He would not let my men go. He wanted his men to lead that attack." Kabay said in his own language. His voice quivered with emotion.

Breena continued to weep. She didn't understand what Kabay had said but she felt his meaning. Tivas picked her up in his arms. Minab's wife would be under his care now. It was difficult to see such a strong personality become as a fragile butterfly. He carried her home and put her on her bed. Breena never felt so much pain before. It was worse than when they had crashed and her father and brother died. Minab had become her life. He was her sanity in a world filled with craziness. Breena wept for days. She stayed in her bed and refused to eat or talk or do anything except cry.

Tivas did not know what to do. "Trela, is this normal for such anguish to last so long?"

Trela had just come from Breena's room. She had tried to get Breena to eat something. "Her kind must feel very deeply. She is with child and the pain is almost too much for her to bear. I am afraid it will overcome the child."

Shirin told Tivas he must go speak with her and tell her of their ways, of Minab's way. Tivas agreed and quietly he walked into the room. Breena had closed the curtains, making the room shrouded from the mid-day sun. He knelt down beside the bed and caressed Breena's hair.

"I have never seen such grief and sorrow before. You must know that you are Minab's forever. You have been bound together for eternity."

Breena looked up. Her face was red and her eyes swollen. "I don't want eternity. I want now. I want Minab to come back to me."

"You must think of Minab's sons now. They need their mother. They need to be reminded of the greatness of their father."

"I can't face them. I can't raise them to be soldiers so they can go off and die like their father."

"It is our way that you become my second. Understand that I must raise seed up unto my brother so his lineage will go on."

Breena sat up slowly. "I don't want to be any body's anything. I'd rather be alone if I can't be with Minab."

"Do you not desire more children for Minab?"

"I have two sons and another child inside me. I don't want to be with anyone else. I could never be with anyone else after what Minab's first wife did to him."

"You do not understand our ways."

"You understand my ways, Tivas. I will only listen to Minab and he isn't here so I must do what I feel is right. I will never again go through what I went through when I first met Minab. You touch me and I will hurt you. I will hurt you bad."

Tivas shook his head. "Your grief talks with much anguish and despair. You are with child, so we will wait until Minab's offspring is born. Then we will continue our ways." Tivas showed her a plate of food. "If you will not feed yourself, feed your baby." He put the plate down and left the room.

Breena looked at the food for hours before she ate it. Why hadn't she died in the plane with her father? If she had never gone on the trip to the pole, she never would have loved someone like she did Minab. She never would have felt such a great loss. A summer at her grandparent's dull little farm sounded very comforting to her now.

Finally, after a week of lamentation, Breena came out of her room. Her sons did not know of their father's death nor could they understand at that age. Breena became a zombie to her everyday life and Tivas began to worry.

"It is needed that you should go to the market and buy fabric to sew clothes for our children." He said to her as she walked by with one of her sons in her arms.

Breena stopped and turned to face Tivas. "My sons are just doing fine."

Tivas held on to Breena's arm. "Go to the market woman. Buy what is needed." He moved around behind her and slid his hand onto her protruding belly. "Life continues."

Breena moved away. She didn't have any desire to fight. It was not a power struggle as it was with Minab. She knew Tivas wasn't as mighty as Minab. "I'll go."

"Be sure to wear the scarf."

Breena put Sheb down and he waddled away on his two little legs. The twins were walking fairly well now. She and Shirin left for the market and Breena deliberately left her scarf at home. It was the color of a widow's and she would not wear it. Shirin had been in the habit of late of letting Breena get away with disobeying the custom, as her heart ached for what Breena was going through. She did not say anything and ignored the looks from the others at the market. Shirin bought Breena a fruit treat and Breena smiled. It brought back many memories. They bought the material and as they headed back, Tivas caught up with them. He had Breena's scarf in his hand and he seemed very angry.

"I cautioned you about the scarf. You deliberately disobeyed." He shook his hand at her, waving the scarf in her face.

"Are you going to hit a pregnant woman?" Breena dared him.

Tivas stood motionless for a second. He tried placing the scarf on her head but Breena stepped back and shook it off. Frustrated, Tivas picked her up in his arms and carried her, squirming, all the way home. He took her up to her room and roughly placed her on the bed. Breena's abdomen was sore from the roughness of the trip home. "It will not be the same as it was with Minab. He was too lenient on you. I am not Minab." Tivas yelled at her.

"And you never will be." Breena sat up on the bed and glared at Tivas.

Tivas sighed and closed his eyes for a second. He opened them and just stood looking at Breena. It was an unkind remark and Breena knew it had found its target.

"I'm sorry, Tivas. I didn't mean that." She bit her lower lip to prevent it from quivering. "I hurt so badly, sometimes. I guess it spills over on to others."

"Soon, your baby will be born and you will be finished with that part of your life. Would you rather be Kabay's second?"

"No. It would be hard to accept. I'll never be able to reconcile myself to this, Tivas."

"You will have to accept it, eventually." Tivas turned and started to walk out of the room.

"Tivas; if I can find a way to return to my home land, I'm going. And I will take my children with me."

Tivas turned around and nodded. "And I would have to stop you. You are Adder now and this is your home land." He left the room before Breena could reply.

Breena looked through her trunk again and found the video camera. She took pictures of her boys and the house and anything else she could think of while the batteries lasted. They had been dormant for over three years but they still had some charge in them. If somehow she found a way to escape this land, and was prevented, maybe the tape would get back to her mother. Even though the play back didn't allow you to hear what was being said, Breena talked to her mother through the whole tape. She told her what life had been like and that her brother and father had died in the crash. She told her the whole story about Minab from the terrifying start to the tragic end. Her mother would understand her love for Minab and maybe, if she couldn't go and the tape made it, someone would come for her.

Time passed and life was full of mundane routine for Breena. There were few arguments as Breena tried to stay out of Tivas' way. She went into labor. It was as long and difficult as the other one and Breena wondered if she would die. Tivas did not stay with her and Breena felt lonelier than ever. Minab would have stayed. After nineteen hours, Breena gave birth to a good-sized baby boy. He had hair like his father's and dark blue eyes. Tivas came to see the baby and told Breena he would name him. But Breena lied to Tivas, and told him Minab wanted the baby would be named after his father if it were a boy. It was his last request as he rode away, she told him.

Twelve days after his birth, little Minab was circumcised and given his official name and a blessing, at a feast given by Tivas. Breena was upset that everyone acted as if it was Tivas' child. But he was to be considered his father now that Breena was a widow and soon to become his second.

Sixty days after the baby was born, Tivas came to Breena during the rain. He told her it was time for her to become his second and Breena pulled out the knife Minab had given her. She told Tivas that he was never to come see her again or she would make Trela a widow. Tivas left the room in a rage but did not return that night.

Trela was expecting a baby now and Breena knew she spent many nights sick to her stomach. It was like morning sickness in reverse, and she slept in the small back room because of it. Breena gave Trela the rest of the herbs Minab had given her but they didn't seem to help. Maybe they had lost their potency, Breena thought; after all, they worked for her.

Tivas had Breena doing chores that she wasn't accustomed to

doing, laundry and gardening and cooking. It wasn't that she minded, but she found herself becoming tired, with the chores and caring for her children. When night came, she welcomed the sleep that found her. It wasn't until the end of the first week, of the new chores, that she realized why he had her over worked. Breena was sound asleep when the door to her room opened and Tivas slowly approached her bed. The curtains were drawn and it was darker than usual in her room. Breena thought that it was unusual, as she stopped pulling the curtains when she came out to be with her children again, after her mourning had softened, but she was too tired to inquire as to who closed them or even to pull them back open. She found sleep quickly.

"Wife, I have returned to you."

Breena was still very sleepy, slowly opened her eyes. "Minab?" She whispered then she hugged him tight and he kissed her passionately. He kissed her again and again until Breena's heart felt it would burst with happiness. She touched his chest. His shirt was off, and she instinctively felt for the scars that she always traced in her mind. They weren't there, and Breena jumped up. She ran to the window and pushed open the curtains. Tivas sat quietly, on the bed, looking at her. Breena wasn't sure what to say. In less than a few seconds, her world had opened again and then shut tighter than a clamshell. Breena touched her lips and wondered if Minab would ever forgive her. She had been deceived, he would see that from his little spot in heaven, she hoped.

"How could you do that to me?" Breena couldn't stand to look at him anymore. She turned and looked out the window. She was still weak from fatigue.

Tivas came up behind her, put his arms around her waist, and hugged her. "Pretend I am Minab, if that will help. I have an obligation to him. You must become my second."

Breena struggled to free herself and couldn't. She started to cry. "He'll never forgive me if I let that happen, Tivas. Can't you see that?"

"He knows that is what must happen."

"No. You don't understand. She hurt him so bad when she chose

Miller over Minab. I can't do that to him. If you loved your brother at all, you'd see it isn't supposed to happen." Breena turned and looked into Tivas' eyes. "I can't prevent you from making me your second, but if any part of what I did to help you get back with Minab counts for anything..."

Tivas picked her up and carried her back to the bed. He sat down and held her in his arms as she wept from fear that he would be as cruel as Minab was at the start of their marriage. "It counts for much, Breena. Do not weep. I will give you a whole year from Minab's death, to work this out in your heart. A whole year and then you will have to submit to our way." He kissed her on the forehead and left.

Breena continued to weep out of relief. A year would help, she thought. Maybe Tivas did understand. Maybe his love for the daughter of Shirin showed him many important things.

Weeks passed and Breena seemed to relax. Tivas was keeping his promise and did not go into Breena's bedroom again. He did however continue the long battle over the scarf that Minab had with Breena. Jaymin came over to the house as Kabay and Tivas were on training maneuvers with some new recruits.

She seemed secretive and motioned for Breena to talk to her in the garden out of the ear distance of Trela. "Breena, I have heard something that could be of great importance to you."

Breena couldn't imagine what was so important. She thought the only thing that would make a difference in her life now was hearing that the months since Minab's death had been a bad dream. "What is so important?"

"Another stranger has arrived. His wagon did not crash and he plans on trying to return to his homeland."

Breena touched her chest. It was almost too good of news to bear. "Where did you hear this?"

"My mother's new husband, whom she is a second to now, has taken him in. She came to visit me yesterday."

"Oh Jaymin. Do you know what this means? I can go home. I can go home and take my babies with me."

"Tivas would never allow that."

"He won't find out until it is too late." Breena hugged Jaymin. "I love you. You are my best friend."

Jaymin smiled. "There is a great conflict in my heart, Breena. I will pretend I do not know, but please I ask that you do not ask me to do anything else."

"I won't." Breena stood up. "I don't have much time. I may have to say good-bye now. It will take me a while to get to Kalat."

"Alone, or with the babies? It is crazy. You cannot make it without a man to guide you."

"I have a compass and a great memory. I used to put the eagle scouts in my city to shame. Don't worry, Jaymin. I'll be there in less than two weeks."

They hugged each other and Breena brought Shirin into her room to talk. "Shirin, I need to ask you something important."

"What is it?"

"You're a free woman now. Where do your loyalties sit?"

Shirin looked at Breena and smiled. "It is with Minab and his wife, always."

Breena almost started crying. "Shirin, I have a chance to go home, my real home. Will you help me?"

"If it is possible, I will do what I can."

"There is a man in Drostom named Fetchmos. I need you to get in contact with him. I need you to take my children to Kalat. If you go to Jaymin's mother's house when you get there, I will find you."

"You will not come with us?"

"I need to get there a head of you to set things up. It is important to move quickly as once Tivas finds out he will surely come after us."

"Indeed he will. Maybe I could have him thinking we are somewhere else for a few days. Is this Fetchmos trustworthy?"

"It is the man Minab wanted me to contact if Portess ever made it through to Chelm. I will give you some money to pay him. I will pay you too, of course."

"I will need to take along the wet nurse for the young Minab. He will need her to feed him as he cannot drink from a cup yet."

"You're very wise, Shirin. Thank you. We must leave on the same day or Tivas will know something is not right. Shirin, why are you helping me?"

"Without Minab, even I know you do not belong here."

They hugged and arrangements were made to contact Fetchmos and the wet nurse and to get supplies. Breena gave Shirin things from the trunk in her room to take and one hundred gold coins for payment to Fetchmos. They both left within hours of each other. Breena took one of the horses Minab had left for her long ago. She was dressed in Minab's clothes. The pants were big and the shirt was enormous but she cinched them up with a strap. It was so much easier to ride in pants than in a dress. Breena figured she wouldn't stand out as much, if she topped it off with a hat.

She had to ride passed Tivas to get through the main gate. She lowered her head and dug her heels into the side of the horse. It reached full gallop as she passed Tivas and although he and a few of his men looked, they had no idea who the crazy man was riding the horse out of the city. Breena rode as fast and hard as she could each day. The horse was strong and only required six hours of rest daily, and that was during the rain. By the third day out, she was two days ahead of schedule. She knew that Tivas would know she was gone by now, but it would take time for him to get supplies and he'd never assume she could ride well. Those boring summers at her grandparents' farm was finally paying some dividends. During the rain, she camped as close to the horse as she could. Wild animals wouldn't attack a horse, Minab had told her. She ached for her baby and longed to see her twins again but soon they would be reunited and on their way back to America.

A day out of Kalat, as she stopped for water by a stream, two men approached her. Breena had brought her knife and her father's gun with her and she was determined not to let anything or anyone interfere with her plans. The two men were not Adder and that bothered Breena. She could possibly reason with them if they were Adder but she knew little of the other tribes' character. Then Breena realized that even if they had been Adder the language barrier would mess things up for her. These men didn't really want anything other than to harass her. She didn't even get a chance to pull out her gun. The attack was quick and while they wrestled, they discovered she was a female. This seemed to confuse them. Breena could have escaped if she wanted to leave her horse behind but her hesitation gave them the advantage and they ended up tackling her and tying her up. At least they weren't going to harm her right away.

They put her on her horse and took her two days west of her destination to a strange building. It looked like a castle from the outside and Breena wondered whose place it could be. It looked, as if the place had been abandoned at one time. It was then set up by the people who now occupied it.

They dragged Breena into the building and brought before a man dressed in animal skins. He was smaller than the men of Adder were but he looked ruthless. Breena wondered who he was and tried to figure out how she could find out. She settled for the use of hand language. Breena stood up straight and proud before him. They undid her bindings. She slapped her chest and told them her name, just Breena, nothing else. The leader grinned, amused at her attitude. Perhaps there was a female race of warriors that would be amusing to overthrow. He slapped his chest and said his name and Breena froze as he spoke it. Portess! This was the man who killed Minab. This was the animal that tortures his prisoners and delights in their suffering. Breena felt a chill run through her. This was the man who ended her desire to live. Breena slowly smiled. It was a friendly smile that deceived him. She brought out her gun and it took all the self-control she processed, not to blow him away immediately. He said something and they all laughed. Breena graciously bowed and then she stood up straight again with the gun pointed at Portess. They had taken the knife, but not the gun. They had no idea what it was. They weren't even sure what she was. Breena, with her blond hair and blue eyes, dressed like a man, but with the shape of a female. Portess laughed again and said something to Breena. It must have been derogatory. He waved his hands and spat at the ground in front of her.

"I don't seem to have your full attention." Breena was not as frightened as she thought she'd be. This was the man who killed Minab, and she was standing twenty feet away from him. The hate she felt filled her whole body and she began to tremble from the adrenaline that was pumping through her blood. She looked around and saw a huge water vase in the corner of the room. One shot made it exploded into a thousand pieces and everyone scrambled from the room, leaving her alone with Portess. He sat with his hands over his ears. The thunderous sound of the gun was beyond his comprehension. Breena pointed the gun at Portess. "You pathetic imbecile! You think I'm a freak with my hair and such? I knew more than you, before I was out of kindergarten." Now all she had to do was justify his death, in her mind. All she had to do was pull the trigger. Too bad he wouldn't explode like the vase. Breena walked over to where they threw her knife and picked it up. She placed it back into its case that hung from her belt. All the time, the gun was pointed at Portess, but she could not fire.

Portess moved towards her and the shot was automatic. He grabbed his side and fell back, bellowing with pain. It would not have been a fatal wound in her world, but Breena knew they did not have the medical knowledge to help him here. "Damn. You idiot! I didn't mean to do that. I wanted it to be an honorable fight. You turned it into a turkey shoot." Breena turned and ran into the hall. The halls were narrow and full of turns and little places for men to hide and jump out at her. She had no idea where she was or how she could get out. Eleven shots left and she had two more clips in her pocket. Breena inched her way along, checking out each new path, she came across. She had to go down. She was on the third level of the building and she knew she had to get to the ground floor. Breena came to a set of curbed stairs. As she proceeded down, two men came after her, their sword drawn. She shot them both, in the thigh, close to the groin. They went down faster than Portess did. At least it wouldn't be fatal with them, no worse than a stab of a knife.

As Breena approached the final stairway, a dark figure grabbed her from behind and pulled her into a narrow pathway. He was so quick Breena didn't have time to react. He pushed her into a crevasse in the hall and up against the wall then he pressed himself up against her so both bodies were enclosed in the darkness of the crevasse. The man was big and Breena felt completely over powered. She could not even get her gun up into a position to fire at him. Warriors ran down the hall, passed them, in their hiding spot. Breena could hardly breathe. After the soldiers passed, the man pulled her out of the tiny crevasse in the wall. He was filthy and Breena almost cringed at the thought of him being close to her. He had a big shaggy beard. His hair, down passed his shoulders, was dirty and a deep, dull black, in color. For a second Breena though he might be Adder but she knew none would be allowed to be here and live. Portess hated Adder. His was clothed in only a pair of ragged pants. There were no boots or shirt and his bare torso revealed scars from the welts left from many whippings. His eyes looked tired and full of despair. Breena knew this man had the strength to kill her with his bare hands, but she felt no fear. He couldn't be one of them, not with those eyes. She tried to remember some of the words of their language but she couldn't concentrate. They heard footsteps coming their way, and the man immediately picked Breena up and threw her over his shoulder. He ran down a long hall and turned; then ran down another and another. Finally, he put Breena down. He pushed on a large stone in the wall. It indented into and then beyond the wall, leaving a hole. He pushed Breena inside and then followed. The man pushed the stone back into place once they were through and the wall looked intact.

Breena looked around at the tiny room. It looked like some forgotten closet, except Breena knew these people didn't have closets. It was dark except for the light that shone through the cracks at the top of the room and around the stone that concealed the passageway into it. It made it possible to see things fairly clearly. The man put his finger to his lips. They could hear the warriors running passed their hideout.

Once the men passed, Breena was instantly pushed down, face

first, onto the floor by the man. Breena wasn't sure what he was doing and she struggled to free herself. He undid her belt and threw it over in the corner, then he started to touch her as if he was not sure if she was female or not. When his hands slid over an area, Breena didn't want him near, she struggled to sit up, and then she slapped him hard, across the face. The man stopped and sat back immediately. They sat staring at each other for a few minutes. The man tried to say something but his voice only produced a hoarse, crackling sound. He pointed to his neck and Breena could see a large red abrasion, like a rope burn, around his neck. It looked as if someone had recently tried to hang him. Instinctively, Breena reach to comfort him, but she realized she did not know this man and he had already been too familiar as it was. She put her hand down. The man jumped on her and started to kiss her but Breena started to scream and he quickly covered her mouth with his hand. His grip was tight and his hand so big that Breena thought she would suffocate. He kissed her neck and Breena hit him on the head with the gun handle. He pushed her away and rubbed his head.

"You stay away from me, you dirty pig, or I'll really hurt you." Breena told him. She knew he wouldn't understand but she held out her hand and told him that way, to keep away. "I appreciate you saving my life but if that is what you want for payment for your deed, I'd just soon as get out of this mess myself, thank you." Breena looked around the tiny room. There was nothing in there except a few cores from some fruit that was eaten. It looked as if he had not been hiding there awhile, a week maybe.

They could hear the rain starting to fall and Breena crawled over to her belt. She put it back on and motioned for the man to follow her. It was the right time to leave this place. She tried to pull the stone back but the man stopped her. He shook his head. He showed her with the use of his hands that they should wait until the following rain. Breena nodded. He obviously knew better than she did. He looked like they had tried to kill him more than once and he had survived. He motioned for Breena to come over beside him and sleep. Breena shook her head and crawled over to the opposite wall. She put the safety on the gun and curled up in the corner to sleep.

Morning brought a repeat of the aggressive behavior of the man, from the evening before. Breena woke to him all over her and she struggled to free herself. He was strong and Breena realized she would soon lose the fight. "No stop. I belong to Tivas, brother to Minab, a mighty warrior. Tivas is a mighty warrior too and will kill you if you touch me again." She said desperately trying to give him names he might recognize.

He stopped and his eyes showed rage. "T...Ti...Tivas?" He managed to say. The attempt to speak hurt his throat and he started to cough and hold his neck.

"Don't talk. We need to get you some water." Breena said as she motioned the same thing with her hands. He nodded.

The man told her to stay, by pointing to the corner of the tiny room. He carefully pulled the stone open and went through, and then he closed it again, leaving Breena alone. Breena knew she was lucky he recognized Tivas' name. She did up the ties on her clothes and waited for him to return.

It was over an hour, it seemed, before he returned. He carried a water pouch and a large piece of cooked meat. They shared the food and Breena wetted down the sleeve of her shirt then gently cleaned the neck of the man. He looked at her but did not touch her. It was almost as if he was surprised at learning the news. Breena was sure if he knew she actually belonged to Minab, before he was killed, the man would really be impressed. Minab's name used to bring respect to people's eyes, immediately. Breena thought about Minab and became very sad. This man in front of her, possibly, knew him. Maybe, he served under him. Why did he live while Minab die? They sat without talking for hours, waiting for the rain to start.

When it did, the man seemed to become invigorated. He pushed the stone away and held his hand out for Breena. They had an understanding now, she figured, and she took his hand. He led her down a series of hallways and stairs, hiding occasionally from a guard.

The castle-like building seemed to be indifferent to them. Breena knew that Portess' men were probably busy, wondering if Portess was going to die and who would take his place as leader.

As they approached the courtyard where the exit was, they noticed four men guarded it. Breena's new partner put forth his hand. Breena shook her head. She aimed her gun, and then stopped. She needed something to quiet the sound. There was an old blanket, meant for underneath a saddle, thrown on the ground. She picked it up and wrapped her hand, holding the gun, in it. She started to walk out to where she could aim better but her partner pulled her back. Breena held out her hand for him to wait. She pointed to the wrapped gun and nodded. Again, he pulled her back.

"Look, I know what I'm doing, buddy. Let me do my part," Breena told him. She thought that maybe her frustrated look would get her message across to him. She walked out again and this time he let her go. Her aim was accurate and all four went down. She had to shoot one man in both legs as he thought he was going to be a hero and attack on one leg. They grabbed two horses that were tied up in the courtyard next to the guards, and rode away.

They rode for hours in the rain, and Breena felt safe. As the rain subsided, they took shelter in a cave. They would hide until they could decide what they should do next. As the man slept, Breena knew they couldn't go on together. He had looked at the gun with awe and a desire to have it. It was a weapon that could destroy many and Breena knew that he would eventually try to take it from her. It was beyond their technology and dangerous for any one tribe to possess. She left him her knife. He needed some kind of weapon to get food if nothing else. Breena slowly crawled over to the horses. She would leave one. She couldn't leave him helpless after he had saved her at the castle. Breena climbed upon the horse and rode. With the use of her compass, she knew which direction Kalat was and the man who would take her and her children home.

It took a day and a half to reach Kalat. Breena was hungry and tired by the time she reached the outskirts of the city. When she dismounted, many stared at her. She was still dressed in man's clothing, but Breena didn't care. Her only interest was talking to the man who flew the airplane onto the same field as she crashed in. She found the house in which he was staying by asking for the English stranger. Breena didn't wait to be introduced; she walked right in on the stranger trying to talk to two members of Kalat's overseer council.

The stranger was average size man for Breena's world, possibly just under six feet tall, but the average man from the tribe of Adder tower over him. His hair was not blond but light brown and his eyes were green.

"I must speak with the stranger." Breena shouted and everyone quickly turned to look at her.

The stranger stood up and smiled. "You speak English?"

"Yeah; I've been told the airplane can still fly. Is that true?"

"Yes. It'll be a rough take off, but it can certainly fly. Only problem is I don't know where I am."

"It isn't Kansas, trust me. The sooner you head out, the better chance you have of ever getting out."

"I don't even know how I got here. My name's Skeller, George Skeller." He held out his hand but Breena shook her head, and refused to accept the handshake.

"I can direct you out of this hell hole but I need to know if you'd have room for me and my three children?"

"I can make room. You must tell me how you came to be here. You have blond hair. You are not one of them, are you?"

"I'll answer all your questions in due time. My children should be here in the city soon. How soon can we take off?"

"I can be ready in a day."

Breena sighed. The overseer councilors were chattering amongst themselves and Breena knew they were upset over her attire. "Look, I'm not really popular with these people; too many rules and customs. I will meet with you at the plane after I find my children. You'll be fine here, as long as you don't break any of their stupid laws."

"How can I keep their laws when I don't know what they are?"

"They're simple, really. Just keep your thoughts to yourself and don't touch any female, under any circumstance, anywhere, anytime, not even me. They have different ideas about that and you could be killed for just a touch. As for the others, ask before you act. Laws for men are different that laws for women."

"You're kidding? Just an accidental touch could get me killed? I guess I've been lucky for the past month. I just thought the women were unfriendly."

"Nope, and I'm not kidding, and you really were lucky. I don't need you getting killed on me so be careful. There are many laws that if broken, could get you killed and I need you to fly the plane." Breena turned and left before the overseers decided she was more than an odd female and disciplined her.

*   *   *

Tivas and his men were only a day out of Kalat. As they made ready to finish their journey, one of the men Tivas had with him, noticed a man on a horse approaching. He was riding a spotted horse that was characteristic of Portess' legion. Tivas and his group of six stood ready, not sure what to expect from the man approaching them. He had on only a pair of pants and hooked on to the waistband, was a knife. It was the same man who helped Breena escape. He didn't look too threatening, and Tivas walked over to him as he stopped his horse and dismounted.

"You look in need of assistance." Tivas told him. The man wavered and Tivas thought he might collapse in front of him.

The newcomer slowly looked up but said nothing. Tivas thought he recognized him, but wasn't sure. He looked foreign in his deteriorated condition, with his long hair and shaggy beard. The man slowly licked his lips as if he was trying to form the words he wanted to say. Suddenly he lunged at Tivas, striking him several times before Tivas could restrain him. Tivas' men pulled him off Tivas and one brought out his knife in defense.

"Halt! Do not harm him. He is just a crazy man. He must have

been a prisoner. Look. He still has part of the chains on his ankle."
Tivas yelled. "Get him some water and some food."

The man seemed to regain some strength. "Tivas..." His voice was
coarse and labored as he tried to form the words.

Tivas came closer. "Do I know you?"

"Where is she?"

"Who?" Tivas' heart jumped as the possibilities of whom this man
was poured into his thoughts.

"She is mine." The man hit his chest with a closed fist.

Tivas stood in pleasant astonishment. He came even closer. "Release
him." His men set the newcomer free. "Minab?" Tivas voice cracked
with emotion. He hugged the man and Minab slowly hugged him
back.

Tivas had his men bring Minab plenty of food and drink. One of
the men chiseled the bolt, on the remaining leg iron, off. Tivas was so
overjoyed to see Minab again; he could not do enough for him.

Minab's voice cleared some as he drank and took in nourishment.
"Where is she?" He said hoarsely.

"Minab, she has been crazy since the day we told her we thought
you dead. She found out another stranger had come to the field outside
Kalat, and she left Chelm for Kalat twenty days ago."

"I saw her. Portess captured her but I helped her escaped."

"She saw you and left you?"

"She did not know me." Minab looked up at Tivas and his expression
was filled with contempt. "She said she belonged to you."

Tivas shook his head. "She refused to become my second. She
threatened to kill me if I forced her. I thought she was crazed, so I left
her alone. I gave her a year to reconcile to our ways in her mind."

Minab slowly grinned. "She is unconstrained by our ways."

"Minab, she had Shirin take the children and flee to Kalat. If this
stranger can leave for her homeland, she plans to go with him and take
your sons with her."

Minab became alert. "We must stop her. She is Adder now."

"That is why I am here, on my way to Kalat."

They mounted their horses and rode briskly towards the city. When they arrived, they went directly to the overseer, and they were told Breena had been there the day before. She was in the city and the stranger had not left but was making plans to leave soon.

*   *   *

Breena had found Shirin. They had just arrived at Jaymin's parents' house, and were waiting for her. She hugged her children and kissed the baby. Shirin had brought along a wet nurse for the little one so he could be feed properly. They all looked healthy. Breena changed into the clothes Shirin had brought in a small sack. They were the clothes Breena wore on the plane trip that carried her to this place, years ago. Breena was pleased that they still fit and it felt good to be wearing jeans and a shirt again. She pulled on the socks and boots and Shirin gasped.

"You wear clothes of the wicked, Breena."

"I can't travel in a dress and the clothes I was wearing are Minab's so they are only held up by twine. It will be all right, Shirin." Breena hugged her. "You are a true friend. When you return to Chelm, I have ten gold coins in my trunk in Minab's room. Take them. Tivas may not be very compassionate to you, for helping me."

"I do not work for Tivas."

Breena took the gun and placed it in the sack that had held her clothes. Inside the sack were written pages of history and culture, Breena had written over the past year. There was also the video tape she had made and information on addresses of people she knew, including her mother. She picked up another sack with food and drink for the trip, in it. "I have to take these supplies to the plane and check on everything. I will be back for the children soon. I'm going to miss all of you but you understand why I'm leaving don't you?"

Shirin nodded. "Yes, I understand. There is nothing here for you and you are not really Adder, no matter what Tivas says."

Breena smiled, then left for the field where the plane was. When she arrived, the stranger was there already, checking out the instruments.

"I was wondering if you would show. You look different from what you looked like before."

"I'm, Breena Keets. I crashed here about four years ago."

"Keets? You're from the felled Max Jared flight?"

"The same."

"Are there others?"

"No."

"Are they all dead?"

"Yes, they died in the crash. They were lucky. Most strangers, who live, are killed over a short period of time, because of one thing or another. This is not an easy culture to survive in."

"You survived."

"I guess I was lucky, if you can call it that. I was forced into a marriage, forced to bare his children, and just when I was beginning to understand the man, and he was beginning to understand me, he was killed in battle. These people are barbarians. They kill off whole cities, including women and children. I've seen so much and I'm barely twenty years old." Breena sat in the co-pilot's seat and explained to the stranger her theory. She explained how they could get back to the North Pole, and their part of the world. He was amazed but receptive to her rationale. Breena placed the sack in a storage compartment. "Look, if for some reason, I don't make it back..." Breena gave a little chuckle. "I'll probably be dead. Anyway, you take off without me and make sure my information gets through. Some of the professors, the information is addressed to, are fairly smart, but they may decide this is not a culture to intermingle with."

"What I've seen, in the month I've been here, makes me not want to return. I've seen someone put a sword through another guy over stupid things. How you've handled it is beyond me."

Breena talked with the pilot for an hour then she told him she'd go back and get her children. She knew the flight would be more than four hours, so she had made a makeshift bottle and nipple for her baby. They might not have enough fuel to make it to a base near the North Pole but the radio seemed in working order and although it would not pick up anything where they were, Skeller was sure it still worked. Breena left quickly and returned to the city. The looks she received were ones of astonishment over her mode of dress and her mannerisms. She dismounted from her horse and walked casually into Jaymin's parent's house.

When she entered, she noticed a look of apprehension on Shirin face. "What's the matter, Shirin?" She looked around and couldn't see the children. Suddenly Tivas stepped out from the adjoining room. "Where are my children?" Breena screamed at him.

"They are in the other room. You cannot have them."

"They are my children, not yours. I don't care what your customs are. They are not yours. You are only their uncle. I am their mother."

"I cannot allow you to leave."

Breena's eyes filled with tears. "Why not? There is nothing for me, here. Damn it, Tivas. Don't you remember what it was like to be estranged from your brother and family? These are not my people. This isn't even my life."

"It would be a mistake to let you go." Tivas turned to leave the room.

Breena grabbed his arm to try to stop him. He was a little surprised that she touched him. "Tivas, please listen to me. Look at me. I'm so far from your kind; I'm nothing but a freak. My children aren't going to be treated like all the others. Their mother is a freak, wife of a dead hero. All I will ever do here is cause trouble for you."

Tivas turned away again, and Breena grabbed his sword. Over the past two years, she had become stronger. She held the blade close to his neck. "Bring my children out to me. I'm desperate, Tivas. I won't play your stupid games. If I have to, I will kill for them. I will die for them."

The wet nurse, with the baby, and the two little boys were brought out. Breena guided them out to the horse, the sword still pointed at Tivas. The young girl who was the wet nurse put little baby Minab into a little packsack type carrier and Breena put it on her back. Shirin lifted the two little boys onto the horse. They had ridden before and weren't afraid. Breena grabbed the saddle and pulled herself behind them. She put her arms around them. "You'll have your own son soon, Tivas. Please don't try to stop me. There is no other way. Understand? None." She threw the sword to the ground, turned the horse, and rode swiftly out of the city and towards the field. She could hear horses behind her but she did not turn around. Her goal was the field. She could see the plane. She was only twenty yards away when she heard someone calling her name. It was clear and Breena was so startled at the familiar voice she stopped and looked back. It was not who she thought it was.

The man calling her name was racing towards her and she recognized him. He was the prisoner from Portess' castle. Sheb slid off the horse and Breena quickly dismounted to retrieve him. "Sheb, come to Mommy." She called and Sheb hugged his mother tight. Tian turned and slid off the horse so he could be with his brother. "No sweetheart. Stay on the horse."

The man was closing in and Breena bent down and hugged her boys. She began to cry as she looked at the plane. Its engines were already started. "Please, let me go. Let us go. You don't understand." Breena sobbed as the man got off the horse.

The man walked over to her and gently took the baby from the packsack. Breena begged him to give her back her little baby, her little Minab. She dropped herself onto the ground and hugged her other sons. Defeat had come by the hands of an outsider. He looked at the baby and it smiled at him. He smiled back and slowly said, "His eyes dance, like his mother's."

Breena looked up at the man holding her son. She was surprised that he spoke English. She stood. "His name is Minab, after his noble father."

"I thought you were Tivas' woman?"

"I lied. I thought you wouldn't care that I was Minab's woman. He died many rains ago." Breena looked back at the plane. "Please, give me my baby. We'll leave and then you won't have to think about us ever again."

"Thinking of you was all that kept me alive, through everything. I could not live if you were to leave now."

Breena stared at the man and slowly shook her head. "I… I don't understand."

"Memories of you filled my days and dreams about you filled the hours of rain."

"Me? You knew Minab? He talked about me?"

"They tried to beat the smile from my face. They tried to hang me, but I remembered my wife's hair full of flour and her dress soaked with milk and the kisses she returned to my lips. I am thankful for a son, who has eyes that dance, like his mother's."

Breena started to tremble. She could hardly form the name with her lips. She reached out to touch his chest.

"Woman, do not touch the flesh that is not of your husband's. If you have become Tivas' second, then you are his, until I go see the church overseer and get you back."

Breena shook her head and continued to reach out to him. Trembling, she found the long scar on the right side, amidst the dirt, just below his ribcage and she traced it with her finger. It was the scar his father gave him, when he was just beginning to train as a warrior. "Minab? Minab!" Breena hugged him and tears rolled freely down her cheeks. Minab placed the baby, back in her packsack and returned her hug. Then he kissed her, gently at first, then passionately, his hands cupping her face as he did so.

"Minab, come with me. We can leave together. We can get out of this crazy place with its violence and its wars." Even as she spoke, she knew that he could never survive in her world. It was a time for the ultimate choice, his world with him, or her world without him. She had tried living without him and she couldn't. This was another chance. Hard as life here was, at least it would be with him.

The plane positioned it-self. The field was level and the take off was rough but successful. It circled the field once then headed north for the land of the cold. With her husband's arms wrapped securely around her, Breena watched until it was out of sight. With the airplane, went her only chance to leave this land, leave the insanity and the lifestyle she would never fully understand. She turned and faced her husband. He kissed her again and any regrets vanished with the sound of the engines of the plane, as it grew smaller in the sky.

CHAPTER TWELVE

IT TOOK AN HOUR for Minab to cut and shave off his beard. Breena sat and watched. She did not want to be separated from him. After, he bathed and changed into clean new clothes. His face was tender but he was glad to be clean, again.

Portess had not known he was a captain. He lost his helmet and sword in the battle that he and his men were captured in, and his men had not revealed his identity. They said their captain was killed earlier in battle.

Portess needed slaves to rebuild his kingdom so he spared his captives, this time. Portess had been cut off from his homeland, and after overthrowing a small city, southwest of Kalat, he established his base there. Using the newly acquired slaves, he fortified the castle-like building that was the center of the small city.

Minab being the strongest and the biggest of the slaves spent the past year building the walls of the castle. Slowly during the time in captivity, one by one, Minab's men were killed because of individual rebellion. They guarded Minab the closest, since they felt he would be the one most likely to organize a mass escape. When Minab did plan and succeed with the mass escape, he was the only one who did not make it out. They tried to hang him but the rope broke and Minab played dead. When they came to check him, he killed his executioners and hid in the very walls he helped build. He stayed there, planning his exit until he spotted Breena while searching for food.

The surviving group of Minab's men, who had escaped, reached the city, on foot, about the same time as Minab and Tivas had.

Minab was upset with Breena's apparel. The jeans were tight and her top showed her form in detail. He could not condone either piece of clothing. Pants for women were disgraceful, and he ordered Breena to change into a dress, immediately. She complied without argument. After all, she had chosen to be with him and that included his attitudes towards women and their place in his society.

Once Minab had cleaned up and Breena had changed, Minab went to find his men, leaving Breena alone. The overseer had offered Minab a room at his house presently, until Minab could return to Chelm.

Tivas walked into the bedroom. She had all three of her boys sleeping in the corner of the room on a small bed.

"You look like a female again, a handsome woman." Tivas said with a smile. "You are even wearing your scarf."

Breena slipped the scarf down to her shoulders. "The scarf was for Minab, but he just left to find the rest of his men."

Tivas stared at her with an intensity that made Breena feel uncomfortable. He walked over to her. "That golden hair! I should have made you my second while I had the opportunity, before the complication of Minab's return. I thought it would only be a matter of time."

"There was never even a chance in a million, Tivas." Breena walked passed him and he quickly pulled her into his arms and kissed her with such fervor that it left Breena almost speechless. "Tivas. No." She tried to break free but he pushed her towards the bed and onto its blankets. He kissed her again and Breena struggled to free herself. "Stop, Tivas. This is wrong." She did not yell. She did not want her boys waking to find their mother in the arms of their uncle.

"Do you know how many men came to me, wanting to make you their first wife?" Tivas started pulling at her dress. "It was my right to have you as my second and I gave you time to grieve, instead."

"Minab is back. He is my husband." Breena began to panic as she realized Tivas' strength was too much for her.

"You can be his, again, but he must talk to the church overseer first. Until then, I still have a right to make you my second. It is my right and no one can prevent it if I want it." Tivas kissed her again on the lips and Breena began to cry as she fought, with all her might, to prevent what Tivas wanted.

When Minab returned, Breena was cuddled up, sleeping on the small bed with her children. Minab found Tivas and asked him if he would ride with him and some of the city's legion to capture the castle of Portess. Tivas said he would be honored, and then he asked Minab if he had seen the church overseer yet. Minab said he had just come from there and that Breena and he were once again, united in marriage. Minab also said that because he had his first marriage with Annek dissolved; Breena was now his first wife, instead of just his second. Tivas smiled and gave Minab a brief hug. He told Minab he would obtain armor and swords for Minab and the remainder of his men, and then he left the house.

When Minab came back into the bedroom, Breena was in the bathing room washing her face.

"Wife. Come greet your husband." Minab called cheerfully and Breena slowly walked out. "Tivas and I will ride with my men and some of the city's legion, to Portess' fortress tomorrow and conquer it. But it is now time to reacquaint ourselves with each other."

"Tivas?"

"Yes. We ride together, as brothers. He has done well, in his care of you. I am indeed grateful."

Breena tried to stifle the tears but they came. "Have you seen the church overseer yet?" She managed to ask.

"Yes, I have. We are one again. I am surprised that Tivas did not make you his second. I would have done so. You are far too great of a prize to keep entombed in a memory of a brother." Minab traced her face with his fingers and gently kissed her tears. "Why do you weep? Are you not happy that your husband returns from the dead?"

Breena wiped the tears from her cheeks with her hand. "What if Tivas had made me his second? I would only have been able to fight as I did with you, and you were much too strong for me. Would you have been angry with him?"

"It is our way. I do not want to think of it. The past is over and mine anger is gone. I am grateful he did not take what would have rightfully been his at the time. Things are now as they should be. All is well."

"Minab, while you were gone. . ."

Minab silenced her with a kiss as he picked her up in his arms and slowly twirled her around. "Tonight as the rain falls, my heart is full. I have my sons and my beautiful wife. Nothing else matters. Nothing can make this time less than perfect." Breena started to say something, but again, Minab silenced her. "You will be happy to know that because I had my marriage to Annek nullified upon her death, you are actually my first wife and not just a second."

A million things tumbled around in Breena's head. She wanted desperately to tell Minab what Tivas had done but she could see it was no longer simple. It would hurt him and their relationship as husband and wife. It could literally, kill Tivas. Would Minab ever forgive her? Breena pulled her sleeves down on her dress so he would not notice the red marks that would soon turn into bruises. By then he would think it was from Portess' men when they dragged her into the castle. "Minab, why did you have your marriage to Annek, annulled?"

"I could not live, knowing my wife was an adulterous." Minab placed Breena on the same blankets, that Tivas had placed her, earlier. "I do not want to think about unpleasant things. My thoughts are only of you."

Breena put her arms around him and kissed him. She only wanted to think of him too. She closed her eyes and pushed the thoughts of Tivas' assault out of her mind.

When Tivas came to get Minab, the next day, Breena held on tightly to her husband and begged him to be careful. She knew she could never persuade Minab not to go, but the fear that he might not return to her was there. Minab touched and kissed Breena in a manner that told those watching them saying good-bye that she was his again. She belonged to Minab. Breena watched as they rode away. Tivas turned and looked back at Breena and smiled. She didn't smile back. Instead, she ran back into the house and hugged her boys.

Minab and his men brutally beat Portess. Breena had not killed him with her gun as she thought she had. Minab, however, finished the job. Portess was surprised to see Minab, and even more surprised when he found out Minab was a captain of a legion. Minab told him as they battled (for his army had let Minab deal personally, with Portess) that the female who wounded him was his wife. Minab told him that Breena was a mighty warrior in her own right, and he was lucky that her magic weapon did not kill him. The duel was not a long battle. Portess was no match for Minab; even in his weaken state from a year of hard labor and torture at Portess' hands. Minab was merciful and did not play with him, too much, before he ended it.

When they returned to Chelm, Tivas immediately moved his wife out of Minab's house into a smaller home. His rank had been restored to him and he could now afford a place of his own. It would be much smaller than Minab's, though. Breena was glad he was gone. She knew Tivas would never tell Minab what he had done and Breena had already decided that in her mind, it had been erased, or at least, stored in an area of locked memory.

The city's officials wanted to celebrate Minab's homecoming. The chief overseer announced there would be a huge feast, with a big party, at his house for Minab and all his friends. Minab had traveled back to Chelm slowly. It had taken three weeks just to return to the city. It had become more of a holiday than a trip. Minab needed the relaxation. By the time they arrived home, Breena was aware that Minab's little army of sons may again, be expanding.

The feast was very grand. Breena didn't feel so out of place with Jaymin and Trela there. At least there were people she could talk to, besides her husband. Minab's mother, the overseer's wife had arranged for musicians to play music and Breena watched with great interest as one of the musician played an instrument similar to the piano. It had sixty keys and sounded more like a keyboard than the grand piano she had back home in America. Breena could play the piano very well and it took a great deal of self-control to overcome the desire to sit down and play a song. Musicians were always men and Breena knew it would cause a stir if she gave into her urges. They played songs that were similar to some of the classical pieces Breena knew. Once the musicians took a break to get something to eat, Breena headed directly for the piano-like instrument. She sat down and found the scale or what was close to the scale, on a piano. She looked around to see if anyone was watching and when she saw that no one seemed to be paying any attention, she began to play a beautiful piece from Handel. It was great fun; and for the first time in ages, Breena really enjoyed herself. She was proud of herself that she remembered the piece and played it without hardly any mistakes. Many started to gather to listen to the strange music that seemed to attract them. They were more than surprised to see a female play the instrument and playing it so beautifully.

Suddenly, Minab placed his hand on Breena's shoulder and she stopped. She looked up at him to see what degree of anger he was showing on his face. There was none, instead, he just smiled.

"Is that the music of your homeland?"

Breena nodded. "It is. We have a variety of types of music but this seemed to be closest to your. What is this instrument call?"

"It is a Quem."

"Our instrument, similar to this is called a piano."

"That is an odd sounding name. Perhaps, if I were to buy you one of these musical instruments, would it make you happy?"

"This would be better than pearls or gold rings."

Minab nodded. He did not understand why the riches of fine jewelry did not appeal to his wife, but unusual and inexpensive gifts, like a Quem, did. "Come; Trela and Jaymin are asking for you."

Breena walked over to the women and Minab went back to talking with the men. It was Minab's new tactful approach with Breena. He had stopped her from playing anymore, without creating a scene. He was quite pleased with the results.

Jaymin hugged Breena. "You look almost radiant. It is very good for you to be with Minab again."

Breena returned the hug and nodded. "It seems that Minab has given me a homecoming present. I'm pregnant again." She whispered.

Trela squealed and touched her own belly. "This is exciting. Now we can be pregnant together."

Tivas walked up to Trela and touched her shoulder, and then he slipped his hand around to the front of her belly. Trela blushed at Tivas' bold actions. "Wife, what has made you squeal?"

Breena tried to signal Trela not to say anything, but it was too late. Trela told him the news and Tivas smiled. "So soon? That is good news indeed. I would not think it possible, with Minab only now, starting to regain his health, but determined posterity will not be denied."

Breena looked around trying to find an excuse not to be near Tivas. "Come, Jaymin. Translate for me while I talk to Minab's mother."

"Wait Breena; I must talk to you. My mother will not mind if you wait a few minutes to speak with her." Tivas let Trela go and gave her a gentle little push away from him. Jaymin told Breena she would go see Minab's mother and wait for her there. She took Trela with her, leaving Breena alone with Tivas.

"I don't want to talk to you. I don't even want to be near you. Leave me alone." Breena started to walk away.

"You have said nothing to him. Were you afraid for Minab?" Tivas spoke quietly.

Breena stopped and walked back to Tivas. She quickly glanced around to see if anyone was looking at them. She felt guilty just talking to him. "If I had said something, you'd be dead."

"If we would have fought, I would have been the conqueror. Minab is still not back to his normal strength. Nevertheless, I love my brother and have done no wrong. I do not wish to fight him over something you have... misinterpreted."

"I didn't misinterpret what you did to me." Breena was beginning to show her anger. She walked away before she said or did something that would reveal her secret.

The rest of the evening went well until it was time to leave. Tivas came up to Minab and told him he wanted to take Trela home before the rain started. Minab said good-bye and Tivas said he wanted to say goodbye to Breena also. By then, Breena was out on the balcony looking at the huge garden that almost surrounded the chief overseer's house.

"I have come to say goodbye."

Breena backed away from him. "I wish you'd go away, permanently. Leave me alone, Tivas."

Tivas smiled. "If I had not been married when we thought Minab dead, than I would have made you my first wife and Minab would never have been able to take you back. You were still his second then."

"Then I am truly grateful to Trela for that, although I pity her for being your wife."

"I treated you well."

"Until you did what you did."

"It was my right."

Breena shook her head. "Maybe in this twisted sick civilization it was your right, but it was still wrong. I didn't want it."

Tivas laughed. "You had no say in my rights. Minab has his sons back and his beautiful exotic wife. He has always had better than I have. Not now, though. You were my second, if only for a moment in time."

"That is over with and we have no bond between us and we never will, again."

Tivas turned to leave then stopped and looked intensely at Breena. "The child you are now carrying is not Minab's. It is mine." He watched Breena's face for her reaction.

Breena could feel the blood drain from her face and she began to shake. The possibility had not even entered her thoughts, until then. She slowly sank down on a small bench that was beside her. Minab strolled out onto the balcony and Tivas told him he thought Breena was ill. Minab thought that the party must have been too much for her.

When they returned to their home Breena thought she should tell Minab that they were going to have another baby before he heard it from Jaymin, or worse, Tivas. She checked on her children and then as Minab readied himself for bed, she chose that time to tell him.

"Minab, after I gave birth to little Minab, I was not allowed to nurse him. Tivas hired a wet nurse."

"He probably thought if you became his second, and had another child right away; it would ease your grieving. He said you grieved very deeply."

"More than I thought possible."

"I am back now and it was not necessary that you become Tivas' second."

"Minab, I think that your little family of warriors may be increasing again. You have given me another child to carry."

Minab pulled her towards him and smiled. "I am truly blessed. Will you give me a legion for a lineage?"

Breena giggled. "I don't think I could give you that many sons in a whole lifetime. Besides; it might be a girl this time."

"It matters not." He thought for a second, "If it is a boy, I shall call him Tivas."

"No." Breena's outburst was a surprise to Minab.

"Do not council your husband, wife."

"Well, I didn't mean no. I meant I just thought it would be nice and thoughtful to name him after your father. Don't you think that would be a good idea?"

"My father?" Minab looked at Breena and his expression softened. "That would be honorable to his memory. You have made an excellent suggestion. His name will be Taru, after my father."

"If it is a female do I still get to name her?"

"A promise is a promise. What would you call a female?"

Breena shrugged her shoulders. "I don't know but I have eight months to decide." She wanted to change the subject so she started talking about something else and soon, Minab was ready for sleep.

It took a few months before Minab fully regained his strength. Breena made sure he ate well. Minab and Kabay spent many days training Minab's new legion. There were still many men from the old legion there, but Minab had lost most of his personal army, to Portess. He wanted to re-establish his personal warriors. They were the ones that Minab trusted. He pulled Kabay out of the section of the legion he was in charge of, and made him Minab's second in command. He put Tivas into Kabay's old position temporarily. Once Minab's private warriors were trained to his satisfaction, Kabay would return to his former position. Training could take months or even years before Minab would have the same faith in their abilities, as he did in his other personal warriors, which were killed.

Breena did not have morning sickness with this pregnancy and it made her wonder if it really was a female. She was as big with this baby, as she was with little Minab, so that really confused her. The baby kicked continually; therefore, Breena concentrated on the fact that it was healthy, at least.

It was difficult for Breena to avoid Tivas. Trela was always visiting or asking Breena to visit her because they were both pregnant and married to brothers. Whenever Breena would visit, Tivas would wait until she was alone and then ask how his son was growing. When Trela's time to deliver came, she called for Breena to come and be with her. Breena arrived to find Tivas pacing outside the tiny back room where Trela was. He was anxious to see his son. Trela's mother was there helping with the birth and Breena comforted Trela by talking with her. The time of delivery was almost ten hours long and then she gave birth to a beautiful baby girl with lots of black hair. Trela looked at the tiny girl and began to cry. Tivas would be furious. Breena told her to nurse her baby; and that she would talk to Tivas. Tivas walked up to Breena, as she came into the room where Tivas waited. He had heard the crying of the baby and wanted to hear the good news, that he had a son.

"My son, how is he?"

Breena put out her hands. "Relax Tivas. It was a long birth and the baby is healthy. She is beautiful and has lots of shiny black hair."

"She?" Tivas' face first showed his disappointment then it showed his rage. He stiffened his countenance and controlled the emotion in his voice. "I will take the female now." He moved towards the door to the room where Trela was. Breena stood in his way.

"Please Tivas; it's just a sweet innocent little baby who will love you beyond belief, if you give her half a chance."

"You have no say in this, woman."

"She is your daughter. That adorable little infant is a part of you." Breena started to panic. She had no right to interfere, yet how could she stand by and let him harm a tiny sweet baby?

Tivas tried to go around her but couldn't without touching her. He stopped and looked at her with deep concentration. He seemed to relent in his attitude. "I will spare the female, if I receive something that will ease my betrayal. I will not harm her if you will do two things."

"Me? What could I do?"

Tivas leaned close to her and whispered. "Allow me to feel my son move. I want to feel his life in your belly."

Breena gritted her teeth. "He... this is not your child."

Tivas looked around and finding no one watching them pushed Breena into the small storage room just off the kitchen. He closed the door behind them. "Minab says you have not been sick with this one. My seed enjoys growing within you."

"It's probably a girl." Breena backed away. It bothered her that Tivas touched her when he pushed her into the room.

"It will be a son. I am sure. I had my doubts about Trela. She was not big."

"Even if this baby is a boy, it isn't yours." Breena gritted her teeth with frustration.

"I know that you and Minab have been bound together forever and it will be his son because of that, but it will not change the seed that grows. He comes from me, and not Minab."

Breena was tired of hearing Tivas' obsessive opinions that he was the biological father of her baby. "I can't let you touch me. I belong to Minab."

"I will go now, and take the female." Tivas headed towards the door.

"No. Wait." Breena felt trapped. "Okay. But don't ever ask again. This is a onetime thing and it will not ever be repeated."

Tivas moved towards her and Breena took a step back. It was not right and she knew it. She took a deep breath, closed her eyes, and waited for the ordeal to be over; as she had done with other unpleasant ordeals, she had to endure. Tivas knelt down and slipped his hands under her dress, touching her bare stomach. The baby kicked and he chuckled. He moved his hands slightly and the baby kicked again. "He lives. My son lives." Tivas marveled.

Finally, Breena could not stand it any longer. She stepped back and pulled down her dress. "No more. This is wrong and I have already dishonored Minab." Her eyes filled with tears. "What is the other thing you wanted me to do? I will not let you touch me again, so it better not be anything like that."

"Take the female and raise it as your own. She is not a female warrior, like your seed would be, but I desire that it be raised by one such as you."

"Trela is her mother." Breena folded her arms.

"You will raise it or it will not live. I will not have it around to constantly remind me of my wife's failure."

"What will I tell Minab?"

"You will think of something to tell him. You are clever. With three sons, a daughter will be no burden. She will not even be noticed. Here, she would be a continuous recollection and I will not have it." Tivas turned and walked out of the room and into the tiny room where Trela was. He picked up the tiny infant wrapped in a blanket.

Trela started to sob. "Please Tivas, have mercy on this tiny baby. I am sorry. I am sorry." She begged him in her own language.

"Do you desire that your failure live?"

Trela nodded. "Yes. Yes. I will do anything. I am sorry Tivas for the shame I have caused you."

Tivas slowly nodded. "Then I will give your failure to Minab's household. It can be raised as a slave or servant or whatever they desire."

Trela cried harder, but she nodded and agreed to Tivas' dictates. It would be the only way Tivas would spare her child. Even as a slave, they would treated her well. Minab cared for his slaves and servants. He was a proper master. Tivas walked out of the room and handed the sleeping baby to Breena.

"Could Trela nurse the baby until I can find a wet nurse?"

"We have sixty days of separation. She may do so if she desires to. I do not care."

"What would you have her named?"

"She belongs to you. Name her anything. Again, it is not my concern." Tivas left Breena and went up stairs.

Breena brought the baby back into Trela. "I'm sorry Trela. I tried to get him to accept the baby. He only offered this as a solution."

"Thank you so much for rescuing her. Tivas was very disappointed. I have failed him greatly."

Breena shook her head. "This isn't right. Look at her; she is a beautiful baby. She is your baby."

"No, she belongs to you now."

"Tivas said you could nurse her for the next sixty days, if you'd like. I won't let her forget who her mother is. Tivas said I could name her whatever I wanted. I would like you to name her. What would you choose for a name?"

Trela started to cry again as Breena placed the baby back into her arms. "I always liked my grandmother's name but I never, in my life, thought I would be able to name a daughter that. Her name was Sumy. Do you like it? It means fortunate. That would be appropriate, do you not think so?"

Breena agreed. It was a perfect name. She left little Sumy with Trela. Tivas had left the house. He told his servants he would be staying at the legion's base camp during the period of separation so Breena wasn't worried he would come back and hurt the baby. Now, she had to go home and tell Minab. When she returned to the house, Minab was eating his meal. He looked up and frowned. Quickly Breena put her scarf back on her head.

"If that is the first time you have properly worn your scarf today and it is now done only for my benefit, you have wasted your effort." Minab sat back on his chair and looked at her. "Shirin says you have been at Tivas' house."

"Trela has given birth."

"Is Tivas pleased?"

Breena knelt down beside of Minab. He turned to face her. "Why are your laces not undone?" She quickly undid his laces and removed his footwear.

Minab stiffened in his chair. "What has happened?" He watched as Breena tended to the removal of his boots. "She had a female. Am I correct?"

"Yes, but..."

"Wife. It is our way and I hope you have not interfered. Tivas is a man and must do what he feels is right, even if it is not the way you would have things done."

"The baby is beautiful. She has thick black hair and such a sweet expression. Tivas did not want her around because he thinks Trela has failed him."

"Her female is not from warrior stock like ours will be. It is just another common female. I cannot change that"

"Minab, it's a baby. It's an innocent little baby girl who's never hurt anyone."

Minab rubbed his forehead. "I have changed my views on female children somewhat, but I am not Tivas. This is not our concern. Even I do not have the right to interfere." He could see by her expression that there was more to the story. "What have you done? I better not have to battle my own brother over this."

"Tivas gave me the baby." Breena said it quickly, hoping he would hear yet not quite understand.

Minab became silent. He folded his arms and looked at Breena. Breena looked up at him and searched his eyes for some sign of emotion. There was none. "I couldn't let him do anything to that baby. Besides, you'd make a much better father for that little girl than Tivas. I'm just sorry poor Trela has been hurt so much."

Minab remained silent.

"She won't eat much, if that is what you are worried about." Breena knew it was not what was troubling him. She had seen him give copper coins to beggars on the street, many times since she had been with him.

"If I accept this infant into my household, it would have to be as a slave."

"But Minab, she's blood relation. You can't make her a slave."

"It would look bad if I were to accept this female as my own. It would be an insult to our ways, as if I assumed her to be of equal value to my sons."

"Females are of equal value. If it wasn't for a female, you would have no sons. Besides, you are a captain, a mighty captain and can do as you please. Minab, you need to send a message to the others that the killing of first-born females is wrong. You know it's wrong."

Minab lifted Breena to her feet. "Tivas gave you the female knowing I would never allow it."

"Well, show him he's wrong. Minab, I could never love a man who would be so cruel to a tiny, helpless baby; male or female."

Minab gave a sigh. "She would have to be bonded to us and become my daughter in the eyes of the church. Then, she will be mine and you must raise her as my daughter, not as if you were just looking after her for Trela."

Breena gave Minab an enthusiastic hug. "You are the greatest man I know."

"I thought that your father held that title."

"Then, it's a draw." Breena gave Minab a kiss. "I know she will think you are the best father in the whole world."

"Enough. You have managed to obtain exactly what you desire, again." Minab placed his hands on Breena's belly. "How is my child growing? It is odd that you have felt no sickness in the morning with this one."

"Maybe I am getting used to having an Adder growing inside me. Maybe it is not a warrior son, this time, but a female, instead."

Minab laughed. "I am not troubled. I will just make more." He picked Breena up and carried her up to his room.

On the twelfth day after Sumy was born, Minab held a very small private party were the baby was given her name, and then bonded to both Breena and Minab as theirs, by the church overseer. Minab made it sound as if it was all Breena's idea and that he could refuse her nothing. However, he did talk of how it seemed hypocritical to practice the immoral tradition of not accepting first-born females, by doing away with them, when they professed to be a righteous people. The church overseer agreed with him and stated that they would be openly condemning the practice. This left Breena hopeful that things would change.

Once Trela's days of separation were over, Breena brought the baby home with her. Tivas returned from camp and was surprised that Minab had adopted the child. He refused to allow Trela to visit the baby. He however visited Minab frequently, leaving just before the rain. Breena was becoming very busy with the children. Sheb and Tian were old enough that they could begin some of their schooling. Minab would speak to them in their language, and Shirin started to teach them to read and write in their language. Breena taught them everything she wanted them to know, in English. Little Minab was just old enough to get into everything. One day as Tivas and Minab were visiting, little Minab came walking into the great room wearing his father's helmet. He would bump into everything because he could not see. It made Minab laugh, and then he called for Breena to come and rescue his son.

Breena took the helmet off little Minab. "He wants to be a warrior like his father, but that will have to wait. It is time to change this warrior's wet pants."

Minab shook his head. "He is far from being a warrior."

Breena picked up the boy. "You started out as a dirty-faced little boy with wet pants." Minab did not appreciate Breena's admonition.

The male children of Adder were much bigger than what Breena remembered little boys from the states were. Every time she picked up one of her sons, she understood why the men were all huge. They started out that way.

"Put my sons to bed and come visit." Minab told Breena as she walked into the back area where the children's' room was.

"She is near her time?" Tivas quietly asked.

"Yes, very soon. She is big this time too. I thought she might give me two again but she says that she only feels one move."

Breena came back into the room after the boys were asleep. She knelt in front of Minab. He had not allowed the servants to undo his laces, so Breena undid them. She didn't really mind the duty. It was a small thing and she now felt it was more of an endearment than a chore. She removed his footwear and remained kneeling, occasionally looking at Tivas and wishing he'd go home.

"Did you witness Trela give birth?" Minab asked Tivas. He knew he had not. Minab was sure no man could give a child of his own away once he had witnessed its birth, even if it was a female.

"No."

"It is a wondrous sight! It is as marvelous to witness new life, as it is vile, to partake in death on the battlefield."

Minab touched Breena's hair and Tivas watched his every movement. It bothered Tivas that Minab had Breena. Most of his thoughts were centered around her lately and it was unsettling him continually. If Minab had not returned, she would have finished grieving by now and willingly become his second. He was sure of it. The year of grieving he had permitted her would have been over. Sure as he was that her baby was from him, he knew there would be no chance of her having anymore from him unless Minab died. That bothered Tivas even more. He did not like having those thoughts about Minab.

Breena closed her eyes and leaned against Minab's legs. "Minab," she whispered and both Tivas and Minab looked at her. She seemed to be in pain.

"Is it your time, wife?"

Breena could only nod her head. The contractions began much stronger than any she had ever felt before, with the others. Minab picked Breena up in his arms and yelled for Shirin. Hours passed as Breena lay in the tiny back room. She kept crying and telling Shirin not to leave her alone. This time seemed different and Breena was afraid. Minab kept coming in and out of the room. Tivas went home, but returned the next day. He found Minab pacing in the kitchen.

"She has not delivered yet?"

Minab shook his head. It had been twenty-two hours since her first pain and Minab was beginning to worry. He left Tivas and walked into the back room again. Breena was breathing heavily. Her eyes were open and she looked exhausted. Minab held on to her hand and kissed her fingers.

"She has managed to rest a short while between the pains. It is not as terrible as it looks." Shirin told him quietly.

"I don't think a little girl would be this hard to deliver. It has to be a boy." Breena's voice manifested her fatigue.

Minab took a small cloth from the table beside the bed, and wiped the sweat from Breena's forehead. "It will be over soon, Breena. Then you can rest."

Breena gave a small chuckle. "Can you believe that I'd forgotten how painful and exhausting this was?" She closed her eyes, and grabbed the bedpost and groaned loudly.

Minab stood up and walked into the kitchen. "Tivas come and witness. Wonder at this miracle."

"I cannot. She belongs to you."

"It is with my permission that I allow this. Come."

Tivas walked into the room. He stood silently, in a corner of the room, out of Breena's immediate view. She did not notice him or anyone else at the moment. Tivas could not believe that he was being allowed to witness the birth of his son. Minab touched Breena's cheek then moved to where Shirin was. Breena was having a terribly difficult time. The baby was big and Breena was greatly fatigued. She grunted loudly, and fell back onto the pillow. Tivas stared at Breena. Had Trela gone through this? Her time had been short. He wondered if Shirin's daughter also went through the pain. She had died because she could not deliver. What if Breena could not deliver his child? Would she die too?

Finally, Shirin became very excited. She encouraged Breena to continue to push. Minab motioned for Tivas to come closer. Suddenly Shirin bent over and lifted up the baby. It was a big male infant. Breena looked at him with amazement in her eyes. The baby must have been close to ten pounds. Shirin put the baby on Breena's tummy and tied the umbilical cord. Breena studied her new son. He had blond hair and she thought blue eyes. His skin looked tanned in color and the face looked more like Tivas' than Minab's. Nevertheless, they were brothers, Breena rationalized. This was Minab's son, and even if it wasn't, it still was.

Tivas watched as Minab kissed Breena and told her she had done well in giving him yet another son. Breena had given birth to a male child and Tivas was exhilarated and frustrated at the same time. He was positive it was his. It even looked like him, yet he could say nothing. The baby belonged to Minab just as Breena did. Those facts did not change his private thoughts. He left the room and silently congratulated himself. When Minab came out of the room, Tivas gave him a quick hug.

"This is a glorious day for our lineage, brother. At least our line will not die with all your sons." Tivas told Minab then he left the house and returned to his own. He found Trela in their room. She was brushing her hair. Tivas grabbed her and roughly pushed her onto the bed. "Minab's wife has given him another son!" He yelled at her as he grabbed her face and forced her to look at him. He squeezed her chin until she began to cry. "I want a son." Trela became frightened and tried to escape his hold but Tivas shoved her back down on the pillows. "You will give me a son or die trying."

Minab was more than ecstatic over the day's events. His house was full of his posterity and Breena had given him another son. Breena was sound asleep when Minab came back into the room. He looked at her as she slept with her new son in her arms.

"She needs much rest, master. It was a very difficult birth and there were moments when I thought she would not deliver. The child is much bigger than the others." Shirin said as she cleaned up the room around Breena.

"I too, worried. Shirin perhaps you should obtain some herbs for her so she may rest from carrying children for a time."

"Is that what you desire, master?"

"Yes. I value my sons but I do not want to obtain a second for her. Breena is all I want. I am troubled that another baby, too soon, could kill her."

Shirin watched as Minab caressed his wife's cheek. Then he left the room. His request was unusual. Most women who died young, died from complications during childbirth, yet the men continued to want very large families, at any cost.

CHAPTER THIRTEEN

REENA SLEPT FOR TWO days, only waking long enough to nurse her newborn son. Minab would constantly check on her to make sure she was all right. He ordered Shirin to make sure Breena wanted for nothing and stayed in bed as much as possible. Breena stayed in bed the whole twelve days that led up to the baby's presentation and naming. She was still very weak but spent the time during the festivities confined to a chair. Shirin held the baby most of the time. The baby name was Taru, after Minab's father.

Tivas gave Minab a slap on the shoulder after the naming ceremony. "It is good that you named the child after our father, Minab. That is what I would have named my first born son."

Breena over heard and looked up at Tivas. "It was my suggestion. But Minab decided that since little Taru is so big, he deserved a mighty name that carried a big responsibility of honor, with it."

Tivas looked at Breena for a second. "He is a large child and the name is appropriate." Tivas then turned to Minab. "Because your wife was in my care while you were in prison, I feel a special bond with all your sons." Little Minab walked by and Tivas picked him up. "Your wife desired that her children become bonded to their father earlier than normal. I spent extra time talking to them when they were under my care and I was surprised to find it entertaining."

Breena did not want Tivas touching her children but was powerless to do anything about it. The wet nurse brought Sumy and Breena took her and held her in her arms. Trela walked over to Breena and gently caressed Sumy's hair.

"Wife; come and hold this male child. Maybe it will cause you to produce one soon, so I may be unashamed." Tivas ordered Trela and she quickly obeyed.

"In my homeland we have many wise men who study the makeup of a human being and they have known for many years, that it is the seed of the father that decides whether a child is male or female. Actually; all embryos start out as female."

"You talk in riddles, woman." Tivas stated.

Breena was becoming angry. "If your civilization could only see beyond its swords and battles and obsolete traditions, there could be many things you could learn."

Minab picked Sumy up and handed her back to the wet nurse. "You need to rest, my wife." He picked Breena up in his arms.

Breena started to squirm, knowing it was futile. "Every time I start to say something your egos can't handle..."

Minab put his lips to Breena's ear. "Our children will be warriors, strong, courageous, and noble but they will also be schooled in the wisdom of their mother. You cannot force people into knowledge. It only serves to make them cling tightly to their old ways." He whispered as he carried her out of the room.

Breena was surprised to find out that it was Minab who asked Shirin to supply her with the contraceptive herbs. She was also surprised at the effect the news had on her, for it only seemed to intensify the desire to have more children for him. The conflict, over Taru's paternity, was a constant in her mind. Every time she nursed him, and every time she watched him sleep, she could see three faces staring back at her, Minab's, Tivas' and hers. Breena had concluded that if she were to give Minab another son it would make up for everything that had happened between Tivas and her.

Trela had become pregnant shortly after her days of separation were over and Tivas was boastful that it was a male child, this time. Trela had become large with the pregnancy and it did look as if it would be a male child. Tivas refused to allow Trela to visit at Breena's house. He told Trela, that seeing Sumy would only increase the chances that she would produce another female. Breena visited Trela though and was concerned over Trela's obsession that the child had to be male. She would constantly tell everyone that it was a male. It had to be a male. Finally, Breena became so worried that she thought it would be best to talk to Tivas.

Breena rode out to camp and found Tivas practicing his knife throwing against a tree in a field just south of camp. She had left a message with Shirin to tell Minab what she was doing, so he would not think she was doing anything improper.

Tivas watched her ride up and he stopped his activities as she dismounted. Breena worn a dress but had pulled it up so the horse could be ridden easily.

"You even ride like a warrior." Tivas exclaimed. "This race of yours must be very peculiar. It is as if it is born in you, and not taught."

"I used to ride on my grandfather's farm when I was a child. It is what happens when you do not restrict a child's learning, no matter what sex she is."

"Will Sumy learn these things?"

"Yes."

"It is good, that you are her mother then."

"I don't get it, Tivas. Trela could have taught your daughter anything you wanted her to. My being Sumy's mother won't change what type of person she is inside."

Tivas smiled. "If I could have my desires granted, you would be the mother of all my children."

Breena sighed. She didn't want to get onto that path of conversation. "Tivas; I came to talk to you about Trela. I am worried about her. The apprehension over the baby she is carrying, being a male is consuming her. If she doesn't ease up, she is going to make herself sick."

"It is not your concern." Tivas threw the knife and it hit the trunk of the tree with a thud.

"Trela is a friend of mine and I care about her."

"Yes, but if she bares a male child then perhaps I will not constantly think about the son you bore, that is mine."

"I want to talk about Trela, not my son."

"Our son."

"Mine."

Tivas laughed. "If Trela bares a female, you will have no say in its future. I will only spare it, if you bare me another child."

Breena threw her hands in the air. "Why can't you be reasoned with? It still wouldn't be your child. It would be Minab's."

Tivas walked over to the tree and retrieved his knife. "At least you would have been mine, once more." He paused. "Do you think I like wishing my brother, misfortune? I gave everything I had to be reunited with him, and now, all I think about is having his wife." Tivas sat on the ground and put his head in his hands. "Go! Go, before I do something that you will not like, and I will not have the power to prevent."

His warning sent a chill through Breena. She mounted the horse and rode away. She did not look back. Nothing had been accomplished for Trela's sake, and Breena wasn't sure what direction her emotions were headed now. She had seen a different side of Tivas. It was the same side that allowed Breena extra time to grieve, when she was under his care. It was a great conflict for him and there seemed little chance things would just correct themselves. Breena was still concerned over Trela. But, deep in her heart, she prayed for her to deliver a son.

When she arrived at the house, Minab was angry. He did not want her to interfere between Tivas and his wife. Minab told Breena the next time she wanted to talk to Tivas about Trela; she should do it when he was there. Breena agreed but she knew that it would be impossible to allow Minab in on a conversation such as the one she had just had with Tivas.

It was disappointing to Breena that she had heard nothing from the pilot of the plane that landed outside of Kalat. It had been over a year and Breena figured either he didn't get out or he told no one of his adventure here. Breena was glad Minab had never questioned her about the gun she had at Portess' castle. She was glad she had put it in the sack that she left on the plane just before she went to pick up her children. It had been taken back to her homeland on the plane, she hoped.

Over the next couple of months as Taru grew and Breena's desires to give Minab another child increased, Trela endured her pregnancy. She was huge, even larger than Breena had been. Tivas hoped it would be twins, as Breena's pregnancy had been but the physician had told him there was to be only one child. Trela was sure it was a male but terrified of its size. Breena would reassure her that the delivery would go well; she would be there for her. Over the past year, Kabay's family had increased also, with the arrival of another son. This only made Tivas more determined to have a son. When Trela's time came Tivas told her she could not call for Breena. He did not want her there if the baby turned out to be female. Shirin had dropped by during Trela's delivery and Tivas would not permit her to leave. He did not want Breena told Trela's time had come.

Shirin had been gone for a whole day and Breena began to worry. Shirin was only going to the market, she had told Breena before she left. Just before Breena was about to ask Minab to search for her, Shirin returned. Shirin was terribly upset. Breena tried to comfort her but Shirin would not allow it. "It is just like Tanisha. It is just like my Tanisha." She cried and Breena did not understand.

Finally, Shirin calmed down enough to relate what had happened. "Trela; she is just like my daughter, Tanisha was. The baby was too big. Tivas' seed grows big within the mother."

Minab came into the kitchen to see what the commotion was. Breena's heart sank as she began to understand what Shirin was saying. "What happened to Trela, Shirin? Tell me."

"She could not deliver. I came to visit, as I knew you would want to hear if Trela's time was near. Tivas would not let me leave. He did not want me telling you that Trela was giving birth. Trela was in terrible pain. She could not deliver. She died."

Breena started to shake as she became enraged. "I could have helped her. I could have done something. He killed her." Breena walked over to where her knife hung in a corner of the kitchen. As she pulled it out of its holder, Minab grabbed Breena's arm.

"Be still, wife. Your passions are ruling your mind."

"This can't go unpunished. He deliberately made sure I wouldn't be there to help her."

"He was probably thinking about what happened last time, with Sumy. Think, Breena. He has lost his wife and child. It was not done deliberately."

Breena began to reflect on Taru's birth. He was at least two pounds bigger than the other boys she had. It was almost that way with her. Breena started to cry as she thought about Trela. If she had delivered, it would have been the happiest day of her life. Minab held her as she cried. He wasn't sure what he should do next. He knew he had to go visit Tivas but he wasn't sure if he should allow Breena to accompany him.

Minab found Tivas sitting on the floor, in a corner of the kitchen, when he arrived at Tivas' home. He sat down beside him and Tivas handed him a large jug of wine. He didn't bother to look over at Minab. Minab took a drink and handed the jug back to Tivas.

"Punishment, Minab. I have waited for the wrath of God, but I did not think I would have my wife and son taken from me."

"It is just life, Tivas. This is not a punishment. You made amends for your unrighteousness, long ago."

Tivas looked over at Minab. He shook his head. "I have done many things that I do not know how to make amends for, and I was not a good husband."

"You cared for my wife and my children when you had to provide for your own household. You are a good man."

Tivas stared at Minab, and then he took a long swallow of the wine. He closed his eyes and rested his head against the wall. His jaw started to tremble and he took another drink of the wine. He shook his head and took another drink from the large jug. A trace of wine, dripped from his mouth, and down his chin. He did not attempt to wipe it away. He blinked quickly, trying to disperse the dampness in his eyes. Slowly, he stood upon his unsteady feet. "I need to leave. I must go to the camp and train. I cannot talk to you at this time."

"Go to Kalat and train with Volcar. He is training his men in the mountains. It will be strenuous, but it will quiet your thoughts." Minab stood up beside him.

Tivas nodded and handed him the wine jug. Then, he slowly walked passed him. He went up to his room to gather his things, so he could leave right away. As he was coming down, Breena entered the house. Minab had told her to stay at home but she could not wait there. Tivas and Breena stood face to face, for a moment, before Minab walked in on them. Tivas wavered, then he walked passed Breena and out the front door. Breena turned to go after him but Minab took a hold of her arm and pulled her to him.

"Leave him. He is in pain." Minab wrapped his arms around Breena and hugged her. Thoughts of what he would have felt if it had been her, shot through him like a scorching iron. He had only felt betrayal with Annek. With Breena, there was pain at the very thought of being without her.

Breena had not expected Tivas to look as he did. She had seen him in anguish when he tried to buy Shirin's freedom, but this was worse. She really hated life here. Just as life began to seem tolerable, suddenly, it would get terrible again. When Minab and Breena returned home, Breena quietly went up to their room and threw the herbs she was taking, down the toilet.

Tivas was gone for five months. Minab had been preparing to instruct his army in the Kipate Valley. It was the closest thing this land had to a dessert. There, his troops would have to learn how to fight and how to survive, when supplies were low. Tivas came to talk to Minab but he was away.

Breena was surprised to see Tivas. He waited to be invited in before he entered her house. "I have come to talk to Minab."

"He is away for the day. He is in the process of preparing to go to the Kipate Valley with his men." Breena offered Tivas a seat in the great room and asked if he would like a meal. He declined the meal.

"I will go with him to the Kipate valley. I will tell him there that I took you as my second, just before he had you returned to him by the church overseer."

Breena froze as she stood in front of him. "Are you insane? You can't do that to me. You can't do that to him. He doesn't know it yet, but I am going to give him another baby. It will make everything all right. It will erase the past between us."

Tivas stood up. "I cannot live with these thoughts anymore."

Breena stood as close to Tivas as she could without touching him. "Well, you better live with it, Tivas, because those thoughts could destroy us all. Please, don't do this. Once this baby is born, it will make up for what happened. It will make up for who Taru may actually be." Breena started to cry. She felt helpless and in the mercy of someone, she couldn't trust. "I didn't choose to have you do that to me. Even if Minab doesn't want to kill me, I'm going to wish he had. I can't hurt him like that. I can't be another Annek to him."

Tivas stood still and watched Breena's strong demeanor dwindle before him. "This must be done."

"What purpose will it serve, except to satisfy your own guilt? Do you think that Minab will just accept it all and forgive us?" They both turned, and watched as Taru waddled into the room. Breena picked him up. "What will it do to him? He's going to be a mighty warrior some day, just like his brothers, and just like his father. But that won't happen if Minab has doubts about his lineage. Taru will grow up wondering why his father doesn't seem to love him as much as he does his brothers. It'll all happen, Tivas. Your culture will insure it does."

Tivas looked confused. He touched Taru's curly blond hair, and then he left the house without saying another word. Breena sunk onto a chair in the great room. She held on to Taru and cried.

Minab returned and Breena greeted him with loving arms. He was happy to see her so affectionate. Breena was relieved that Tivas had not talked to him, yet. She helped him pack the few belongings he would take, and struggled to think of things to say that would remedy anything that might be said to him in the future. She told Minab how much little Taru looked and acted like him. She reminded him that she loved him, and missed him so much, when they all thought him dead. She told him to be careful, as she could not survive such a horrible time like that, again. Breena also told him that if either of them ever was to die she wished it would be her first. Minab was filled with joy as he thought of how devoted Breena had become and that she seemed to have forgiven him for the manner in which he had claimed her as his, years ago. He knew that it had caused her heartache when he first made her his second, in Kalat. Breena pampered Minab through the evening as she served him his favorite foods and then washed his hair. The next day, just before he left, he told her he was reluctant to go, as he felt much like a king in his own home. Breena almost asked him not to go but knew that would draw him into a pool of thought about her behavior. He kissed her and the children, then left, looking very gallant upon his mount.

Breena did not hear from Tivas for the three weeks Minab was gone and she could not find out if he had joined Minab's men at the Kipate Valley. One evening, just before the rain, Minab surprised Breena as she came down the stairs on her way into the kitchen. Minab looked tired, as if he had been riding for a long time. He was still in full uniform and he had a funny look on his face.

"Minab; you're home. I didn't expect you for another week." She said to him with some caution. He was staring at her and not saying anything. It made her feel something was wrong.

"Did you miss me?"

Breena was almost ready for bed, but was on her way to the back room, behind the kitchen, carrying an armful of clothes for the morning wash. She put it down on a nearby chair and came over to him. "I missed you very much. I told you once before, Minab, that I was afraid of loving you because I thought I would lose myself. I lost myself in you long ago and now I am a part of you." She put her arms around him.

"You belong to me." The authority in his voice made her feel like a possession.

"There is no question of that. I know who I belong to."

Minab picked Breena up in his arms. "You desire no one else?"

Breena shook her head in response, and Minab kissed her roughly. He carried Breena up to their room and fell with her, upon their bed. He did not remove his sword or armor and continued to roughly kiss and hold her. His affection turned harsh and severe and he pulled at her gown. It frightened Breena and she began to squirm. Minab ignored her subtle protest and continued. Breena silently began to cry. She knew what brought about Minab's actions and she had no idea how to correct the damage that was done. Tivas must have talked to Minab. As Breena submitted to Minab's frustration, she buried her face in the shoulder pad of his armor, and wept. Suddenly, there was a voice calling from down stairs. Minab turned to listen and he heard his name. He left the room and Breena followed. Minab walked halfway down the stairs and yelled out Tivas' name. Breena stood at the top of the stairs and wiped her wet cheeks. As she held up the shoulders of her ripped nightgown, she watched the two faced each other.

Tivas stood at the bottom of the stairs. He too, looked as if he had ridden for a long period of time, without rest. "This is between you and me." He glanced beyond Minab and saw Breena's messy hair and the torn nightgown. "Your woman has nothing to do with this."

Minab turned around and looked at Breena. Breena slowly walked down towards Minab as he yelled, "She is nothing but a stranger in her blood." His anger echoed in his voice and Breena wondered if he meant what he had just said. Minab grabbed her arm and his grip was exceedingly tight. Breena tried to loosen his grip as she watched them both. "If she desires you, then she may have you. It means nothing to me." His words were curt. Minab pushed her towards Tivas and Breena could not secure her step. She fell forward down the stairs, landing at Tivas' feet. She groaned, then became still. Minab and Tivas both stood in stunned silence.

Minab raced down to her and Tivas bent down beside her. "Touch her not, or I will kill you." Minab told his brother. He turned her over, onto her back. Breena's eyes were closed and she was limp in his arms. "Wife, open your eyes and talk to me." Breena was silent and Minab checked her breathing, which was normal. "Breena?" There was no response, again. Minab carried her upstairs to their bed. Tivas followed.

"You must call a physician." Tivas said as he stood slightly back from the bed.

Minab stood up and faced him. He drew his sword. "This is your fault. Defend yourself or I will cut you to pieces." Minab lunged at Tivas, knocking him off his feet and onto the trunk that was against the wall of the room.

Tivas slowly stood and drew his sword. "I do not want this, brother. I do not want this at all."

Minab swung his sword and Tivas defended himself but did not return the swing. They battled for a length of time, as Minab countered and Tivas defended. Breena regained consciousness and slowly sat up. It took her a few seconds to realize what was happening around her.

"Stop! Stop this, please!" Breena sat up on her knees on the bed and yelled. There was terrible a pain shooting across her hips and down her legs and she could hardly keep from buckling over.

Minab glanced over at Breena and missed a swing at Tivas, and Tivas shoved Minab to the floor, tackling him. As he jumped on top of him, he held his sword to his throat. "No more, Minab, stop."

Breena bent over and cried out in agony. Tivas released Minab and he quickly came to Breena's side. "I meant you no harm, Breena. What is causing you pain?" Minab asked.

Breena continued to cry and rock herself, as she tried to escape the pain she was feeling. Tivas disappeared for a few minutes, and then he came back into the room. He had sent someone to bring the physician back to the house. Minab had wrapped Breena in his arms and she leaned her body against him but continued to moan with pain. Tivas started to bend down towards Breena, but stood again as he saw the expression on Minab's face, darken. He then, just paced the floor, occasionally wiping his face with his hand. He suspected what was wrong and wondered why Breena said nothing.

Finally, the physician came in and Minab released Breena into his care. She whispered to tell him, that it was the baby. The problem was the baby she was carrying. Minab relayed the message to the physician, and then stood, almost motionless, beside the bed as the physician checked Breena. When Breena began crying harder and then buried her face in the pillows to conceal her grief, Minab turned and stormed out of the room, knocking over a table with a water jug on it, as he left. Tivas followed Minab down stairs, and out into the garden, at the back. Minab took his sword and slashed at the bushes, screaming out his frustration as he swung. Tivas watched in silence. At last, Minab turned and faced his brother. He did not speak for a while, as if he was desperately trying to control his emotions. "You had a year to take her as your second. Why did you wait? It would have been your right and I would have accepted it, then, but after I had returned?" Minab closed his eyes and swallowed hard.

Tivas shook his head. He started to speak, and then stopped, as his emotions also began to spill from his heart. He threw his sword down at Minab's feet. "I thought she would stop grieving on her own. When you returned, I was joyful that I had regained my brother, but saddened that I had lost her back to you." Tivas fell to his knees. "Be merciful and end this, brother, for I am unable to stop my thoughts, and they are saturated with her."

Minab stared at Tivas and blinked back the tears he had been denying. Slowly, he gripped his sword with both hands and raised it above him. Tivas closed his eyes, bent his head down, and waited. Minab's breathing was labored and he began to shake. For many moments, Minab struggled to hold the sword above him, and then he lowered it and placed it back into its sheath. "Take yourself back to the Kipate Valley. I cannot deal with this. I cannot stand to look at you." He brushed Tivas with his shoulder as he walked passed him and back up to the bedroom where Breena was.

Breena was curled up, on her side, on the far side of the bed. The physician had just finished giving Breena some herbs and Shirin had just changed the bedding. Minab walked over to the other side of the bed and sat down. He put his hand on Breena's shoulder and she buried her face in the pillow so he could not see her tears.

"I have killed Tivas. Will you mourn him?"

Breena looked up at him with shock in her eyes. "You have killed your brother?"

"Does that bother you?"

Breena's lower lip trembled as she fought back the emotions she that overwhelmed her. "If I had gone back to my homeland, none of this would have happened. You have murdered your own brother and you ask if it bothers me?"

"Did you desire him? Were your thoughts as filled with him as his was with you?"

Breena pulled herself up to a sitting position. "I stopped taking the herbs so I could give you more children. It felt as if my heart had been ripped from my body when I was told you were dead. I stayed here with you, when I could have gone home, and I wanted to go home, so much. My thoughts are filled with love for Sheb, Tian, little Minab, Sumy, and Taru. I am always thinking about you. The only thoughts I had about Tivas, was that he would tell you and you would hate me, like you do." Breena closed her eyes and whispered, "This place is brimming with carnality, murderers, hypocrites, and thieves. Each day, I pray I'll wake from this nightmare, and each day I am reminded, that, this is my reality. I will grieve for the waste of life and for the things we can't change." She covered her face with her hands.

Minab sat quietly as Breena talked. He gently rubbed her shoulder and then leaned over and kissed her forehead. "Why did you not mention that you were with child?"

Breena put her head back down on the pillow. He was talking so casually that she thought that maybe he had not realized how somber the events of the day were. "I wanted to surprise you, when you returned from the valley, with your troops. I thought you would know how deep my love was, then."

"Who sired Taru?"

"You did."

"He looks like Tivas."

Breena looked at Minab and wondered if she ever really knew this man. "You look like your uncle."

"I look like my father."

"Then your uncle must have looked like his brother, just as Tivas looks like you."

"You have lost the baby?" There seemed to be no remorse in his voice and that offended Breena greatly.

"Yes. This house is full of death today." She replied.

"I must return to my men. Things must be resolved."

"Will you return to me afterwards, or am I like Annek in your eyes, now? I didn't want Tivas' attention, ever."

"I will return. You are my wife and this is my home. It is filled with my family." Minab left and Breena did not attempt to stop him. She had some resolve to find in her heart also.

Minab returned to his troops. He was disappointed that Breena did not ask him to stay. He wanted to show her that he was the only man she needed, but she never seemed to need anyone. Minab silently cursed the independence of the strangers, as he rode along. She was his wife and belonged to him but it bothered him that she seemed to handle life well without him. Strangers were survivors. Miller adapted, survived, and would have lived well, if Zorban had not killed him. Minab smiled as he remembered how stubborn Breena was when he tried feeding her when he first took as his second. He didn't want anyone else.

When he arrived at the camp, he sought out Tivas. His brother had arrived just an hour before. Minab walked up to Tivas and Tivas took a defensive stance. "I have no need to fight with you, brother." He said in English so most of the others would not understand. "I know it is I, whom she desires." He started to walk away then stopped. "You are not welcomed in my home, and if I ever see you near my woman, I will cut your head off and feed it to the dogs." Minab looked at Kabay. He was standing off to the side of the whole scene, watching, and not quite sure how to handle the situation. He would not have interfered in a fight between his best friend and Tivas; but it would have been difficult, as blood brothers were meant to be closer than any friends should ever be. It would have been a bloody battle and no one would have won in the end.

"We will take my personal guard out during the rain and they will be required to climb to the ridge before the rain ends." Minab ordered him.

Kabay nodded and readied the personal guard for departure. Tivas was not part of the personal guard. He would stay behind with the other men. This would give Minab time to think about other things. He could forget, at least for a small moment, the continual failure of his brother to the obedience of their moral laws.

Minab stayed with his men in the valley for another month. He deliberately worked Tivas harder than any of his other men. Minab knew his brother had the ability to be a great warrior, much like himself, but he lacked the selfless judgment that would make him great. Just before they departed the valley, Minab sought out Tivas for one more application with the sword. Tivas did not want to fight, but Minab asserted his request. Minab was surprised how Tivas' skills had sharpened from the time when they fought at his house, a month ago. It was possible that Tivas could have beaten him, had Tivas not insisted on making it an offensive battle; but Minab rationalized it to being too passionate at the time. Now, he had to know if his brother's skills were as good as they appeared to be. Minab pushed Tivas into a circle that some of his personal guard had made. They fought, and this time Tivas did more than just defend himself. Minab was impressed as Tivas matched him blow for blow upon their shields and against the blades of their swords. It took deep concentration for Minab to beat his brother, by finally knocking him to the ground and placing the tip of the sword to his ribcage, just underneath his breastplate. Tivas threw down his sword and conceded. Minab helped him up and looked his brother directly in his eyes.

"You are good, very good. I would have you in my personal guard but I might wonder if it would be wise to turn my back on you."

Tivas picked up his sword and sheathed it. "If I desired to destroy you, I would have had many opportunities, already, and I would not have confessed my peccadillo to you."

"Peccadillo?" Minab sneered. "Yes brother and we both know your limitations towards what is mine, now. I would like you in my personal guard but I am indecisive towards your loyalties." He had mentioned the recruitment twice, and Tivas knew what he really wanted to know.

Tivas knelt on one knee and bowed. "It is to my commander, first and always."

"And what to your brother are your feelings directed?"

"He knows of my bass imperfections and yet, he still shows love towards me. I will not disappoint him any further."

"My decision, as to your non-acceptance in my home, still stands."

Tivas nodded, then Minab took out his dagger and Tivas held out his arm. Minab cut a series of incisions in his upper arm, consisting of three long lines that joined at the bottom. Tivas showed no pain in his face and only nodded his response as Minab placed herbs over the wound and rubbed them into the blood. It was the mark of Minab's personal guard and only those who belonged to that elite group had it on their arm. The herbs would heal the wound, leaving a blue-tinted scar in its place.

*   *   *

They divided into three groups before they departed for Chelm. The first two groups were Minab's general troops and specialty troops. The general troops fought in open warfare, hand to hand and were good combat soldiers. The second group was comprised of the troops who specialized in weapons such as the bow and sling. The final group was Minab's personal guard. They were his best, excellent in any weapon, and loyal to Minab and the Adder civilization. Each legion had such divisions and always fought with similar tactics. The foot soldiers went in first followed by the specialists, then the personal guard worked behind the scenes or in other areas as they sought out the enemies' weaknesses and attacked them there. Minab sent his foot soldiers and his specialist's home to Chelm, first. He kept the personal guard behind to plan the next training session. The personal guard consisted of approximately two hundred men. They would have a planning session and then depart for home in the morning, after the rain stopped.

As they slept, a small group of men entered the camp, and swiftly attacked them. They caught Minab's troops off guard and the battle was intense. It was more relentless than it should have been, but they were not on a strict sentry. Being so close to home, they had not imagined an attack such as this. They defeated the group, but during the battle, Minab was stabbed in the upper thigh so severely, that the physician worried, that if he moved before the leg had started to mend, Minab might lose his limb. The leader of the enemy group lived long enough to tell Minab his people were on their way to Chelm to destroy his posterity and prevent Minab's family from living to revenge the attack. Minab was frantic as he tried to mount his horse and ride for home.

"Minab, I will go and hide your wife and children until we can locate and destroy this threat to you." Kabay stated as he pulled Minab from his horse and placed him upon the ground. "You can do nothing for your command if you do not heal."

"I must save my wife. Nothing is more important to me."

"I will take twenty of the guard and we will ride like the wind."

Minab nodded as he realized he could never make it home in time. "Go. Take our best. Protect my family as if it were your own."

Kabay nodded and quickly gathered the twenty men. "Come Tivas. Minab has requested his best." Kabay mounted his horse.

"I cannot." Tivas looked back at Minab as he rested on a blanket. He appeared very agitated and Tivas knew he would be no help here, but Minab would not want him near Breena. "I will go if Minab permits." He walked over to Minab. "I ask for permission to protect your family."

Minab glared at him then he nodded. "If my family dies, they will kill Taru also. Protect my children, Tivas. Protect them as if they are your sons and daughter."

Tivas ran to his horse and leaped upon it. They rode fast, exerting the horses to their very limits. Minab knew Tivas would be the one to send to protect his sons. They were as important to Tivas as they were to him. Tivas would keep his distance from Breena. Kabay would make sure of it.

As they approached the city, Kabay told the men from the guard to disperse and seek out the enemies that were surely within the city, by now. He and Tivas rode on the Minab's house. They dismounted and ran into the house shouting for Breena and the children, but Shirin was alone with the children. Breena was out in the fields helping with harvest. Minab would have been angry that Breena was with the servants working in the fields but Breena often helped when Minab was away. It gave her satisfaction to keep up with the others and reminded her that she was not above them. They were equal. Kabay had Shirin gather the children and quickly place them in a wagon that he would take to a small village outside Chelm, where he would hide them. Shirin was crying for Breena. Shirin was afraid that Breena would be found, and killed.

"Since you are protecting the children, I will search the fields and find Breena." Tivas said with regard to why they had been sent.

"No. You must not go near her." Kabay ordered as he put his hand out to stop Tivas from leaving.

"I know, but there is no other way. You speak only our tongue and not that of the stranger. She will not understand you."

Kabay thought for a moment. He needed Shirin with him to look after the children and time was running out. This was a dilemma that needed to be solved with haste. The assassins may be very close by now. "Go. We will resolve this after she is safe. That is what is immediately important."

Tivas swiftly mounted his horse and rode out of the city, towards the fields. Breena was in the cornfield gathering corn in baskets. It was heavy work but it helped Breena keep in shape, physically. Being female, she was not allowed to exercise outside the home and even if she jogged on her way to the market, she found it cumbersome in a dress and sandals. She looked up and saw someone riding towards the fields, but she assumed it to be one of the servant's masters, so she paid no attention. It wasn't until Tivas was within twenty feet of her, that she looked up again. Tivas had no difficulty spotting Breena. She was the only one without her scarf up, which made her sparkling blond hair easily seen, in the sunlight.

Breena wasn't sure if she was happier to see him alive or more frightened to have him near her. Minab had lied about his death; perhaps she felt, to check her reaction.

"Breena, you must come with me. You are in grave danger." Tivas told her. He was out of breath and confused as to how the situation should be handled.

Breena stepped back. "I am not. You go away, Tivas. I will not have you ruin my marriage. Minab said he would return and things would be all right."

"Minab has been wounded during a battle with a group of men who have sworn to kill his family."

"Where is he?"

"Back in the valley. The physician feared the loss of his leg, should he move. He has sent me to protect you."

"Now I know you're lying! Minab would have sent Kabay or anyone else, but you."

"Kabay is with your children. I came here because I speak your language and Kabay does not."

Breena put down her basket and brushed the hair out of her face. "I can't trust you, Tivas. Go away!"

Tivas took a step closer to Breena. "We do not have time for this, Breena. There could be great danger all around."

"What should I tell Minab? That I went with you because you just showed up here and told me I was in danger? Minab would never believe that lame excuse and neither do I. Leave me alone."

Tivas looked around at the others who stood watching them argue.

He was beginning to get frustrated. "This is not a deception. Assassins will try to kill you. They may be here, in this field, at this very moment. How could Kabay have made you understand that? How could anyone who does not speak your language, make you understand?"

Breena thought for a moment. "He would have brought Jaymin."

"There was no time!" Tivas shook his head, and then he grabbed Breena and threw her over his shoulder. "You have to come with me now and we will dispute the matter, later."

Breena fought as hard as she could and Tivas had a difficult time holding down her arms as he walked towards his horse. He put her down but still held on to her arm. Then, he mounted his horse and lifted her up in front of him. Breena tried to scream but Tivas covered her mouth with his hand. He used her scarf to tie her hands then rode off into the woods as quickly as he could, holding on to Breena securely, so she would not squirm off the saddle. After several hours of hard riding, Tivas stopped to give the horse water from a riverbed. Breena tried running as soon as her feet touched the ground, but Tivas caught up with her and pulled her back by the scarf that still constrained her wrists.

"Stop this foolishness, woman! I will not allow you to wonder off into the wilderness by yourself, even if there was no danger coming after us."

"I am capable of taking care of myself. You forget I rode to Kalat alone." Breena tried jerking her hands free from Tivas' grip but his hold was secure. "Release Me!"

"No. I cannot trust you."

"Trust me?" Breena laughed, mocking him. "You are absurd."

Tivas did not like being talked to in that manner, especially by a female. He pulled her close, too close and Breena felt uncomfortable. She looked up into Tivas' eyes and became silent. "If I really wanted to have you, you would be mine already. I came to protect you, for my brother."

Breena looked away; uneasy by the intense look Tivas was giving her, and unsettled by the feelings she was experiencing. "I don't believe you. If you really wanted to do something for Minab you would have found a way around my language barrier."

"Perhaps you are correct, but I did not have time to reason it out in my mind. You are in jeopardy and whether I am protecting you for Minab, or for you, or even for myself, it matters not. You are here, and out of danger's path."

"Kabay is protecting my babies?"

"He said he was taking them into hiding in a small village outside of Chelm."

"Sumy too?"

"All of your children are in hiding." Tivas stopped talking and looked at Breena's blue eyes. He took a deep breath and released his hold upon her. "I will not bind your hands if you will vow to me, that you will not run."

Breena stood still. Vows, oaths, and promises were very important to those who were Adder. It was not something you gave knowing you would violate. In most cases, it was punishable by death. She looked down and remained quiet. She could not give that promise. Tivas gritted his teeth and shook his head.

"Then I cannot loosen the scarf that secures your hands. Come. We still have a distance to travel before we rest." Tivas lifted her up on the horse again and got up behind her. They rode along and Tivas told Breena he would take a second so that he may have a lineage, but he would be selective this time. He would seek a second whose family history contained large babies at birth, and he would not love this woman, as he did Trela. Tivas could not withstand another trial of death, as he had experienced with Trela.

"How could you not want to love the woman you take as a second? How could you live without love?" Breena didn't understand his reasoning.

"Trela loved me and one day when Minab is old and passes away like our father did, you will grow to love me also. That is all I require to make me content."

"Tivas, please, stop this obsession."

"Oh, you have taken what I said, incorrectly. I will not do anything that will harm Minab. I love my brother, but he is very much like our father. If I am patient, then his fate will be as our father's was and you will be left in my care once more. You are still very young and even by then, you will still be able to bare children, so I will acquire my children, through you. Until then, I will be the best brother-in-law and the best uncle possible, and it will seem natural to love me."

Breena bowed her head and became quiet. He could not be reasoned with and she did not want to provoke him. They doubled back a short distance then crossed the river and traveled on for another hour or so, until they came to a cave. The clouds were gathering and the rain would soon begin. Tivas brought Breena into the cave and left his horse to graze on the green grass just outside. He went into the cave, far enough in so that light from a fire could not be seen. Then he tied Breena to the heavy saddle he had brought in. "I will obtain food for us. I am sorry that you have forced me to bind you to this saddle but I see no other way." He ripped a strip of fabric from the hem of Breena's dress and gagged her. "If you were to cry out, it might attract the wrong people." He touched her cheek and left her in the shadows of the scanty fire.

Breena rested her head against the saddle. At least it was more comfortable than the rocks around her. If Tivas was lying, Minab would find them, and this time Tivas would not escape punishment. Breena fell asleep and started to dream about Minab. He was beside her and everything was safe and assured, in her life. He began to kiss her and love her and Breena felt wonderful in his arms. In her dream, she kissed Minab and he kissed her, but then Minab changed to Tivas and Breena continued to kiss him.

Tivas came back into the cave and Breena woke with a start. She stared at Tivas as he slowly undid the gag and she continued to stare as he skinned and cooked the small animal he had killed. He kept looking up at her and Breena wondered if her dreams showed in her face. She put her head down on her knees and shed silent tears as guilt flooded her. Could she be responsible for her dream, she wondered?

Tivas handed her some meat and Breena refused it, as a small form of self-punishment.

"If I bring Minab a starving wife, he will be exceedingly angry at both of us."

Breena shook her head. "I'm not hungry. Thank you."

"Nevertheless, you must eat. I do not know when our next meal will be." He offered her the piece of meat again and Breena took it. After the meal, Tivas took the blanket from the back of his saddle and placed it over Breena. She refused it, also. "Why are you so obstinate? I have trained in the rain and have slept in the rain. You are a delicate female and are not used to the harshness of nature, like the breeze that is coming from the entrance of the cave."

"Just because I am a female, doesn't mean I'm some weak pathetic puppy dog. I can stand a tiny breeze." She tossed the blanket over to Tivas. "If I can handle having my hands tied, what's a little breeze?"

Tivas shook his head again. He curled the blanket up and used it as a pillow. Breena curled up against the saddle and fell asleep. The breeze, from the entrance of the cave, was an icy draft that sent chills over Breena's body. While she slept, Tivas covered her with the blanket, but she continued to shiver. He moved over to position himself beside her. Soon she had snuggled up to him and her shivering stopped.

When Breena woke, she was stunned to find herself cuddling up to Tivas and that he was watching her. She pushed herself away immediately but the scarf wrapped around her hands had put her whole arm asleep. She groaned. "Tivas, I can't even feel my hands. You're going to have to untie them before I lose all circulation and damage them completely."

Tivas undid the scarf and began to rub her wrists. It sent a tingling feeling through her hands and arms and Breena jerked away. Tivas grabbed her hands again and continued to rub them. "Your hands need to be rubbed in order to regain the feeling in them. You do not know everything. You said you would not be cold but you lay shivering all during the rain."

"I thought you were Minab. That is why I didn't move away. My mind plays tricks on me when I sleep."

"I know." Tivas remembered the time she thought he was Minab, returned from the dead, when she was under his care before. He continued to rub her hands and wrists.

Tivas tied the scarf around Breena's waist, and on to his belt. Breena could not move more than four feet away with the scarf linking them together. As they were coming out of the cave, Tivas spotted something and quietly led his horse into the cave. He motioned for Breena to be silent. Tivas undid the scarf at his belt and crawled to the entrance. Breena followed him. She wanted to see who was out there. Maybe it was Minab. There were six men approximately fifty yards from the cave and Tivas pulled Breena down beside him out of fear that they would see her golden colored hair.

"If Minab was protecting me, he would have attacked them." Breena whispered.

Tivas pulled her close to him, so that he was almost on top of her. "Even Minab would not be so foolish as to attack six men at once." He whispered back.

"He would battle them all and be conqueror."

"You may continue your exaggerated fantasy of Minab if you like but I would never fight as he and risk your virtue in such a way."

"How is that risking my virtue?"

"If I were to die in battle with them, they would come after you and I am sure they would not be respectful before they killed you."

Breena shuttered at the thought and ceased to criticize Tivas about his handling of the situation. She did not like being so close to Tivas and she initiated a slow shimmy away from him. Tivas stopped her with his two hands being placed firmly on her upper arms. He looked into her eyes and studied her expression. "If I were to kiss you, would you cry out and commit us both to death?"

"I would not want to live, knowing I had deliberately betrayed Minab with a kiss."

Tivas smiled. "If you kiss me, I will take you to your husband and allow him to protect you in this matter."

Breena did not move. She wanted to be with Minab very much but she could not trust Tivas. "Will you swear to me that you will take me to my husband immediately and will you also swear that you will not suddenly become overwhelmed with guilt and tell Minab of our minute bargain?"

"Yes, I swear by my love for you." Tivas did not wait for Breena to agree to their negotiation. He leaned over her and kissed her with such passion it made Breena light-headed and weak. In all her life, she had never even dreamed of a kiss such as that. When it was over, she remained still, trying to control her emotions and wondering how she could ever push what had just happened from her mind.

Tivas slowly moved away from Breena. He whispered to her to watch the men, and tell him if they come closer, or if they left. Then he packed up the blanket and few supplies and attached them to his saddle. As he was saddling his horse, the men outside seemed to be satisfied that whatever they were looking for was not there and they left. Breena told Tivas, right away.

"I can take you to Minab but we will have to head north then east and then west again, to avoid running into those men again, or I can take you to your children. I do not know if Minab will still be in the valley and I am sure Kabay is worried Minab will find him with the children and know that you are with me. What would you prefer?"

Breena knew that Minab would never tolerate Tivas' protection of her rather than Kabay's and she was worried Minab would punish Kabay for allowing Tivas to come after her. "Take me to my children. I want to see for myself that they are all right. Do you know these men who want to kill us?"

"No, but as a captain of a legion, many enemies are often made. It is possible that even Minab cannot remember from which fight they seek vengeance."

They rode all day and took shelter during the rain. By late afternoon the next day, they came to the village where Tivas thought Kabay had hid the children. Tivas made a few inquires and eventually found Kabay. If Tivas had not been a warrior, he would have not been able to acquire any information about Kabay at all. The town did not talk with outsiders. When Breena was reunited with her children and Shirin, Kabay took Breena into another room away from Tivas. With the help of Shirin, he asked Breena if Tivas had done anything that was inappropriate to her. Breena told him she was hungry and tired but nothing had happened and she was thankful to be with her children again. She told Kabay that she wanted to be with her husband and asked Kabay to take her to him. Kabay said he would arrive soon but could only travel slowly, because of his injury.

When Minab finally arrived, it was just at the time that Breena and Tivas were arguing. Breena wanted to take a horse and go to meet Minab and Tivas refused to allow her to go. She had asked Kabay each morning for the last three days, where her husband was and if he thought, someone should go find him just in case whoever was out to kill him had sent more men. Kabay would just say no, without any explanation. That would drive Breena crazy, so finally she decided to take a horse and go look for him, herself. She knew Kabay would send men after her and that way she would have protection for Minab, but her plans were foiled.

Breena yelled at Tivas and then she picked up a clump of what she thought was dirt and threw it at Tivas. "Let me pass. If you and Kabay aren't worried about Minab then I'll go without you."

Tivas put his hands up to deflect the clumps that were being chucked at him. He was not impressed with Breena's rebellious attitude and the insult of having her throw things at him, annoyed him greatly. "You are such a foolish woman. Just go back and tend to your children." He waved his hand in the direction of the small cottage where the children were.

"Don't tell me what to do, Tivas. You think that just because you're a man and have all those muscles, it makes you right and me, wrong. I really hate this male, superior attitude around here." Breena picked up another clump and threw it at Tivas.

"Stop this behavior!" Tivas stepped closer towards her and Breena folded her arms in defiance.

Minab and his men had ridden silently into the town and Minab sat upon his horse watching, amused at the dispute. He could hear what was being said and he was glad to see Tivas at the center of Breena's hostility. Slowly Minab dismounted from his horse. It was obvious that he was still hurting from his wound and the long ride had caused much pain and stiffness in his leg. Breena did not notice Minab and his men ride up, but Tivas did. He nodded to him and Breena turned around to see to whom the nod was directed.

"Wife. Why are you throwing dried horse dung at a warrior?"

Breena thought it was just dirt but she smiled at the thought of its true identity. She was so glad to see Minab, and she ran up to him, jumping into his arms. "Oh Minab, I've missed you so much. Why are you punishing me by staying away so long?"

Minab laughed as Breena's leap almost knocked him over. He gently put her down on to the ground. It did not hinder her though, in staying close to him. She kept her arms wrapped around his neck. "Your behavior is inappropriate for my men to see. You are the wife of a captain. Conduct yourself accordingly." He was silently grateful that her love for him was not damaged by his previous actions.

"I don't care what your men think." Breena remembered Minab's wounded leg and she immediately fell to her knees. "Oh, Minab; what can I do to make your leg feel better?" She touched his thigh and could feel the bandage under his pant leg.

"Stand up, wife."

Breena smiled. "Is this embarrassing you?"

Minab knew that Breena liked to embarrass him that way, and he was careful of his answer. "No. I just did not want you to make me desire you so much, that I must tell my men that I require a nap, in the middle of the day." He replied softly.

Breena stood but leaned into his ear. "Go ahead."

Minab stood looking at her. What he thought was odd, when they first met, was now the object of his desire. He loved her golden hair and her blue eyes. He could look at them for hours, as they seemed to relay every emotion she bore. Minab grabbed her and picked her up in his arms. "I will check on my children first, but I have, indeed, become very much in need of a nap." He walked into the cottage with Breena and they were greeted by Kabay. He looked at them disapprovingly.

"I am glad to see you again, Minab. As you can see I have faithfully carried out your request of protecting your family, but we have not captured all the assassins." Kabay pulled over a chair for Minab. "You must rest."

It was in their language and Breena did not understand much, only the part about resting. She giggled as Minab sat down. He had not released her. "Tell Kabay I need a rest too." She pretended to yawn and said the word 'rest' in Minab's language.

Kabay frowned. "This is a time to be on our guard. A warrior shouldn't be concentrating on trivial things, such as females. If your wife is tired, it is because she has been busy being a burden on our minds since we found her, and brought her here."

Minab laughed. He knew Kabay was probably right. Breena would want her own way, even at a time like this, and Kabay would not want to give in. He thought Minab pampered Breena. Breena placed her head against the side of Minab's head and Minab turned his lips to hers and kissed her. "You would deny a dying man the pleasures of a beautiful woman?"

"She is beautiful, indeed, but she is like a mule and a wildcat, combined. I am sorry I suggested that you take her as yours. She has put a spell on your heart and you cannot see passed those eyes of hers. If you were a dying man, the last thing you need is this woman."

"She has been difficult?"

Kabay rolled his eyes. It caught Minab off guard, and he chuckled. Kabay was not customarily sarcastic. "All I can say is if she was my woman. . ." He shook his head as if the thought disturbed him.

Minab whispered to Breena to apologize to Kabay for the problems she had caused him and Breena shook her head. "I haven't done anything that I don't do normally. He gets upset over everything. He's just angry because I gave him a few suggestions as to how he could trap the men who are still after us."

"Did my wife suggest a plan to trap the assassins?" Again, it was spoken in their own language.

"Yes, with her as bait. If something went wrong, you would not have cared if it were her idea, as you slew me with your sword. She does not think before she speaks and neither does your maidservant, Shirin or she would never translate half the things your wife says. I would wish to know only two phrases in this language of hers; keep silent, and stupid woman, do not interfere."

Minab laughed loudly. "I will teach them to you later."

The door to the back room opened and Minab's children came rushing out. The two older boys were carrying Taru and Sumy, and Breena was pleased to see how they seemed to be protective of their younger siblings. Minab junior crawled up on his mother's lap as she sat with Minab.

"Father, we were so worried that you were hurt." Sheb said as he touched his father's shoulder pad.

"We would protect mother and the others for you. You didn't need to send Kabay." Tian added. Their attitudes seemed a great deal older than they were. They were approaching their eighth birthday and Breena had instilled a strong desire of family in them. They knew soon they would spend much more time with the males of their culture but they had no desire to be separated from their mother or brothers and sister.

Minab tenderly touched each of them and he could see Kabay frown, out of the corner of his eye. It did not bother him though, as he did not care as much about that tradition as he once had if it meant his family, especially Breena, would be hurt. The older boys would soon be required to go on training sessions with him. He had preconceived ideas about how it would be, as he had seen others handle their sons, but he now wondered if it would be that easy. Breena had not only instilled a strong bond between her and their sons but also between him and his sons.

Tivas stood outside, away from the family, as he knew Minab did not want him near them, now that he was there to protect them. As Tivas pondered his future, his mind kept wandering back to the cave and the kiss he experienced. He was worried that Minab would find out, he was the one who had brought Breena to the village. He knew Kabay would not tell but maybe one of the children say something. Breena's children talked more with their parents than other children did. In his mind, in an effort to control his thoughts of Breena, he went over the prospects he had for a second. He had already narrowed the search down to two. There was Maylo, the daughter of an old friend. She was a candidate. She had good body posture and was a large baby herself at birth, but she was not pretty and Tivas knew he would not like looking at her much. Then there was Bashimah. She had a pretty face with a dimpled smile but she was already a little plump and Tivas knew she would eventually become fat from having children. Still, he realized that was the reasons the two women were not chosen as first wives, and were eligible to become seconds. He decided upon Bashimah. At least with her, he could look at her smile occasionally, and maybe his son would have a dimpled smile.

CHAPTER FOURTEEN

THEY STAYED IN THE village for almost a month. It wasn't until the last week that they were there, that Minab's guard found the last six men that were after his family. The men had returned to Chelm and they were too curious about the location of Minab's family. By then, the city was aware of the threat and everyone was looking for the outsiders. Minab returned his family to their home once the danger was gone, and life resumed as normal.

Tivas took Bashimah to wife, but did not spend much time at home. Bashimah was very friendly and could speak a little English. Breena invited her over to the house many times, as she knew Bashimah was lonely. Minab assumed that with Tivas' decision to take a second; he was over his feelings for Breena. Again, Minab extended his hand towards Tivas and welcomed him into his home to visit.

Tivas took great effort not to even look at Breena and to focus his attention on Minab or the boys whenever he was there, but he was curious that Breena had not conceived another child. He figured that with the accident that caused the loss of her last child, she would want another one right away. As Tivas was visiting, on one occasion, he saw Shirin put an herb into Minab's drink and Tivas waited until later to speak with Shirin. Tivas waited until everyone was busy before he walked into the tiny storage room where Shirin was. "Shirin, you are very knowledgeable about herbs. What is it that you have been giving Minab lately?"

Shirin froze. She was mixing something in a small bowl and she discreetly pushed it under a shelf at the back of the counter where she stood. "It is nothing."

"Tell me old woman, or I will make life difficult for you. I know that you still visit the idol worshipping priests, from that religion you profess not to believe in anymore."

Shirin looked at Tivas. "It is for my master's wife. My master killed her baby when he pushed her down the stairs and he does not deserve to have more sons right now. She needs time to heal in her heart."

Tivas knew that Breena's fall down the stairs was an accident, the fault of no one. "Breena asked you to do this? She does not seem to blame Minab."

"I do it on my own. She is too forgiving. My master's wife means a great deal to me. She honors me as if I were her mother."

"So you have taken it upon yourself to pass judgment on a great man like Minab?"

"I am no more judgmental of him than you are."

Tivas smiled. They understood each other. "Do these herbs really work?"

"Yes. My master's wife is not with child and it has been ten months since she lost the last baby."

"How long will you give Minab these herbs?"

"He leaves for camp with the two older boys next week after their entry celebration. I will have to stop then."

"Tell me. Do you have herbs that will cause sleep to be very deep and full of dreams? My second is not easy to approach."

Shirin smiled and reached for three small pouches. She mixed a handful from each and placed them into another tiny pouch. "This will cause a deep dream-filled sleep. She will think her dreams are better than her reality." Shirin handed it to Tivas and he left.

Sheb and Tian turned eight the following week. Minab held a big celebration for them. They were brought before the church and the ceremony of entry was performed. Then they went back to Minab's house for a big party. Many important people were there and the boys were introduced into the male society as pre-cadets. They would go with their father the following week, to be presented to his camp and to learn the very basics of manhood, such as hunting and protection. Breena had made them wooden swords when they were five, and they had battled in many imaginary wars since then. Now, they would be given metal swords, not as big as the real swords, but ones that they will practice with, until they are twelve.

During the celebration at the house, Tivas sought out one of the young female slaves. He pulled her into one of the vacant rooms and the young girl stood looking up at Tivas. She was shaking with fear.

"Do not tremble little mouse. I have not brought you in here to trespass against you. I want you to do something for me and I will pay you. Have you ever touched a gold coin before?" The young girl shook her head. Tivas held out one gold coin. "Here. Touch it. Hold it. See how it sparkles like your master's wife's hair?"

The young girl took the coin and examined it carefully. She smiled as she ran her finger around the edge of the coin. She put it up to her eye and touched it carefully to her eyelashes. "It is beautiful. What can I buy with such a coin? Can I buy my freedom?"

"No, but you could buy passage way back to Kalat with it. That is where your mother lives, is it not?"

"Yes, but I could not run away. I am a slave to this household."

"They would not come after you. You are a tiny mouse in this city and would not be missed." Tivas reached out and took the coin back. "Maybe you do not want to go back to your mother."

The young girl's eyes pleaded her answer even before she spoke. "Oh, yes. I do want that very much. What is it that you require of me that will reward me with this shiny gold coin?"

Tivas handed the girl a tiny pouch. "You are to put this in your master's wife's food at the evening meal, every night that your master is gone. Divide the contents of the pouch into seven portions and use one portion a night. No one must see you or find out. If they see you, I will not give you the coin and if they find out who has requested this deed, I will kill you with my own two hands. Do you understand?"

The young girl nodded and slowly put the pouch in the pocket of her dress. "I will not fail at this task." She left the room.

Tivas smiled. His plan was progressing easier than he expected. For an instant, he almost hoped that it would have been thwarted. Thoughts of Breena were, overpowering his judgment, once more. He said good-bye to Minab and the two boys but he did not talk to Breena; then he found Bashimah and went home.

The next day, Minab and his two oldest sons left for camp. All males spent time in camp during their adolescence no matter what their career ended up being. There in the camp, they were taught things all males learned in the art of supplying food and protection for their future families.

The day Minab left, the little slave girl started putting the herb into her master's wife's evening meal. The first night Breena dreamed she was home with Minab and all the children. It was a wild dream of how Minab reacted to all the modern things that happened in her society. Breena could not believe how vivid the dream was.

The second night, during the rain, Tivas climbed up one of the trellises that were on either side of the balcony just outside Breena's room. He went into her bedroom, and Breena, again, had vivid dreams of Minab returning to her after Portess had captured him. Breena had similar dreams for the next four nights and they seemed so real. She couldn't wait for Minab to return as she missed him terribly.

As the rain began to subside on the seventh evening, Tivas climbed back down the trellis. Hearing a noise, Shirin came out to investigate. She thought a stray dog that was digging in the flowerbeds around the neighborhood, during the rain, caused it. She spotted Tivas as he put his feet upon the ground below Breena's balcony.

"Master Tivas. What have you done?" Shirin whispered in tones of scorn as she stood, with an oilskin held over her head, in the drizzling rain. She immediately suspected what he was doing there while the master of the house was away.

Tivas turned and faced her. He was not surprised to see her; neither did he seem ashamed of his actions. "I have only done the deed that you made accessible to me. I have given your mistress what she desires, and what Minab could not possibly provide, thanks to your herbs."

"I have not done anything that would sanction you to do a thing such as this." Shirin was not unaware of the symptoms Breena had shown all week long. Breena had talked about having unusual dreams and she was still very tired each morning, even though she slept so soundly Shirin had to go wake her. Usually, before Breena woke on her own, shortly after the rain stopped. Shirin quickly understood the meaning of Breena's puzzling actions. "How could you do such a thing as terrible as this blasphemous trick you have done to your brother and his wife?"

"Your mistress has not been beguiled."

"She does not know of this trickery! She would think you to be her husband and only in a dream, if anything."

Tivas smiled and gave a slight nod in agreement. "Yes, but I have made her happy this past week. I imagine Minab does not make her smile in her sleep, as I have." Tivas' attitude was completely arrogant. He folded his arms and waited for her reply.

"You have shamed us all. When will this disgrace end?"

"I have spent the last six nights in paradise, and I do not care what some worthless old woman thinks. No one will ever know, except you, and I know you will never tell." Tivas was smug in his replay. He casually brushed his now damp hair out of his face with his hands and then smiled a boyish grin.

"I should tell my master and let him slay you!" Shirin turned to go into the house but Tivas grabbed her arm tight.

"Think of what he would do to you, old woman. You have been giving him herbs for months now and it was you who gave me the herb to camouflage my liaison." Tivas put his hand on her neck and Shirin began to fear for her life. "Tell me what your master would do to his wife? For I am sure, he would not believe she slept through the liberties I took with her, not only once, but six times!"

Shirin lowered her head and began to cry. She loved Breena like a daughter and she knew Tivas was right. Only those who understood about herbs would fully believe in their influence on people.

"Do not weep, silly old woman." Tivas removed his hand from her neck. "This will put an end to Minab's doubts about Taru and his wife's devotion to him. When your mistress has another child, which is just like Taru, Minab will believe both children are his. After all, I have not even spoken to Breena in months. There would be no other conclusion to believe." The rain had stopped and Tivas stood still as he watched Shirin scurry back into the house. He turned and silently left the garden through the back gate, thinking this achievement would be enough to satisfy his lusts.

Shirin let Breena sleep until mid-morning before she woke her. Breena tried to tell her about another weird dream she had but Shirin did not want to listen. She told her to bath quickly and to dress, as Bashimah was coming to visit. Breena had promised to teach her how to make the tiny sweet cakes that were served at the boy's celebration.

Breena was concerned for Bashimah, as she seemed very sad for someone who had just been given as a second. Bashimah's English had improved greatly over the past month. Breena showed her how to make the tiny cakes and Bashimah began to confess her unhappiness.

"I do not understand why I was chosen by Tivas. I think he dislikes me, greatly." Bashimah said as she stirring the mixture.

"I'm sure he is just not over the terrible time he had after Trela's death. He wouldn't have chosen you if he didn't want you or like you." Breena tried to sound sincere but she could not help remember Tivas had told her he would not love a second as he did Trela.

"I think not. He keeps calling me by the wrong name when he talks to me and that is not often. He calls me Trela, and your name, and sometimes, Tanisha. He also has slept in the back room since I came to his house. For the past week, he has left the house just before the rain and has not returned until the morn. He must prefer the company of his friends to mine."

Breena could see the tears forming in Bashimah's eyes. "Well, that shows he cares. He just doesn't want to be with you until he can resolve his feelings about Trela. He blames himself, you know." Breena hoped she sounded convincing. "Give him time. He's not a cruel man. He would not hurt you on purpose."

Bashimah nodded. "I must learn to bake this special treat. Tivas said he likes them and maybe if I do well and please him in this, he will talk to me more."

"I'm sure he will." They spent the day making a variety of treats Breena knew how to make and Breena showed Bashimah how to curl her hair by using a hot iron rod that she warmed in the stove. She showed her how to braid her hair too.

When Bashimah came back home she found Tivas in the kitchen. He was eating some fruit. "How can my wife make me a meal when she is not here?"

Bashimah quickly put down the basket containing the treats she had made and knelt in front of Tivas to undo his laces. "I have been over at Breena's house learning how to make tiny cakes. I have brought home a basket full for you." She removed Tivas' boots and then quickly started preparing the meal.

"Do you like Breena? She is a stranger and her ideas are very odd." Tivas sat watching Bashimah work.

"She has been very nice to me. She seems to be nice to everyone."

"Well, she hates me. She was under my care when we thought Minab was dead and she thinks I was improper in my actions towards her, concerning becoming my second."

"She does not understand our ways."

Tivas walked over to a corner shelf and took down a jug of wine. He drank it right from the jug. "She will be under my care again one day and then I will not care how she feels. It is my right and our way." Bashimah placed his meal before him and another plate of food in front of where she would sit. Tivas gave thanks quickly then began to eat. All the while, he kept drinking out of the jug of wine. He pointed to her plate and chuckled. "You must stop eating such a big plate full or others will think you are with child before you become that way."

Bashimah looked down and slowly pushed the plate away. "I will do whatever pleases you, my husband."

Tivas shook his head and pushed the plate back towards her. "I am in a bad mood that is all. Smile for me, so I may see those dimples that make your face sparkle."

Bashimah smiled. It was as close to an apology that an Adder man ever gave. Bashimah did not know Tivas very well, and her smiles were the only thing she was sure he liked about her. Tivas took another drink and smiled back at her. He drank more than he ate and that night he did not spend it in the back room.

Minab came home with the boys, and Breena was at the door to greet them with open arms. As the boys entered the house, they did not hug their mother.

"Where are the boys I kissed and hugged, before they left for camp with their father? Minab, you did not bring me back my sons. Who are these outsiders, you have brought home instead?"

Tian shook his head. "No Mom. We are the same sons. It is not our way to hug as much as you do." She liked that they called her Mom instead of Mother.

Breena frowned. "Well, you should find out the truth about what is really our way. You both came from your mom and from your father. Your way is only half Adder. The other half is from my stranger side. Did you think you got the blue in your eyes from your father?"

"No Mom." Sheb shook his head too.

"Well then, you get your stranger half over here and hug your mom, before she gets upset and spanks your stranger-side butts."

The boys ran into their mother's arms and hugged her. Minab stood watching, with his arms folded. "You may have a difficult time spanking them when they are older, my wife."

Breena looked up and smiled. "Oh, I have that all figured out. I will just challenge them to a sword fight if they won't hug or kiss me."

"They will not fight you. They might injure you."

"Then, they will have to hug me or I will lay a beating on them. I have been practicing with the sword." Breena grinned and walked over to Minab and put her arms around him. "I have missed you terribly."

Minab looked at his two oldest sons and smiled. "I am the husband. This is my right." He leaned over and kissed Breena passionately, and the two boys chuckled.

"Maybe she will spank you too, if you don't kiss her good." Tian said and the two boys ran off to find their brothers and sister.

"I have missed you also, my wife. How is it that such a tiny female can take up such a big place in my thoughts?"

Breena guided him into the kitchen where the table was full of food and treats she had made. It was like a small feast to celebrate their homecoming. Minab sat down and Breena undid his footwear. The two boys told their mother endless tales of what they had done and Minab sat back quietly and enjoyed the food and the stories. He was very pleased with his two sons and their behavior during their session with his troops. They had tried very hard to succeed at their training and Minab was satisfied with their effort. He had seen other fathers with their sons and Minab was sure Sheb and Tian had done as well, if not better than any he had seen. He watched Breena act excited over each tale, as if she had never heard or experienced anything as unique as her sons' experiences. He silently chuckled at the story of the boys' hunt of the wild beast. To them, it was a ferocious monster, when in actuality it was a young feral boar. Breena did not become squeamish at the sight of the boar's teeth, souvenirs from the hunt, and that pleased Minab. Breena suggested putting a hole through each of the teeth and making pendants out of them. The boys were satisfied that their mother now thought of them as young men, not just babies any more. When she asked for another hug from her future warriors, before they went to rest for the night, they gladly complied. Breena was a little saddened that her young warriors felt they no longer needed to be tucked in at night, but she understood and reminded them to give thanks for their adventure, before they fell asleep.

Breena turned her attentions to her husband as Shirin cleared the table. "Pedra has disappeared. I am worried about her." Pedra was the young slave girl, Tivas had made a deal with.

"I will make inquiries about her tomorrow. Sometimes the young ones will miss their mothers just before they come into the age when they can wed. Perhaps she has run away to her mother's family. They are back in Kalat. If so, I will have some of my men find her and bring her back."

"If that is the case maybe you could just let her be with her family? She is so young."

"If I did that, I would have no slaves left. They would all leave. It is our way, wife. You know I treat them well and it is better that they be enslaved than what would have happened in times of war."

Breena nodded. There were less and less customs, she could interfere with. She was, after all this time, finally beginning to understand the code of ethics, her father always stood behind concerning non-interference in cultures. They had to develop naturally, and Breena could now see what could be changed and what could not be changed without damaging the normal development of the society. Some of the things she did not like, she learned to close her eyes. As long as she did not partake in them, her conscience was clear.

Weeks went by and Breena discovered she had finally conceived once more. This time she told Minab only a week after she had realized she was pregnant. Minab was again thrilled that he would have another offspring. This time, he told Breena he hoped it would be a female so Breena could have a daughter. Breena already thought of Sumy as hers, and she could see her influence on her as she played with her brothers.

Pedra was indeed, found in Kalat, and returned. She was not happy about being brought back but did not fight against what was right. Minab had bought Pedra's mother from her master in Kalat and she returned with Pedra. Now that the household would soon have another child in it, Minab was concerned that Breena would feel compelled to do more and more of the chores. He did not want that.

Bashimah told Breena things had changed at her household and

Tivas no longer avoided her. She too, was with child. Breena was happy for her and Minab was pleased to hear the news, as it meant that Tivas was not dwelling on his past mistakes.

As Breena's pregnancy proceeded, she was pleased that she had not had any morning sickness with this one. Shirin had become devoted to Breena and the children. She spent many hours teaching the children reading and writing skills while Breena continued teaching other subjects. Breena often brought the children over to see Minab's mother, which thrilled Karisha. Not many women with her standing had visits from their grandchildren. It was considered too imposing, but it often left the grandmothers feeling lonely. Karisha was proud of her son's big family and pleased that his wife's lineage made them all different, yet accepted.

Bashimah visited quite often and Minab had softened his attitude towards Tivas. With Tivas in his personal guard, they often did things together, away from Chelm.

CHAPTER FIFTEEN

ONE DAY AS BREENA and Shirin were busy drying meat that Minab had brought home, a messenger came to the door. He had news that another plane had landed just outside of Kalat and that strangers were journeying to Chelm to visit Breena.

When the strangers finally arrived, Breena was pleased to see four men and one woman. When the woman came close enough for Breena to see her face she almost collapsed with shock. It was her mother. Breena ran to her and hugged her and they cried together for a long time. It was found that leaving the area for the north pole was no problem and was easily done by the last pilot with the instructions Breena had given him, but unfortunately returning took a great deal of effort and much luck. The only way that it was possible was if a storm as big as the one that hit Breena's plane would develop just as they were in the sector Breena's plane had been in. Many expeditions were sent to the North Pole only to return after almost using up all their fuel flying around the area where the other planes were lost from radar. The two components of a storm and the planes ability to survive the storm were the only elements that allowed for a successful journey. After years of efforts and hundreds of thousands of dollars, the effort had been called off. Breena's mother had put up the money for this trip. She had received the journal and video from Breena and had written a novel about her. It had become a best seller and had brought in millions of dollars for Breena's mom. She hoped to be successful in finding her daughter with this trip and she was commissioned to write a sequel upon her return.

Breena kept touching her mother as if she could not believe her senses. Finally, she introduced her mother to her family. Breena's mother was thrilled with meeting her grandchildren. It was a different attitude when Minab returned home.

"Minab, please come quickly. I have someone I want you to meet." Breena grabbed Minab's hand and pulled him into the great room.

Minab could see the resemblance right away. "Another stranger? Is she your sister?"

Breena was beaming with pride. "My mother. They came in a flying machine and landed near Kalat, two weeks ago. They asked about me and came here right away. I will introduce you to the others in a minute. I wanted my mother to meet you first."

Minab looked at Breena's mother. "Are you also a stubborn female?"

"Are you the man that violated my daughter?" Breena's mother hit Minab with her fists. It did little but made a noise on his armor.

"Mother." Breena grabbed her mother and held her back.

"I do not understand your mother's reaction. I have done nothing to harm you."

Breena's mother composed herself. "My daughter was barely seventeen when you forced her to become your wife. And what have you done for her since? She has become your own personal baby factory."

Minab laughed. "The females of your race have odd ideas about what a female is supposed to do. Men cannot have children. How else are we to obtain a lineage?"

Breena hugged her mother. "This isn't going to change anything, Mom. As you can see, I'm pregnant again. I like having babies. I'm good at it."

"You're a human being, and can do lots of things. You're good at a lot of things." Breena's mother began to calm down. Her daughter's hug told her they would talk later.

"She is my woman and I allow her to do many things. I will not allow her to fight like the men though. She is a mother and that is her role in life."

Breena could see her mother's temper rising. "Minab, did you know that my mother can cook just about anything and she was the best mother in the whole world?"

"Then it is from her that you have obtained your ability to nurture. She has raised you well."

Now Breena's mother didn't know what to say. She had predetermined she would reprimand Minab's people for their behavior of her daughter, but things had not turned out as she thought they would. She did not know Minab had been captured, and not killed. She was expecting to find Breena in the Tivas' household. She was coming to take her daughter home.

Breena read the novel her mother had written and was surprised at the contrast between what people really were like and what was in her writings. The story itself seemed to be accurate, although Breena blushed at the descriptions of some of the events that took place within the pages of the book. She had not realized that her mother could imagine such things as passion and love. The description of Zorban was amusing, as he became a very sinister looking man when in reality he was better looking than most men were. Minab, in her mother's writings was almost an Adonis, and much younger than he really was. Maybe her mother could not imagine her daughter being married to a man fifteen years or more, her senior. Although Breena now thought of Minab as being handsome, at their first meeting she would have described him as too old and much too rugged to ever appeal to her. The women's description made Breena chuckle, as they all sounded like hefty country farm girls with no grace to them at all.

Minab organized a feast for the strangers and invited many. It would be a grand dinner with many different foods to eat and good conversation.

The evening meal was relaxed and enjoyable with everyone being served in the great room. Tivas had not visited Minab's home in months. He had seen Minab other places and Minab had visited Tivas at his home but Tivas had deliberately avoided coming to any place where Breena was. He knew she was pregnant but made no comments about it. Minab had invited him to the house with the others.

"Mom, this is Tivas, Minab's brother." Breena noticed Tivas' peculiar attitude but dismissed it in her mind. "Tivas, this is my mother, Karen." Breena gave out a small uncomfortable giggle from speaking her mother's name. To her she was just, Mom.

"I recognize him from the video. It's nice to meet you." Karen held out her hand but quickly withdrew it. "Sorry. I keep forgetting the no touching policy you have."

Tivas gave a quick nod of the head, in recognition. "You are very exotic, very beautiful, like your daughter."

Karen smiled and gave her daughter a wink. "Just what a modern widow needs, a civilization full of huge muscular hunks who speak superbly flattering words."

Breena became uneasy, and then she looked up at Tivas. "My mother can no longer bare children, so don't get any ideas." She turned and walked away leaving her mother confused and feeling a little awkward.

"Minab's woman has never gotten over our ways concerning seconds. She was in my care when we thought Minab was dead, and she did not understand or like what had to be."

"My daughter has ideas of her own. I am flabbergasted she has adjusted to this way of life as easily as she has."

Tivas turned and watched Breena as she talked with some of the other guests. "She is in her glory when she is with child, so beautiful and magnificent. She carries them well and produces children that are fine to look at."

Karen stared at Tivas and an uneasy perception of him filled her mind. "Your wife is also pregnant?"

"Yes. She is the big one over there. Children will add to her size but it is necessary. Not many can survive the birth of the children I sire." Tivas pointed to Bashimah. "She is my second. My wife died while trying to give birth to my second son."

"I'm sorry. This is Breena's fifth pregnancy, isn't it? I never thought she ever have children. I never thought she would make me a grandmother. Is your first son here?"

Tivas looked at her intensely, then smiled, but did not answer. He turned and walked over to Bashimah. He put his hand on her belly and she seemed overjoyed at his touch. Bashimah looked up into Tivas' eyes and smiled. Tivas smiled back at her and then touched her cheek. He closed his eyes. A scowl spread across his face and he left the room, heading towards the back garden.

Karen walked over to Breena. "Breena, sweetheart, can I talk to you?"

Breena nodded and handed her mother a plate of food. Karen liked the unusual food offered in her daughter's world. "You must find this whole thing bizarre." Breena said to her mother.

"It is like walking onto a movie set of a film about the Roman Empire, except nothing clicks. Do you know what I mean?"

Breena chuckled. "Exactly; nothing clicks as normal. It's as if I've been living someone else's dream for years. Sometimes it's a nightmare."

"I think I might have said something wrong to Mr. Tivas."

Breena smiled at her mother's polite proem of Tivas. "It is just Tivas, Mom. The civilization doesn't seem to get big enough to need last names or titles such as mister whatever. Whole cities are wiped out in battles. I guess it's their way of controlling the population. The Adder civilization is the biggest, I think. I'm not Mrs. anything; I'm just Minab's woman."

"I certainly don't like that implication. It's like you're not an individual."

Breena shrugged her shoulders. "I've fought it for almost ten years, Mom. It isn't going to change. Besides, you change your attitude when you want or need protection. I belong to Minab and he will protect me even if it costs him his life. That's been lost in our society." She signed. "I actually like belonging to Minab. He belongs to me, too, but it's never spoken like that."

Karen shook her head as if it was beyond comprehension. "What is it with Tivas? The others I have met seem straightforward but he is different. I think I upset him. He told me about his wife dying while giving birth to his second son and when I asked him if his first son was here, he just gave me a strange look and walked away."

Breena looked horrified at the information. "He's not normal. He... I will tell you all about it when we are alone. Maybe you should stay away from him."

Karen agreed and the evening continued. Breena waited for the opportunity to talk to Tivas, alone. It came near the end of the gathering as Minab became engrossed in a conversation about weaponry with one of the strangers. Breena found Tivas in the kitchen. He was nibbling on a piece of the large cake Breena had made.

"This food you have made is delightful to the taste. The white cloud-like substance, on top, is very sweet." Tivas complimented her.

"Why aren't you in with the others? They are talking about your favorite subject."

"Are they talking about you?"

Breena placed a few empty crumb-filled plates in one of the buckets on the counter. "Where did that come from? I thought things were well with you. Bashimah is with child and it definitely looks like it'll be a boy."

Breena tried to lift the bucket down to the floor and Tivas quickly took it from her and placed it on the ground. "Things are well, but nothing seems to dull the mind. Sometimes the images are so clear, they scream at me. I have stayed away because I cannot control my thoughts. Soon, I must leave, before my urges overpower me."

"Tivas, you need help. You need to go see a physician or a holy man or someone."

"There is no cure for what afflicts me, I fear. I can only wait for fate to deliver you to me."

"Tivas, stop it! You have Bashimah and soon you'll have a son. Why did you tell my mother that Trela died giving birth to your second son? Taru is not yours and I want you to stop this conflict. Do you want me to end up hating you?"

Tivas' eyes watched Breena's every move. It was unwavering and Breena turned away from him. He reached out and touched her belly and Breena slapped his face with such force the slap seemed to echo through the house. Tivas closed his eyes and began to breathe hard as he tried to control his temperament. Breena stepped back. She was sure if they had been alone in the house, he would have struck her back.

Suddenly he opened his eyes and they were like fire. "You will never be able to drive me away. I am your fantasy. I know your dreams. I am the one who made you smile at night. You thought it was Minab, who whispered in your ear that his love was incessant. You thought it was Minab that made two hearts beat louder than the clap of thunder, united, during the rain; but it was I. We are the ones who flew in the sky like the falcons, with our blood burning through the veins of our bodies."

Breena's mouth dropped open and she could feel a crimson blush sweep over her face. Had she talked in her sleep, and had Tivas heard her at one time? Breena turned away and covered her mouth with her hand. Even if he had heard her talk in her sleep, how would he know the things she had dreamed, the things left unspoken? Breena burst into tears and sunk to the floor. What had happened? What had Tivas done and why could she not remember what was real?

Tivas left the house immediately, just before Minab walked into the kitchen. He bent down beside Breena. "What is wrong? Is it the baby?"

Breena looked up at Minab and shook her head. "Keep him away from me. I don't want him near our children, or my mother or even our home. Please Minab. Tell him never to come here again."

Minab lifted Breena to her feet. "What did Tivas do?" Minab's face darkened with rage as his suspicions mounted.

"He told my mother, Trela died having his second son. I hit him Minab. I slapped him in the face, as hard as I could."

Bashimah walked into the kitchen and Minab glanced at her, then he stormed passed her into the other room. Bashimah walked over to Breena and hugged her. Breena hugged her back. She knew Bashimah knew what was in Tivas' heart, and for whom that heart yearned for. Minab walked back into the kitchen with his sword and Bashimah burst into tears. She fell to Minab's feet and begged him for mercy. She told him she would make Tivas forget his desires, if Minab would just give her a little time. Minab looked at Breena, and then he pushed Bashimah away with his foot. He left the house in pursuit of Tivas. Breena looked at Bashimah as she sat crying on the floor. There was going to be a battle and Breena knew she could not stay in the house and act as if nothing was going on. She walked out to find Minab and Bashimah followed her.

Minab found Tivas near his house. He called out his name and Tivas stopped. Tivas casually looked back at Minab. His face was still reddened by the slap Breena had administered. "You have come to slay an unarmed man, brother?"

"I have come to put an end to your torment." Minab walked around him, sizing up his strengths and weaknesses. "You have a second and soon will have a son. Why do you relentlessly torture what is mine?"

Tivas smiled. "You have no idea what it is like to be defective as I am. You received all that was good from our father. I was only given his passions."

"That is not true. You have the ability to be mighty, but you choose unwisely at almost everything you do. You let your carnality rule you. Whatever excuses you decide upon, it does not change what evils boil within you." Minab threw down his sword. "Now we are equal, both unarmed."

Breena could see them from a distance and Bashimah soon caught up with her. As they watched their men fight, Bashimah begged Breena to stop them. Breena shook her head. "No. This needs to be done."

As the men brawled, fighting hand to hand, Breena watched and slowly she began to feel nauseated. This was what she hated the most about this place. There was always violence; and yet now, she was condoning it. They were parallel in strength and skill. They almost seemed to take turns knocking each other down, throwing each other against fences, and stairs, and the sides of buildings. Minab finally threw a blow that landed on the side of Tivas' head. It sent him back against the outside wall of the Tivas' house. It was an opportunity that Minab could not ignore. He grabbed Tivas, with one hand, around his neck and throttled him. With the other, he continued to hit him with mighty force. Breena suddenly felt afraid. She did not want Tivas to die. She did not want anyone to die. She only wanted Minab to make him leave them alone. Bashimah could see the seriousness of the blows and she began to scream.

Breena stepped closer to them. "Stop! This is enough. Minab, stop. He is not worth the blood on your hands, if you kill him." She knew Minab would never forgive himself for uncontrolled rage.

It took a few seconds for Minab to comprehend Breena's words, but finally he loosened his grip. Tivas, still fighting for air and his life, lunged out at Minab. He knocked him over and Minab fell onto Breena, sending her against the wall. She hit her back with such a thud that it halted the men in their tracks. Breena fell over in a hump on the ground.

"Breena!" Minab screamed out as he realized what had happened.

Tivas could hardly stand. He painfully looked at Breena through swollen eyes and a blood soaked face. Minab did not look much better. Quickly, Minab scooped Breena up in his arms. Tivas told him to bring her into the house, and then he yelled for Bashimah to run for a physician. Minab brought Breena into the house and placed her on a couch in the great room of the house. Tivas picked up Minab's sword and followed them into the house.

"Breena, Breena, my love, my life." Minab touched her face and stroked her cheeks, and then he kissed her gently.

Tivas stood back a bit and remained silent. The physician finally hurried into the house, followed by Bashimah. He looked at the two men, as they appeared to need his help more. Minab called for him to attend to Breena. The physician told Bashimah to get a basin of water and a cloth. He checked Breena's eyes and felt for movement from her baby. He wiped Breena face with the wet cloth and then felt around her head for bumps or visible cuts.

Breena stirred and Minab gave a sigh of relief. He turned to Tivas. "Take your second and leave Chelm. You have almost killed the only thing that means anything to either of us. You are nothing but an obstacle to our happiness. I do not want to see you until you are over your obsession. Go before I declare I have lost my brother, again."

When Minab brought Breena home, Karen was very upset. "What kind of world treats their women like this?"

Minab was by Breena's side on her bed and Breena hugged him close. "I am all right. Minab, I love you." She buried her face in his shoulder and Minab stroked her hair.

Over the next few days, Breena was watched carefully. Shirin made her stay in bed. Karen stayed close to her daughter's side. "Tell me about Tivas. We are alone and I'm curious."

Breena had Karen close the door to her room to ensure privacy. "Tivas is Minab's brother and for a long time Minab denied he even existed because of things he had done in the past."

"Like what?"

"He fell in love with a slave girl in Minab's house. In this culture a slave girl is from another class system and mixing is not allowed."

"That is not right. You should know that, Breena."

"I do Mom, but it isn't something I can do anything about. Slaves are slaves as an alternative to death. When a tribe overthrows another in a city, they usually put everyone to death. Some are spared if they agree to become slaves. In this case, the slaves are idol worshipers and that makes them definitely taboo, among the Adder tribe."

"So Tivas fell in love with someone who was taboo?"

"Yes. They don't mix tribes often, but they never mix religious ideas, especially with what they consider a pagan."

"You never used to believe in any one type of religion. How is it that Minab married you?"

"At least I didn't worship idols, and their religion is not filled with mystery and hocus-pocus. It is complex, yet easily understood, all at the same time. I wrote about it on some paper I had left. We can talk about that later. I met Tivas in the market place. I thought he was Minab, from the back and he looked so much like him I knew they must be related. Tivas made amends for what he had done with the slave girl."

"Did he marry her?"

"No. He thought Minab would allow him to marry if she was with child, so he got her pregnant. Minab did not allow it and the girl died giving birth. Tivas sires large children."

Karen shook her head. "You're beginning to talk like them. You never would have used phrases like sire, back home."

Breena shrugged her shoulders. "Tivas bought the girl's mother, Shirin, her freedom as a token of his desire to make things right with Minab. He also gave up his rank in the army and enlisted under Minab as a subordinate."

"So what happened that made you not like him?"

"Minab went into battle against Protess, a mighty leader in a vicious army. He was captured and we thought he was killed. When a husband is killed, the wife becomes the property of the brother. If there is no brother, then she falls under the care of a close friend of the husband."

"That's terrible."

"It is done so that she does not become destitute and her children still have a father. It is a better welfare system than anything we have, but it'll only work if all the men in the culture are responsible. The men are taught from an early age that values such as honor, loyalty, and responsibility are very important."

"So you became the property of Tivas. He had a wife then, didn't he?"

"Yes. He had a child also, but it was a girl first and that is looked down on as very undesirable. He gave the little girl to me and Minab to rear."

"That's Sumy? I thought she wasn't yours. She looks too much like Minab's race."

"She's mine now. Anyway, I was so upset with the thoughts that Minab had died that I wanted to die. It was awful. I never hurt so much in my life."

"You really love Minab, don't you? Even after all he's done to you and how your marriage started out, you can love him?"

Breena nodded. "I love him with all my heart. The culture is different Mom, what happened at the start was what only could happen when two total different cultures collide."

"Even after he forced himself on you? I'll never forgive him for that."

Breena looked down. "Even if you look at it from his view? Here when a second is picked, the female is usually very grateful. The stigma of her not being picked as a first wife is gone and she is treated well. I was from a conquered city and he compromised a great deal. He didn't kill the rest of the people or even make them slaves."

"He, in turn, received a one of a kind woman. No, not even a woman yet, you were still a child, practically."

"I agreed to become his second and give him a lineage. He expected me to keep my word. After all, he had kept his."

"Okay. I don't want to discuss that any more. It is too upsetting. Tell me what happened with Tivas."

"He gave me a year to mourn when we thought Minab was dead, and then I was to become part of his household as his second."

"He already had a wife."

"A second in this case is different. Any children out of that union are bonded to the second's first husband. It sounds confusing but they are very precise about lineage and family lines, on the male side."

"You said the year was almost up in the video you sent back in the plane."

"Yes, and I planned on going back on that plane with my children, but at the last minute, I found out Minab was alive and had escaped. I couldn't go and leave him."

"Why didn't you have him come with you?"

"Mom, you've been here for almost two months. Honestly, do you think Minab could survive in our world? He'd hate it and he'd feel like a caged animal."

"You survived in his world."

"Maybe women are more adaptable. In any case, I chose to stay here with Minab."

"So how did that work, with you being in Tivas' household?"

"Minab had to go see the Holy man and have the records changed or something but while Minab was away talking with the Holy man Tivas decided to exercise his right to make me his second." Breena looked at the closed door. "Never tell this to anyone. I think Taru is Tivas' child. I could do nothing. Tivas was as strong as Minab and overpowered me. I never told Minab."

"Why not?"

"I thought he would have killed Tivas, and Minab would have been in the wrong. It was Tivas' right until I was given back to Minab, in the eyes of the church."

"What a ..." Karen's words faded off into a vulgar description of Tivas. Breena was a little surprised at her mother's choice of words. It had been almost ten years since she had come close to even hearing something like that.

"Tivas has been obsessed with me ever since. About two years ago, he told Minab that he had taken me as his second just hours before Minab had the Holy man reinstate me as his wife. That was the time I lost a child I was carrying. Minab had forgiven Tivas, until the other day." Breena closed her eyes, and covered her face with her hands for a second. "He said something to me that was really upsetting, Mom."

Shirin came into the room carrying a tray with drinks for the two women. She gave Karen a bad look, as if she thought she was upsetting Breena. Karen became quiet as if she was afraid Shirin might hear what they were saying. Breena thanked Shirin for the drinks. "Don't worry about Shirin. She is my confidant, my true friend and substitute mother, and knows more than anyone knows. I bet she knows more about Tivas' activities around here even better than I do. Isn't that right, Shirin?"

Shirin froze in her stance. "He is a terrible man."

"He bought you your freedom. Doesn't that make you feel some charity towards him?"

Shirin looked Karen directly in the eye. "My loyalty is to my mistress."

Breena touched Shirin gently on the arm. "I'm afraid Tivas has done something in this house that I am not aware of, Shirin. He spoke of my dreams. Did you tell him about those unusual dreams I had months ago?"

"I cannot tell, Breena. I will not have you think poor of me. Tivas is a master of manipulation."

"What has he done?"

Shirin looked at Karen. "In my heart, your daughter is as much my daughter. I would do nothing intentionally to hurt her."

Breena closed her eyes and lay back on the pillow. "I must know, Shirin."

"My herbs do many things. Trivas inquired about herbs to give to his second, as she was not easy to approach, he said."

"When was this?"

"Just before my master and his sons went out to train on the manhood session." Shirin started to cry.

"Please Shirin, don't cry, it's going to be alright. Just tell me what he did. Did you give him herbs for that purpose?"

"Yes. Those herbs cause deep and unusual dreams."

Breena became silent. She sat up and shook her head. "No. I don't think I want to know. Please tell me the truth is that he used them on Bashimah."

Shirin slowly shook her head. "I witnessed him descending from the trellis that is on the side of your balcony."

"Impossible! I didn't take any herbs."

"You may need to question Pedra as to where she obtained coins to aid her escape to Kalat. She insisted on serving you while the master and his sons were gone."

"What is she saying, Breena?" Karen asked her daughter.

"Nothing I want to hear. Shirin, did you speak with him when you saw him on the trellis?"

"Yes, but you may not want to hear the words that he spoke to me as it rained."

"No, I do not want to hear them, but I must."

"He stated that when you have another child, Minab will no longer dispute in his mind who sired Taru, for they shall look alike and Minab would think both where from his seed."

Breena cried out and put her head in her hands. She was silent for a long time. Karen and Shirin weren't sure if they should speak. Finally, Breena looked up them. "This never happened. I don't believe it happened. It is just a story, a fairy tale with a wicked wizard and innocent people in it."

Shirin understood and nodded. "As you wish."

Shirin left the room and Karen turned to her daughter. Breena shook her head and put her hand gently to her mother's lips. "You will go back and I will stay here, with my children and my husband, whom I love. Say nothing of what was spoken. My life is in your hands, Mom. Minab would never believe I was innocent in this, and the penalty for adultery is death."

"You can't stay here, Breena. What if he found out?"

"Then, I will die by the hands of the man I love. I won't leave him. No matter what happens. Tivas will never tell, no matter how guilty he feels this time. There would be no forgiveness for a deliberate act such as this, and Minab would kill him. I have seen Minab kill over things that were less of an evil."

*   *   *

More time passed, and Minab was told that Tivas had moved his home to Kalat. He had joined Volcar's legion. Breena regained her health and was soon preparing for the birth of her child. Karen was slowly learning the culture and although she did not like it, she was thankful for the chance to be near her daughter. The expedition planned to leave after Breena gave birth. By then, they hoped to have acquired enough information and historical facts to make a judgment as to the origin of this civilization. Karen knew she would return with them and was greatly disappointed that Breena would not even consider going with her, but she understood that this was her world now. Maybe Karen could return to visit, but the chance of another storm to take them into the exact coordinates, in the near future was unlikely, so another visit may not be for a long time.

Minab was very aware of Breena's pregnancy this time and he told Breena he noticed there was no morning sickness with this child. She knew it had eased his doubts of Taru's lineage. She watched, as Minab seemed to become closer to Taru. He sat talking with him and allowed him to touch his sword. Once, he gave Taru a ride on his stallion with him and Breena wept at their bonding. Taru spent hours talking about his father to anyone who would listen. Their love was strong. Minab was the mighty one in his eyes and now that Minab had begun to pay attention to him, it was like a dream come true.

Breena was huge with child and Minab spent more time at home as her time approached. She went into labor and Karen and Shirin assisted each other with the labor preparations. The delivery was as long as the rest and Karen felt helpless as she watched her daughter struggle. Minab paced the kitchen floor and the other children tried to distract him. Finally, as the birth drew closer, Minab entered the little back room. He sat down beside Breena and whispered in her ear, that he was sorry for the pain he had caused her when she lost her other baby because of the fall down the stairs. Karen was amazed at the change in Minab's demeanor. He had gone from a serious, coarse man, to one whose gentleness poured over his wife and the love he had for her was so real it could almost be felt, like a gentle breeze. Breena finally gave birth to another large male child. She was exhausted and it took a great effort to nurse the baby. Minab was thrilled with his new son. The baby looked similar to Taru, but his light colored hair and blue eyes reflected Breena's characteristics. Minab took the baby out to show the other children, and especially Taru. When he brought him back into his mother, Breena motioned for Minab to come close.

"This child is ours and there is no doubt about that. He looks like Taru, Minab. So do you now doubt who sired Taru?"

"No. I have no doubts in my mind or heart and I will prove it to the world. I shall call this one Tivas. He shall bear his uncle's name, and everyone will know I would not call him that if I had my doubts."

Karen and Shirin looked horrified at Minab's suggestion. Breena gripped herself and smiled. "If that is what my husband wishes that is what I wish also. Are you pleased with your increase?"

Minab touched Breena's face. "The sons of Minab will change the face of history. We will become a great nation of our own and many will wonder at how great our people are. You are working a fine accomplishment of teaching them to be right in the eyes of their God."

Breena's heart filled with remorse over what she could not reveal. After the betrayal of Minab's first wife, Breena knew the truth would not only result in heartache and mistrust but Minab would kill Tivas and maybe her. She smiled back at Minab. She would fill the rest of her life working at that accomplishment. Minab would never doubt her love.

EPILOGUE

THE EXPEDITION WENT BACK to Kalat and departed by plane with no difficulties. Karen returned home with more of Breena's journals, many pictures, and a few hours of video. She wrote a sequel to her book and it too became a best seller. It took almost another fifteen years before another successful trip back to the land of the tribes, was ever made. By then, things had changed dramatically. Breena had given Minab three more sons, Voltek, Kabeth, and Tertan, and finally a daughter. Her name was Paru, which means, born to be mighty. She had sparkling blue eyes and beautiful dark red hair. Obviously, her coloring was a throwback to Breena's ancestors. Minab had died from wounds received in a mighty battle to defend all of the Adder territory against the Zebrons, and destroying them. Breena held him in her arms as he passed into the next world. He counseled her not to fight against their way, if only for the sake of their children and that he was grateful for a wonderful life and for the extraordinary and faithful woman by his side.

Tivas had changed. He had spent many hours working to serve his people. He had spent years working with the holy men and striving for forgiveness. Bashimah had only borne him one son, but had given him six daughters. She died giving birth to the last child and his only son died in an accident while he was learning to ride a stallion. Tivas was now chief overseer and had taken Breena as his second, immediately after Minab's burial, fearful she would reject him completely. She bore him one son and no more. The boy was born eight months after Minab's death and although it was thought the child had been delivered early, Breena alleged that he was really sired by Minab. She insisted they call him Alexander after her father. Tivas always had his doubts about the boy's real lineage. She told Tivas she would never love him and he vowed to spend his days trying to change her mind, but forgiveness for the betrayal of Minab and her agonizing silence for many years would not come easily in this life.

Her sons had all become warriors in their own legion. The older ones became the father-figures for the younger sons. None of them was ever defeated in any battle. Their legion, was known as Minab's Warriors and because of their unusual physical distinctiveness, and large stature, they were considered a nation unto their own. Breena went on to win battles of her own, changing many customs for the better. Women were still wives and seconds but they now received better education and had a say in the government. When Shirin was ill and on her deathbed, Breena searched for her sons and Shirin received the one gift she most desired. Her sons gave her many hugs before she died.

Breena's life after Minab's death was as turbulent as her days when she first came to the land of the tribes. Karen didn't write another sequel, though. She figured no one would believe it. She would wait until Paru grew up. She had the tenacity of her mother, the skill of her father and the loyalties of her brothers. With the attention and pursuit of two great warriors for her alliance in marriage; Zorban's only son, Zoran; Kabay's oldest son, and also Maclesh; the son of a king from the south, that would be a book unto itself.